D1132736

For the veterans of World War II

JAN 1 9 2016

Guarded
by Angela Correll

© Copyright 2015 Angela Correll

ISBN   978-1-63393-136-7

All rights reserved. No part of this publication may be reproduced, stored in a retrieval system, or transmitted in any form or by any means – electronic, mechanical, photo-copy, recording, or any other – except for brief quotations in printed reviews, without the prior written permission of the author.

This is a work of fiction. The characters are both actual and fictitious. With the exception of verified historical events and persons, all incidents, descriptions, dialogue and opinions expressed are the products of the author's imagination and are not to be construed as real.

Published by

◀ köehlerbooks™

210 60th Street
Virginia Beach, VA 23451
212-574-7939
www.koehlerbooks.com

Guarded

ANGELA CORRELL

VIRGINIA BEACH
CAPE CHARLES

THE FARMS on MAY HOLLOW ROAD

Jake's Cottage

The Wilder Farm

wall cross

← To Somerville

Betty & Joe Gibson's

N

Cemetery Hill

Swimming hole

The Old Stone House

Beulah's House

Gibson's Creek Road

May Hollow Rd.

Chapter One

THE OLD STONE house looked solemn in the September afternoon. Even the birds were quiet, as if in respect for its suffering. Annie stared at charred stones, glassless windows, and a scorched chimney jutting into the blue sky, all evidence of the fiery injustice done only weeks ago.

Glass in the fanlight window over the front door was gone, a casualty of the water pressure that night as men guided hoses to the fire in the upstairs room. There was no time then to think of collateral damage. The goal was to save the house.

The door stood slightly ajar. Annie slipped inside, her running shoes crunching on pieces of glass, the stench of smoke still heavy in the air. They had left the house just as it was after the fire, not daring to move anything out until the insurance company had done its own investigation. Now it was disappointingly over, with no prize at the end of the waiting. The check her grandmother received was a fraction of the repair estimates.

"Well, that's that," her grandmother had said.

For all her love of heritage, home, and family, Annie knew Beulah was ultimately a frugal realist. To counter her own disappointment, Annie went for her daily run through the barn lot, following the farm lane to the stone house, as if the house might tell her how it could be saved.

The downstairs rooms had damaged plaster and warped wood floors from the water. She went carefully up the stairs and looked into the room where Stella, the renter, had left a candle burning. The fire had leaped up a curtain near the chimney, burning a hole in the roof.

Amidst the destruction, Annie closed her eyes and imagined the house as it was in her childhood, before her mother's illness, before the house went into the hands of whoever needed shelter and offered cash by the month.

Windows open, curtains dancing in the honeysuckle-scented breeze, and a vase of lavender on the bedside table. Clinking pans in the kitchen, the smell of savory cooking, a crackling fire in the great stone fireplace. In the summer, her mother tended to her small garden, or the patch of lavender just beyond the back door. In the winter, the rich brew of coffee warmed and comforted the adults sitting around the fire. Story after story fueled laughter, while Annie and her childhood friend Jake occupied themselves with a game or puzzle nearby.

The house offered no answers and only fueled her discouragement. Outside in the fresh air, she plucked a green walnut off a tree and breathed in the scent that whispered *summer is over*. If the house was not repaired soon, the fall rains and winter wind would invite even more destruction.

Annie set off on a run back to the house she shared with her grandmother, this time crossing the wooden bridge spanning Gibson's Creek and then onto the tree-lined road bordering the branch. Once she reached May Hollow Road, she relaxed as the rhythmic thumping on macadam cleared her head. After a half mile, she turned right into her grandmother's long and winding driveway just across from Betty and Joe Gibson's small bungalow. The white plank fence lined the curving driveway, newly repaired and painted, the result of her hard work this summer after losing her job as a flight attendant.

Betty Gibson's faded pink Cadillac was parked in the driveway. Annie slowed her pace, not in a hurry to see their nosy neighbor, especially today. Betty had taken to stopping by a couple times a week since Annie had moved home. Betty's smothering interest in her personal life had grown annoying. The screen door creaked when Annie opened it and the chatter of a female voice stopped as soon as she stepped into the mudroom just off the kitchen.

"Is that you, Annie?" Betty called. "I was telling Beulah the zinnias are beautiful. If the frost holds off, they'll be perfect for Scott and Mary Beth's wedding."

Annie steeled herself, remembered her customer service training as a flight attendant, and smiled before entering the kitchen.

Betty was sitting across from her grandmother at the farmhouse table, her curly blonde hair held back by two barrettes, her eyes wide with interest. They were both drinking iced tea, empty dessert plates in front of them.

"I surely hope the weather is good," Betty said. "Evelyn is about to work herself to death."

Annie busied herself with pouring a glass of iced sweet tea.

"But I really don't understand why Evelyn is goin' to all this trouble. I mean, Scott and Mary Beth are no kin to her," Betty said. "I know they met while taking Sunday dinner with you and Evelyn on your mission of mercy to the local single folks, but she's acting like they are her own children. Here's her own son, Jake, nearly about to marry Annie, and she won't have nothing left over to give."

"Jake and I aren't even engaged," Annie said. "Evelyn will have lots of time to recover from this one."

"You know Evelyn loves a party," Beulah said.

"It's a mighty big expense," Betty said, with a disapproving shake of her head. "How much you expect she's paying for all this?"

"Scott and Mary Beth have good jobs. They're paying for the wedding," Annie said. "Evelyn's hosting it."

"Well, I'm glad to hear it," Betty said, leaning back in her chair. "I did wonder."

Annie felt like she had thrown a mouse to the cat.

"Would you like a piece of Betty's derby pie?" Beulah said, pointing to the pie on the counter.

"Kentucky Nut Pie. You know all that trademark business," Betty corrected, with a dismissive hand wave.

"Sounds good," she said, her opinion of Betty softening. The pie plate was still warm, and Annie's mouth watered as the knife cut through the pecans and soft chocolate morsels.

"Speaking of you not being engaged," Betty said. "It's time enough with you and Jake, don't you think? Why, you two have known each other since birth. When we gonna hear weddin' bells around here?" Betty said, her head cocked to one side.

The chocolate chips were still warm and melted in Annie's mouth. She closed her eyes, enjoyed the sweetness, and ignored Betty's question.

"I showed Betty the estimates for fixing the old stone house," Beulah said.

"Higher than a cat's back," Betty said. "What do they think coming in with prices like that? Law have mercy! Joe and me were talking about it last night and he told me there's a fella over in Rutherford who has a business selling salvage from old houses. He pays good money to take an old house apart. They take out all the good wood, the trim work, and the fireplace. Why, Joe said there's no telling what he'll pay for the stone house with all those old limestones to be reused. Just think about it, Beulah. You get the money from the insurance, little as it is, and then you get paid again to haul off all the pieces and parts. A bulldozer can take care of the rest and there you've got a nice place to build a new house, if Annie and Jake ever get married."

"That so?" Beulah said.

"Don't you like the idea, Annie? Your age group is all so interested in recycling and such. Repurpose; isn't that what they call it today? I heard the word on *The Today Show*. You know, I used to love Matt Lauer; I could have sopped him up with a biscuit. I've gone off him lately. What do you think, Annie?"

"About Matt Lauer?"

"No, honey, about salvaging a house for recycling," Betty said.

"Houses should be used as houses whenever possible," Annie said, and glanced at her grandmother.

"Well, I better get supper started," Betty said, and pushed back her chair. "Joe comes in at four-thirty hungry as a bear, and if I don't have something on the table, he goes to paw at the refrigerator and mess up my organizations."

Beulah stood.

"Don't get up, I'll see myself out," Betty said. "See you tomorrow night, Beulah."

The screen door slammed behind her. Annie turned to her grandmother.

"How do you stand her? She's always digging for something."

Beulah laughed. "She doesn't bother me. You have to understand, Betty was the Tobacco Festival queen for three years in a row when she was young. In fact, when Hollywood came 'round years ago to film a Civil War feature, they picked her to be a stand-in. Life has never quite measured up since then, so she has to hunt down her own excitement."

"It's no excuse," Annie said. Though it did shed a glimmer of light on Betty's personality, not to mention her buxom features and straight white teeth. "She makes tearing down the house look pretty attractive, but will you give me some time to see if there's any other way we can save it?"

Annie searched her grandmother's face for softening, just like she had done when she was young. She saw nothing there to give her hope. In times past, Annie would have gone to her grandfather, knowing he would see her side, and then work on her grandmother in the way only he could. But Annie was an adult now, and there was no one else to do the work for her.

"I've been doing some thinking lately," Beulah said, her tone measured and calm. "You know I want to leave you this farm intact. It's one hundred forty-three acres of well-watered land, what with Gibson's Creek running through it and several springs. I've told you before it's paid off. I have savings as well, but I'm getting older, and we don't know what the future holds."

Her grandmother paused before going on. "The stone house gave me rental income and helped with my living expenses. Now, I've lost the income, and we're looking at many thousands of dollars to fix the house. I can't imagine how we could make up the difference between the insurance money and what they're saying it will take to fix it. I hate the thought of losing that old house. It's been in my family since the beginning. However, you need to understand that if I have to choose between saving the farm or the old house, I'll choose the farm."

"I understand," Annie nodded. "But Grandma, give me some time to try to find another solution. Please!"

Beulah looked at her like a teacher looked at an errant student.

"We have to do something before November. With the roof burned through in the one room upstairs, the fall rains will destroy what's left to save," she said.

"That's only two months from now," Annie said.

"The salvage company will need time to get everything out before the rains start if you don't find a solution. Let's see where you are in two weeks. Then we'll make a decision."

"But Grandma, two weeks . . ." Annie said.

"Two weeks," Beulah said firmly.

Chapter Two

BEULAH WENT UPSTAIRS to bed, and for a long time Annie sat in the den, curled up on the faded polyester couch, and fingered loose frays from a cushion. The room was comfortable, in a well-worn and familial way, but there were no luxuries. The bulky television, used only for the evening news and the occasional basketball game, was built long before technology streamlined screen size. The braided rug in front of the fireplace was the same rug from her childhood. The oversized lamps on the veneer end tables provided the only light in the room. It was a room from the 1970s. Now that she thought about it, she could not remember one time when her grandmother bought something new for the house—except for her grandfather's recliner.

Annie remembered the day when the recliner was delivered. After grunts and groans, two men finally wedged it into the living room. Once the paperwork was signed, her grandparents stood back and marveled at it. Each of them took a turn sitting in it, raising the leg rest, and leaning all the way back. Beulah gave her a stern look when she brought the leg rest down with a thump. "Be careful; it was expensive," her grandmother had admonished.

It was only a few months ago when her life in New York City crashed and she moved home to Kentucky. Living with her grandmother was like falling back in time. The dated furniture, the quiet of the country, the deferred maintenance, all seemed to smother her at first. Her grandmother's frugality agitated her, from the cheap coffee to the lack of connectivity to the outside world. There was no subscription to satellite or cable, and certainly no wireless Internet. But during the last several months at home, Annie had grown to appreciate her grandmother and her heritage. Nearly all of her grandparents' savings preserved the farm that had been in their family for generations.

She understood her grandmother's position on the old stone house. If only there were a solution to repair it and keep her grandmother happy on finances.

There was her own savings account, but despite Annie's best efforts to search out a job in Somerville, there was nothing to be had. She would eventually need to buy a car, something she had not needed in the city. But here in the country, there was no way to have a job without one. Jake had fixed up her grandfather's old farm truck, but it had already broken down on Annie twice. And if she had to look as far as Rutherford, or even Lexington for work, reliability was even more crucial.

She went to the kitchen and put on a kettle of water for tea. The insurance check and the restoration bids were still on the kitchen table. She laid the estimates on the harvest table side-by-side. There was the local contractor's bid, another from a company out of Rutherford, and a third from a large construction company out of Lexington. Each bid was within a few hundred dollars of each other, and all well beyond the insurance check.

Each bid included demolition, roof, plaster, woodwork, plumbing, electrical, replacement windows, glass repair, HVAC, and fixtures.

So much to be done, Annie thought. Yet tearing down the house would be a regrettable decision.

After a cup of tea and staring endlessly at the papers, she stood and turned off the lights before making her way up to her bedroom. As she eased into the soft cotton folds underneath the worn and frayed quilt, an idea came. Tom Childress' name was recently in the Somerville Record for attending a state historic preservation meeting. His daughter, Lindy, was Annie's new friend. She would call them tomorrow and see if they could help.

***

Lindy Childress sat behind her desk in the law office where she practiced with her father. Her blonde hair fell around her pixie face as she leaned forward and tapped the desk with a pencil.

"So you see," Annie said. "I thought since it is an old house, maybe there are some grants out there for historic sites at risk."

"We need to talk to Dad. I know there are tax credits at the federal and state level. There might be some grants available, but there'll be research to do, and lots of forms to complete. And far more than two weeks before you will know anything."

"I don't think Grandma wants to tear it down, but losing the income was discouraging, and then finding out the insurance payoff was so skimpy made it worse. She reduced the insurance after my grandfather died to cut expenses. After sitting there for two hundred years, she never dreamed about something happening," Annie said.

"Let me see if Dad can come in for a minute. He had some clients, but they may be gone now."

Annie admired Lindy's office. It was in an old Victorian building with tall ceilings, wood floors, and a gas log fireplace she imagined her friend enjoyed in cooler weather. A red and gold Persian rug covered most of the floor, giving the room a cozy feel.

"Hello, Annie." Tom Childress entered the room, glasses in his left hand and his right extended to her. Lindy followed and sat in her chair behind the desk while Tom folded his large frame in the chair next to her.

"How's Beulah?" he asked.

"Remarkable," Annie said. "You'd hardly know she had the knee operation just a few months ago."

"Good," he said. "And Jake is closing on his house this weekend, I believe?"

"Tomorrow. Then he will be home for good," she said, not even trying to contain the smile.

"I've enjoyed meeting with him. He's a fine young man, and our community will be better for having him back here. And Evelyn?"

"Thrilled to have Jake back."

"Good, good. Well, Lindy told me about your situation with the old stone house. It's a common problem in the preservation world. How do we save our treasures and make them economically viable? I have some tax credit information for you to share with Beulah. There are papers to fill out and certain criteria, of course, but I believe she could get some help there. Who have you talked to about doing the work?"

Annie listed the contractors and the bid amounts.

"Uh huh," Tom said and then wrote down some notes on a legal pad. "How are you at research?" he asked, looking at her over his reading glasses.

"I don't know—I've never done any, other than college papers."

"That house is rumored to have an interesting history, although I don't think anybody has ever dug into it."

"Really?"

"Oral history says it is the first stone house built in Kentucky. If you could prove it, that could mean special historic status and might qualify for a grant from a national organization." Tom flipped over a sheet on the legal pad and continued writing.

"I'm listing several organizations here you should look into for grants. I'm also writing down the name of an elderly lady who is in Richwood Manor; her mind is sharp as a tack. You should go see her about the house. She knows everything about the county and might give you some ideas on where to look for the historical information. I'm also writing down the name and number . . ." Tom reached for his phone and scrolled through his contacts. ". . . of a guy who is the best at restorations. He's also very reasonable and has low overhead since he works for himself. His name's Jerry Baker. He's from Rockcastle County, a true artist who loves his work. I think he will give you the best price. Maybe between that, whatever grants you might qualify for, and with the tax credits, you can convince Beulah to restore the place."

Tom smiled and tore off a couple of sheets and handed them to her.

"I'd be glad to work on it," Lindy said. "Especially the research; I love that side of things."

"Let me know what you end up applying for. I have a few contacts at the national level. I'd be glad to make some phone calls if it would help." Tom stood and looked at Lindy before leaving the room. "Still on for three o'clock?"

Lindy nodded. "We're just going to lunch and I'll be back in time to prepare."

"I can't thank you enough," Annie said.

"If you can manage to save the old stone house, I'll be thanking you," he said.

***

Just two blocks down the street, a red and white striped awning marked the entrance to Bill's Diner. She pushed open the plate glass and metal door, which jingled the bell above. Bill was in the back at the grill and threw up a spatula in greeting.

They slid into opposite vinyl-covered seat benches where checked curtains hung in the windows. Whenever she ate here, she always remembered her waitressing days at the diner during high school. Bill and Viola had given her a chance at her first job. It was hard to think of sweet Viola now in the throes of Alzheimer's and Bill needing to sell his restaurant so he could stay home and take care of her. She had even considered asking Bill for a job, but she knew he was fully staffed at the moment. And with his plans to sell, it would be short term.

"Has Jake heard anything on the diner?" Lindy asked.

"Not yet. A chef is interested in doing a farm-to-table concept, but he hasn't made a decision yet."

"I hope it works out. It'd be a sad loss to the town if it shuts down."

"Tea?" the waitress asked.

They both nodded. "Need a minute to order?"

"I'm ready. I'll take the burger," Lindy said.

"Same for me," Annie said.

The waitress gathered the menus and left.

"So, Jake's back for good after this weekend?" Lindy asked.

Annie nodded. "Now we finally get to see what it's like to

be around each other every day. He's been back and forth to Cincinnati so much getting his house ready to sell and moving."

"I'm so happy for you both," Lindy said, and smiled. The diner doorbell jingled behind Annie and she saw Lindy's smile freeze. She turned in her seat. In the doorway stood a man with skin tanned to a golden brown under a faded T-shirt stretched across his muscled chest and shoulders. Annie saw his long auburn hair was pulled back into a twist as the guy turned to shut the door. Ragged shorts and worn sandals: *a Goodwill Adonis*, she thought.

Annie turned back to Lindy and saw the frozen smile had thawed to wide eyes and mouth forming the word *What?*

"What's wrong?" Annie asked.

"That's Rob. My ex-boyfriend."

"Are you okay?"

"I thought he was in New Zealand. Or at least he was, the last I heard," Lindy said.

Smiling, Rob spotted Lindy and glided over to the booth.

"Hey, Lin," he said, sliding into the booth next to Lindy in one catlike motion, then leaned in to give her a gentle kiss on the cheek. He turned to Annie.

"Rob McElroy." Annie took the extended hand and noticed callouses and a strong handshake.

He looked back at Lindy, who had yet to say a word to him, the longest stretch of silence she had ever witnessed from her friend.

"I stopped by your office and they sent me here," he said.

"I thought you were in New Zealand?" Lindy said.

"I was, but I'm done and headed to El Cap. Got a little guiding job there for a while. Are you busy later? I thought we could hang out when you get off work."

"That would be great," she said, smiling now.

"Brilliant. I'll pick you up. Maybe a little dinner in Lex?" he said, easing out of the booth. "Nice to meet you," he said to Annie, and then was gone.

"He's your ex?" she said. "He didn't act like an ex."

"He's my weakness," Lindy said. Her face glowed.

"Where or what is El Cap?" she asked, just as the waitress brought their plates.

"Rob's a rock climber. El Capitan is a vertical rock formation in Yosemite National Park. He's well known in that group. Climbing Magazine did a feature on him once."

"That's his job?"

"Sort of. Sometimes he gets guiding jobs and sometimes he gets sponsors to do a certain climb for events. It's a simple lifestyle with lots of travel and adventure."

"Which is why you are broken up."

"I don't hear from him for months and then he just shows up. This is even stranger because I didn't think he would come back until spring."

With a generous dollop of mustard on her burger she took a bite. *Ah, perfect.* "So he shows up and you hang out."

She could see color rising in Lindy's face. "Well, sort of," she said. "It's complicated."

***

The back door of Evelyn Wilder's brick Italianate was usually unlocked during the day, like many other houses on May Hollow Road. She called a hello and followed the responding voice of Jake's mother into the kitchen where the scent of cinnamon hung heavy in the air. Evelyn, always elegant even in blue jeans and polo, twisted dough into buns at the kitchen counter. She turned and smiled.

"Annie, you came at just the right time."

"Yum, Cinnamon rolls," she said.

Evelyn laughed. "If you stick around for another thirty minutes, we can enjoy one of these on the back porch with some coffee. The sun should just be going down about then."

"Sounds good. Sure you don't mind if I use your computer?"

"Of course not. I told you, anytime. I have some coffee brewing if you'd like a cup while you work."

The steaming mug was in her hand when she sat down in the small maid's room just off the kitchen. While she waited for the computer to boot, she looked at Evelyn's menagerie of photographs on the desk. One in particular caught her eye. It was of Annie and Jake, leaning against a white plank fence next to her grandmother's house. The picture was taken when she had just arrived home after losing her job and Jake had just come home to sort out his future and choose between banking and farming. Annie had freshly broken up with her old boyfriend Stuart and Jake was dating Camille.

Camille, the daughter of Jake's Cincinnati friend and mentor, was Jake's intended until he brought her to the farm for a visit. Annie was grateful for the jealousy that had reared in her own heart, catching her off-guard, and making her realize Jake was much more than just a childhood friend. As bad as it was at the time, her feelings had forced a confrontation with Jake that led to his breaking off with Camille and their eventual honesty with each other.

When the computer was ready, Annie typed the names of the organizations Tom had given her into the search engine. When she found something interesting, she printed it out. One site led to another, and she lost herself in the search until Evelyn called to her from the kitchen. "Rolls are ready."

"Coming," she said, pulling together all the printed papers and putting them in her notebook.

Evelyn had served each of them a steaming roll with drizzled icing on top.

"I'll bring these if you don't mind to grab a couple of afghans off the couch and bring them outside," Evelyn said. "It gets a little chilly now when the sun goes down."

Annie fetched the colorful hand-knitted afghans from the living room couch and followed Evelyn out to the back porch.

"I may need to come back. So many things need to be printed out," she said. "I'll bring a ream of paper next time."

Annie tore off a piece of the sweet bread and popped it in her mouth. *Delicious.*

"Anytime; and don't worry about the paper. I hardly print anything off—maybe a recipe or two once in a blue moon. What are you working on?"

"Historic preservation grants for the old stone house. Did Grandma tell you about the dismal insurance check?" The two widows talked every evening on the phone and Annie was sure Evelyn was informed.

"Oh yes, disappointing. Have you talked with Tom Childress? He's awfully good at anything involving history."

"As a matter of fact, I talked with him today. He suggested I go see a lady in Richwood Manor who knows a lot about local history. And he gave me some organizations to contact. I don't know if she told you, but Betty Gibson is pushing a salvage company that will pay for the architectural pieces," Annie said, rolling her eyes. "I know Betty means well, but sometimes I wish she would stick to her own business."

Evelyn laughed. "There's a reason we are told to 'love your neighbor.'"

Annie sighed. "I only have a couple of weeks to come up with some sort of plan. I understand where Grandma is coming from, but it's not much time."

"Don't worry. If you can meet her halfway, I am willing to bet she will do what she can." Evelyn took a sip of coffee. "Any luck finding a job?"

"None. My friend Janice is coming to visit the first week of October, so at this point I might wait to expand my search to Rutherford and Lexington until after she leaves."

"Tell me about her," Evelyn said.

"Janice is like the sister I never had, yet we're so different. She's 100 percent New Yorker, and a full-blooded Italian on top of it. My first day on the job out of training, I was assigned to work a flight with her, and I was so nervous I spilled coffee on a passenger. The man yelled at me and complained to the crew chief. I cried in the galley, and then Janice yelled at me for crying."

Annie pulled the afghan tighter around her.

"I guess she felt bad later and she asked me to come home with her for dinner. After being in New York for a few months and not knowing anybody, it was so nice to be with a family. After dinner, she apologized, but she told me I needed to toughen up if I was going to survive the city." Annie smiled at the memory. "Janice was right, and I did toughen up. We've been best friends ever since."

"Those kind acts when you are vulnerable mean so much," Evelyn said. "Beulah took me under her wing when I was a young bride and new to the farm. I remember that first summer I had a pile of green beans on the table and a canner on the stove and no idea what to do in between. Beulah stopped by to check on me, and when she saw the mess I had she took over and helped me with my first batch of green beans. My mother taught me all about etiquette and how to set a table, but we didn't know anything about farm life."

"Janice wants to experience nature," Annie said. "Her mother-in-law is living with her so it's been a little stressful lately. She mentioned learning to can. What's in season now?"

"There are persimmon trees around the graveyard. We have some pawpaws in the back of our farm. Both ripen about then so you could make jam," Evelyn said. "Are her kids coming?"

"No, but it's why she's free. Her sister invited them to spend the week with her because they have a short break at school."

Annie held the coffee mug in both hands and breathed in the rich aroma, enjoying the comfortable silence between them. "How's the wedding coming along?" she asked.

"Mary Beth was trying to keep it simple since it's a second wedding for her. But, it's Scott's first and he has a big family in Alabama, so the guest list is already up to a hundred. The church will have a reception for them after they return from the honeymoon, which smoothed over a few ruffled feathers with not inviting all the church members out here for the wedding and reception."

"I told Jake I would help him organize his house for the wedding guests from Alabama," Annie said.

"Thank goodness. I was worried about him ever getting those boxes put away before the wedding. For all his good qualities, he can live in a barn stall and feel like he's staying at the Ritz." Evelyn laughed. "He's just like Charlie. Could care less about tracking in mud or keeping things neat. I have to confess, I was somewhat relieved when he decided to stay in the servant's cottage."

Annie smiled, thinking about the difference in Jake and her old boyfriend Stuart, the compulsive neat freak.

"It's getting late, and I want to digest all this grant information so I better go home." Annie stood and gathered up the dirty dishes.

"Annie, what do you think about a dinner party next weekend to celebrate Jake's official return to Somerville? I was thinking around twelve people. Scott, Mary Beth, Woody, Lindy, Betty and Joe, Tom Childress—I'll see if he wants to bring a date—and the four of us."

"I'll be glad to help," Annie said.

"I think I can manage it. Saturday night?" Evelyn asked.

"Looking forward to it," Annie said, and walked out the back door.

Chapter Three

THE NEXT MORNING, Annie found her grandmother in the kitchen, bent over the oven. Beulah wore a cotton work dress with a faded blue apron tied around the waist and her "sensible shoes," as she called the particular brand of flats.

"Grandma, do you know a lady named Vesta Givens?"

"Sure do," Beulah said, standing and turning to face her.

"Tom Childress suggested I see her. He said she knows about history in the area, particularly related to the old stone house."

Beulah rolled her sleeves up past her elbow and began working dough for a pie crust. "Vesta's bound to be in her nineties now. Her people were from just over the hill behind the May Family Cemetery."

"She's in the assisted-living section of Richwood Manor. I think I'll drive over there this morning, unless you need me for something. Later, I'm meeting another guy who might be able to work on the stone house for less than the other bids. Tom recommended him."

"Give Vesta my regards," Beulah said.

***

Richwood Manor was a red brick building that sat atop a leveled hill with a smattering of young trees. It was on the highway to Rutherford, just beyond the Somerville city limits. Annie imagined the planners selected the site for easy access to both communities since no such place existed in Rutherford.

There were two wings of Richwood Manor: one side was a nursing home facility for residents who needed more care; the other was for assisted living for those desiring more independence.

When she inquired about Vesta, the silver-haired woman at the reception desk looked at her watch. "This time of day, she is likely in the common room."

"Thank you," Annie said and headed in the direction she pointed. If she were honest with herself, a sense of dread accompanied the assignment. In her few experiences, nursing homes were filled with the heavy smell of urine, the sad sight of residents in various states of decline, and the lack of adequate staff.

Richwood, or at least the assisted-living side, seemed cheery and clean. Skylights invited natural light and the interior colors were warm instead of the cool blues and greens so long associated with institutions. It smelled fresh, as if the windows and doors were open, allowing the autumn breeze to cleanse the hard smells of aging.

In the common room, residents sat on couches and chairs, some watching television, some playing cards, and some reading magazines. A young woman shelved books on a far wall and Annie approached her.

"Excuse me," she said. "I'm looking for Vesta Givens."

"She's right there," the worker pointed to the living area, but there were nearly ten ladies sitting around.

"Which one is she?"

"Well, she's the only one reading Tolstoy. And, she's the only black lady in the room right now." The girl smiled at Annie.

"Tolstoy?" she said.

The girl nodded and raised her eyebrows.

She made her way over to the woman who sat with her back straight, despite the confines of the wheelchair. "Mrs. Givens?"

Bright almond eyes looked back at her through crystal clean glasses.

"I never married, so it's still Miss Givens." She shut the book and placed it in her lap.

"*Anna Karenina* . . . Tragic story," Annie said, and pointed to the book.

"Yes. I keep reading it, hoping she will not do it. But she always does."

"I'm Annie Taylor."

"Taylor," Miss Givens said, and closed her eyes. "Ah, yes. We had a state legislator by that name. He got into a bit of trouble as I recall."

"My father's uncle, but please don't hold it against me."

After ten years in New York City, Annie had nearly forgotten how people in small towns used last names to connect. And the Taylor name wasn't associated with good things in Somerville.

Miss Givens smiled. "I don't make judgments. It does give us perspective to see the whole. Are you here to see me? Or are you interested in talking about the Russians? I would love to have someone with whom I could discuss literature."

Annie smiled. "I have read *The Brothers Karamazov*, but that and *Anna Karenina* are the extent of my knowledge."

"It's a lovely start," she said. "However, I think you are here on another matter?"

"Tom Childress gave me your name," she said.

Miss Givens smiled. "A good man. Very bright. He was one of our best students."

"You're a teacher?"

"I was the Somerville High School librarian. After integration, of course. Before, I was the librarian at the Bonaparte School."

"Tom says you are the most knowledgeable person about history in the area."

"Maybe the most knowledgeable still alive," Miss Givens laughed, a high tinkling sound like delicate crystal clinking together. "There were others, but they're all in the town cemetery now."

"I'm interested in learning anything you might know about the old stone house, the one on Gibson's Creek Road. We had a fire a few weeks back, and it badly damaged an upstairs room. The water used to put out the fire did even more damage. If we know the history, it might help us save it."

"You're a May?"

"Yes. My grandmother is Beulah Campbell. She was a May."

"I know it well. What do you want to know?"

"I've heard it might be the first stone house built in Kentucky. If we can prove it with historical documents, a grant is possible," Annie said. "I was hoping you could give me direction."

Miss Givens sighed. "Call me Vesta. You know, when someone offers you his or her first name it's a gift. These days we're all so informal, we use someone's first name without allowing them to offer it to us."

"And you can call me Annie." She liked this woman even more.

"I've always heard it was the first stone house in Kentucky. Oral tradition is not likely to be taken well on a grant application. There are the Draper papers, although I don't remember seeing much related to a house, unless it was in a deposition, so I don't think I would spend time there. Let me think," Vesta said, tapping her finger on the arm of the wheelchair.

Annie tried to envision Vesta behind a reference desk in a library or teaching a class.

"There are diaries of early pioneers. Oh, that's it," she looked at Annie, her eyes shining. "Joseph Crouch wrote extensive letters back home to his family in the East. Through those he chronicled the early frontier in this area. That's where we should start."

"Where are the letters?" Annie asked.

"The Kentucky History Center, not far from the state capital building in Frankfort. You'll be looking at copies of course, probably on microfilm."

Annie scribbled the name down.

"If you come up empty handed, let me know and we'll try another route," Vesta said, looking at her over the glasses.

"Thank you," Annie said, grasping Vesta's arm. "This helps so much."

"Come back and let me know how it's going."

Annie stood. "You can count on it."

***

Plunking over the plank bridge crossing Gibson's Creek, Annie parked her grandfather's old farm truck under the shade tree next to the old stone house. Every time she saw the house now, Annie was surprised by its condition. *It's like what Vesta thought reading Anna Karenina,* she thought. *The ending always turns out the same, and the reader always hopes for something different.*

In the same way, she almost expected to see the old house as it was before the fire.

When Annie got out of the truck, a cool breeze blew, hinting at cooler weather to come, and a reminder that time to save the house was running short.

While she waited on Jerry Baker to arrive, Annie walked around behind the house and saw where Jake and Joe Gibson had put up a new fence to keep the cows from tromping into the creek from the adjoining pasture. Jake was intent on cleaning up the creek so the water quality would improve.

Sunlight filtered through the leaves on the bank of Gibson's Creek, and as she stood there enjoying the peaceful moment, Annie remembered when she and Jake were children. They were playing in the creek, catching tadpoles and skipping rocks, when a summer storm blew up. Her mother called from the back door, but they were just about to catch the biggest tadpole they had seen all day. When her mother called again, this time using her whole name, Annie May Taylor, and even Jake's whole name, Jacob Willis Wilder, Jake grabbed her by the hand and pulled her up the bank. They ran into the yard, laughing, until they reached the threshold of the old stone house. Lightning bolted from the sky and struck a tree on the creek bank, where they had been only seconds before, splitting it in two. Jake's blue eyes were wide, and he had stopped laughing. Annie had swallowed hard. Her mother was angry.

"Annie May, when I call you to come in, I mean right now!" Dark shadows appeared heavy under her mother's intense and angry eyes. Her frail hands reached for Annie's shoulders and shook them before she pulled her into the hallway.

"I'm sorry, Mama. We were just playin'."

"Sorry, Mrs. Taylor," Jake added.

It was unlike her mother to be so harsh. Her mother was frightened and now, as an adult looking back, she knew the fear had run much deeper than an eleven-year-old could comprehend.

"You two just sit quiet in the living room until this is over," she said, a trembling finger suspended in mid-air. Annie and Jake had gone to the living room, meek as lambs, and talked quietly until the storm passed. It was the last summer in the old stone house, the summer before her mother's diagnosis.

***

The slam of a car door jarred her from the past and she turned to see a shiny white truck. A sixty-something-year-old man with pressed pants and a starched shirt smiled a greeting. Jerry Baker, she assumed, but she had pictured him in blue jeans, cotton work shirt and redwings. Instead, he looked like a banker. She smiled and extended her hand.

"Thanks for coming."

"Nice to meet you," Jerry said, in a twang that hinted of a mountain heritage. "Let's see what you got here," he said, and looked up at the damaged house. "I'll just be taking some notes while I look around." He pulled a clipboard with a legal pad attached out of the cab of his truck.

Jerry stepped into the suffocating stench of smoke and ashes. They walked through the two downstairs rooms original to the house, and then the kitchen and bath, which had been added later. Upstairs, they first looked at the room untouched by the fire and then made their way to the damaged room. Charred ceiling beams went to nearly nothing near the chimney. Annie imagined the flame from the candle in the window touching the curtains and setting them ablaze. Walls were blackened and the wood floor was bowed in places from the water damage.

"Pretty bad, huh?" she said. Jerry nodded and wrote notes on the note pad. When he finished, he looked up and smiled.

"Why don't we go outside where it smells a little better?"

They were quickly refreshed by the clear blue skies and crisp air. Jerry lowered the tailgate on his truck and laid his clipboard on the makeshift desk.

"We'll need to remove sheetrock and plaster. The insulation needs to come out to expose the structure and make sure everything is okay underneath. We need access to everything in order to kill the smoky smell. Then we'll need to check the stones and make sure the fire didn't loosen the mortar joints," he said. "I can do the carpentry and stonework. I'll need to hire out an electrician and a plumber. What about the kitchen and bath? Usually folks want to upgrade at a time like this."

"Not at this point. We're trying to keep the bid as low as possible," she said.

"I like to use materials from the local lumber supply. You might save a bit from the big box companies, but you'll use it up in running back and forth."

"We agree with that. I was wondering if you could bid the job in parts with the first one focusing on the roof and windows, whatever we need to do to keep it sound and then outline what we need to make it livable."

"Sure. We'll bid what it takes to get it in the dry. The more specialized work like plumbing, electrical can go in phase two. We can add carpentry and all the finish work in the third section. You decide how much you want to do," he said.

After Jerry gave a promise to mail his bid in a few days, he got in his truck and drove away. She watched him go and then went back inside the house to examine the downstairs kitchen and bath. Annie had not thought of upgrading. Now she saw the Formica countertops were in bad condition. The linoleum on the kitchen and bathroom floors buckled. All the appliances needed to be replaced. Her spirits sank.

Another car door slammed and she went to the front window. A man was standing next to a gray Tahoe and staring up at the house.

"Hello, can I help you?" she said, stepping out of the front door.

The man had a wide mouth and a hawk-like face with the largest teeth she had ever seen.

"Randy Wilson," he said, extending his hand. "Fine Architectural Salvage. Are you the owner?"

"Annie Taylor," she said, feeling herself bristle. "My grandmother is the owner."

"I believe her neighbor, Betty Gibson, called and asked me to come over and take a look at the house and give an estimate of what I could buy from you good folks. Mind?" He pointed toward the door.

Annie nodded and followed him inside, feeling the anger rise up like hot lava. *Betty Gibson.*

"Ah, real nice mantle. I could place that tomorrow," Randy said, moving his hand along the wood. "And these poplar floors, look how wide the boards are; you don't get that these days," he said, and squatted down to examine the wood. A childish urge to kick the seat of his khaki trousers washed over her.

"I'll wait outside for you," she said, and left before she acted on the desire.

Next to her grandfather's old truck, she rubbed her temples, closed her eyes, and leaned against the metal for support. The house meant nothing to him. It was all just wood, fine carpentry, and dollar signs.

In a few minutes Randy Wilson came out the front door grinning like an old rat in a corncrib.

"Real nice. I'll write up the estimate. What's the address?" he said, and pulled out his note pad.

Annie hesitated and then gave him Evelyn's address. It would only delay things a day or two if she was lucky, but she needed every single minute.

Chapter Four

BEULAH REACHED FOR the cane leaning against the back door. It was a smooth piece of oak with rubber on the bottom and a gently curved top making it easy to hold. It had helped her navigate the uneven ground many a time, but it also made her feel old. She set aside her pride to avoid a fall. Truth was, she needed it, and probably would for another few weeks.

Carefully, she used the stepping-stones to the chicken house and then she took a grass path to the vegetable garden just beyond. Tomatoes were still coming, and she made a point to get every last one until frost. They were smaller this time of year, but they were good and ripe. She dropped seven in the pocket of her apron and then eased down in the metal chair next to the garden and surveyed the kale, turnip and collard greens planted just a few weeks ago.

The September growth and the cool weather greens were the last gasp for the garden until it was put to sleep for winter. Kentucky was a sight to behold in autumn with all the red and yellow maples dotting the hills, hollows, and knobs. Beulah couldn't help but feel a little wistful for the warm weather and the green and growing plants. She dreaded losing the garden to cold. It was like saying goodbye to an old friend and wondering if it might be for the last time.

The garden was a place of restoration for her. And it must have been for the Lord as well, since he was always going to the garden to pray. As peaceful as it was, she couldn't seem to shake the unease settling around her, like the cold dread of some unpleasant task.

Her relationship with her granddaughter had been going fine the last few weeks as they were getting along better than ever. But now the old stone house had caused a rift between them. *It's understandable why Annie latched onto the house,* Beula mused, as she shifted her hip to a more comfortable spot in the seat. Her grandchild was abandoned by her father when she was only a baby, him coming in and out of her life when it suited his needs. Annie was only twelve when her mother, and Beulah's only daughter, Jo Anne, died. Just a couple of years ago, there was the loss of Fred who had doted on her and had connected with her in a way Beulah had never been able to understand. This all led up to this past fateful summer when her granddaughter came home after losing her job in New York City where she had lived for ten years. It was no wonder she needed to hold onto something solid that represented happier times.

Beulah thought about her own emotional attachment to the place, it being in her family all the way back to pioneer days when her ancestors had laid the stones. It was where she grew up with her mother, her father, and her older brother, Ephraim. It was on the stone step outside the front door where she hugged her brother and said goodbye when he left for the Army. Little did she know it would be the last time she would see him on this earth. There were happier memories, too, like meeting Fred and his brother when they came around after the war to help Daddy with the tobacco crop.

How else am I to approach the dilemma? She couldn't use her savings on it when there was no telling what the future held. It had taken Fred and her a lifetime to save money. No, whenever God decided her time on earth was done, her granddaughter would need every penny to keep the farm going if anything was left.

The thump of tires hitting potholes caused her to look up in time to see Fred's old farm truck spew gravel before sliding to a stop. The door slammed and then there was Annie, barreling toward the house, looking fit to be tied.

"Out here," Beulah called.

Annie turned to her voice, her thick, dark ponytail flying in the breeze behind her change of direction. She almost heard Fred's voice saying, "Little thoroughbred filly." It had been his nickname for their grandchild and it fitted her both in looks and in demeanor. Long legs and fast movements, she was a beauty but awfully high strung, like the racehorses.

"Grandma, do you know what that woman did?" she stopped several feet in front of her with one finger raised in the air.

"What woman?"

"Betty Gibson," Annie spit the name out like it was tobacco juice.

"Did Mr. Wilson catch you at the house?" she said.

"You knew about it? But you gave me two weeks!"

"You still have the two weeks. Betty suggested he come on over and look at the house so we would at least have an estimate of its value. I thought it was a good idea."

"He was like an old buzzard, pecking around and drooling over the mantles and the floors. Betty Gibson needs to mind her own business."

"Now Annie," Beulah heard the hardness in her voice, but it had gone far enough. "I need facts in order to make this decision, and I can't go on what we *might* get from the salvage company. I need to know. Betty Gibson was being nothing but neighborly. I'll grant you her neighborliness sometimes goes too far."

Annie's shoulders slumped and she looked on the verge of tears.

"Grandma, do you really want the house picked apart and torn down? Once it happens, we can never get it back."

"You know I don't."

Annie raised her chin, calm now, the flashing heat of anger over.

"If I find a promising solution before the two weeks, even if it's not a guarantee, will you consider another option?"

"I'm trying to be reasonable."

Annie nodded and set her jaw in that determined way Beulah knew well, and started toward the house.

"Would you take these tomatoes for me?" Beulah said. Annie came back and took the tomatoes and the apron as well. Beulah watched her walk away, ponytail swaying, the screen door slamming behind her. If Fred were here now, he would chuckle into his pipe at Annie's fiery spirit. Beulah and Annie were too much alike, Fred had always said. If that were true, shouldn't they understand each other?

It wasn't long before the sound of crunching gravel broke her reverie. Gently, Beulah pushed herself up from the metal chair and waited for the faded pink Cadillac to park.

***

A trip to the Country Diner was their Saturday night tradition for going on fifteen years, starting back when there were six of them instead of four. It was a time of fellowship with Beulah's across-the-road neighbors and her best friend and next-door neighbor, Evelyn Wilder.

Beulah knew to wait for Joe as he turned around in the gravel drive so they could pull straight out when she got in the car. Joe Gibson was one of those drivers who always backed into parking spaces, so he could be ready to go. He said it was due to his service on the rescue squad years ago. Possibly, she observed, people were either backers or pullers, just like there were savers or spenders.

Joe hopped out and opened the door for Beulah, his wiry frame as agile today as it had been thirty years ago, even though he and Betty were just a decade behind her in age. *Being thin has such advantages,* Beulah thought. It seemed like everything worked a little better when there wasn't such weight to drag around. Beulah eased her own size sixteen carefully into the seat, always wary of the twisting to her knee with a sudden move.

"Beulah, did you get that blouse at Penny's? I declare they have the best end-of-summer buys going on right now." Betty's small eyes peered out from the fullness of her round face, admiring her shirt like it was a coconut cream pie.

"I got it last year," Beulah said. "I haven't bought a thing lately and I reckon it's all picked over now."

"I've been shopping for fabric and I wish it would go on sale. I was hoping to find something nice to decorate the tables for the wedding reception," Evelyn said.

"Terrible big job you've got." Betty said, clucking her teeth and craning her neck to make eye contact from the front seat.

Evelyn sighed, "I can't get Mary Beth to make any decisions. She tells me whatever I decide will be fine, but it's her wedding for goodness' sakes. Scott's the same way. They should go off to Gatlinburg and be done with it, but his family is all coming up from Alabama and they want the reception so everyone can meet."

"Surely you're not hosting a wedding *and* a houseful of company," Betty said.

"It's just his parents, his brother, and an aunt and her husband," Evelyn said. "It'll be fine."

"Well, I hope Scott and Mary Beth appreciate what all you're doing," Betty said, arching her left eyebrow at Evelyn before turning to face forward.

Beulah shivered at the thought of planning a party and entertaining a crowd to boot, but she and Evelyn were cut from different cloths when it came to entertaining.

Evelyn smiled and thought before she answered.

"Honestly, I love it. With Jake and Suzanne being gone for the last several years, I haven't had the opportunity to throw many parties for them. Of course, after Charlie died, I hadn't really been in a party mood."

"Well, it's a mighty good thing you do love it since you've bit off a chunk of hard work," Betty said.

Joe sat silently and drove, probably not even listening to the chatter. After being married to Betty all these years, and with her overabundance of words, he was likely thinking about cows, tractor engines, or crops—maybe even how to persuade Betty to sell the pink Cadillac. Anything but a wedding.

The road to the Country Diner wound this way and that, up and down hills, until they finally arrived at the red metal building on the side of the road in Chicken Bristle. It was just after five in the evening, but the parking lot was filling up. Saturday night was all you can eat catfish, seasoned and fried, freshly reeled in from Lake Cumberland by the owner's son.

The air inside the diner had vastly improved three years ago when smoking was banished to the deck out back. Beulah was still surprised to see that day come to rural Kentucky, where most everyone she knew had made their living off tobacco. But times had changed and folks were aware of the harm it could cause. She did wonder if the buyout hadn't come around, which put most tobacco farmers out of business, might there still be smoking allowed inside?

Annie had gone with them one night to the diner. She had complained about the fluorescent lights, saying it needed more atmosphere, and the food was too greasy. It was all the atmosphere a body needed, but not the kind Annie liked. The food was a bit on the greasy side, but everybody knew a little grease made both man and machine function a bit better.

They greeted friends as they passed through the room to their usual table. Patsy, the waitress, stopped by the table and said, "Same as always?" When everyone nodded, she swished off for the sweet tea.

There was something very pleasant about a routine, she thought. No surprises, no disappointments, just pure comfort and familiarity. A few new faces appeared now and then, but overall it was the same crowd nearly every Saturday night.

Betty leaned in. "Well, now we've got one wedding underway, any news on Annie and Jake?" The question was addressed to both Beulah and Evelyn, her bright eyes darting back and forth between the two of them. When she looked at Evelyn to answer, her friend simply nodded the question back in her lap.

"It's only been a few weeks," she said. "And Jake's gone back and forth to Cincinnati moving and getting his house ready to sell. I'm not sure they've quite settled in yet." Betty looked at Evelyn.

"I agree—it's too early. Even though they grew up together, there's ten years to catch up on while Annie was in New York and he was living in Atlanta and then Cincinnati."

"Seems time enough to me," Betty said. The waitress brought their teas and small bowls of finely chopped coleslaw.

"I'm sure she misses her life in New York City with all that fast pace and fast talk," Betty said, as if she had some inside knowledge of Annie's feelings.

"She does, but she's awful happy here," Beulah said.

"Well, she hasn't landed a job yet, and I just wonder if she might be tempted to go back and work for the airline," Betty said, looking from her to Evelyn as if they were the ones responsible for her granddaughter not getting a job.

"It's not for lack of trying," Beulah said. "After her friend Janice comes for a visit in October, she said she would start looking in Rutherford, or maybe even Lexington."

"One of her old roommates?" Betty asked.

"No, Janice is her married friend," Evelyn answered, rescuing her from the hot seat. "Annie told me all about her. She's Italian American," Evelyn said.

Joe reached for the saltshaker and made his only comment, surprising Beulah he was actually listening. "I had a good friend who was Italian when I was in Vietnam. He was from New Jersey and could tell stories that would make you cry laughing so hard. I liked him real well."

"You must have picked up some of your tales there," Evelyn teased.

"He give me some good ones," Joe said.

"What about the old stone house?" Betty asked. "Did Randy come over and do the estimate? Sounds like good money to me. What about that Stella woman who burned it in the first place? She 'ort to give you some money for the trouble of it all," Betty said.

Beulah finished her slaw and put her fork down.

"She doesn't have any money. It's why she came running down here from Chicago. Jake's been helping her get connected with a money counselor up in Chicago. She's working on getting herself straightened out," she said.

"Talked to Woody the other day," Joe said. "He was headed up to Chicago looking to buy a horse."

Betty cut her eyes at Joe.

"Joe Gibson, you didn't tell me! Why, you know Woody only has one reason to go up to Chicago. The sparks flew when he and Stella met after all that fire and missing persons ordeal. He hasn't gone up there to buy no horse. Who would leave Kentucky to buy a horse when we've got all the horses right here?"

Beulah saw Joe grinning into his iced tea, pleased with

himself for holding out information Betty would have wanted to share herself. She brought her napkin up to her own mouth and acted as if she were trying to wipe something off so she could hide her grin while Betty's full lips pouted.

"Wouldn't it be nice? Woody's been a bachelor so long, I thought he never would marry," Evelyn said. "Maybe there's something in the water."

"If there is, I'm not drinking out of it," Beulah offered. "One man was enough for me."

The waitress brought the fried catfish platters with hush puppies and an ear of corn and a container of homemade tartar sauce.

"Me too," Betty said. "If somethin' ever happened to Joe, I mean. Some days, one man is too much," Betty said and then cut her eyes over at Joe again before allowing him a faint smile. Joe grinned back, like someone would do with a wayward child.

Beulah noticed Evelyn's silence after both she and Betty had chimed in on not marrying again. Evelyn stared at her plate, cutting up the catfish with the precision of a surgeon.

Surely catfish didn't require so much concentration.

Chapter Five

ANNIE STARED AT the papers spread out in front of her. Preservation grants were available from different organizations, most outside of Kentucky, but none would be awarded until after the first of the year, and some not until spring. Just as Lindy anticipated: far too late for her grandmother's timeline.

She leaned back and twisted and untwisted her hair as she thought. If the history center gave her a shred of indication on the house's age, anything to shed light on its history, it was well worth a trip to Frankfort. Her phone vibrated on the wooden table and Jake's name popped up on the screen.

"Are you awake?" Jake's deep voice both soothed and excited her.

"I've had enough coffee to keep me up all night. Where are you?"

"Walking through the barn lot. I didn't want the car to wake Beulah. Meet you out back."

Jake was home, sooner than expected. Annie jumped up and took a quick peek in the bathroom mirror, then dabbed on some powder and lip-gloss. She grabbed a sweater hanging on a peg in the back room before going out.

Once her eyes adjusted to the dark, she saw his shadow, silhouetted against the stock barn's security light, moving toward her.

A hug and a long kiss, and then he took her hand and led her around to the front porch.

"I missed you," he said. They sat on the old porch swing and she leaned into him.

"How did it go?" she asked.

"The closing went well. I ended up going out for an early dinner with the guys, and I couldn't see spending another night there on somebody's couch when I could come home and see you."

"Did you have a good time with your friends?"

"Yeah. They messed with me about leaving town for Green Acres and old MacDonald's farm. I actually think they were a little envious. One of my friends pulled me aside and asked if I needed any help on the farm," Jake laughed. "I told him it'd be a while before I can pay myself, much less him."

She squeezed his hand, enjoying the sound of his voice and the warmth of his body next to hers.

"Did Camille's dad come to the dinner?" she couldn't help but ask. He had been a mentor to Jake and wanted his youngest daughter to marry Jake. When the relationship broke up over the summer, her father was understandably disappointed. Jake's relationship with Camille's father seemed to be the real casualty, since Camille had apparently moved on to a New York real estate executive.

"No, but he sent a note wishing me the best. It's just as well." He reached over and pulled a strand of hair away from her face.

"I wonder ... What if we had not ended up here last summer?"

"I don't know. I guess it was meant to be," Jake said.

"Grandma says that all the time. I wonder about it. Are things meant to be *despite* human choice? Or, are they meant to be *because of* human choice?"

"Maybe it's both," Jake said. "I think entire theologies are formed around those questions."

"So when did you know you wanted to come back and live here?" she asked.

"When Dad died," Jake said, his voice just above a whisper.

The answer surprised Annie and she sat up straight and turned so she could face Jake. "Five years ago," she said.

"It's taken me a while," Jake said.

"Why then?"

"Dad wanted me to come back to the farm after college. I'd had enough of dairy farming and I liked finance, so I took the banking job in Atlanta. The Cincinnati promotion came along after that. Everything was going my way until Dad got sick. I took a leave from work to help on the farm since the doctors said it wouldn't be long. He was gone within a month," Jake said.

Annie remembered she was taking flights from New York to Dallas and Chicago at that time. Knowing what it was like to lose a parent, she had reached out to Jake and they talked two or three times during his dad's short illness. When her grandmother called with the news that Charlie Wilder had passed, she was sitting on the edge of a bed in an airport hotel in Dallas.

"After he died and I went back to Cincinnati; I was in a weird place. I felt guilty about not helping him more, not spending more time with him. It was like being haunted with all the things I should have done for him. There was no way to fix it and I hated myself for it. There was a girl I was dating at the time," Jake's voice trailed off. "I didn't treat her very well."

His blue eyes looked deep into hers, as if seeking her forgiveness for some past sin.

"I understand. Guilt mixed with grief can do terrible things to your mind," she said. They were silent for a few moments before she gently said, "Then?"

"Camille's dad helped me through it, meeting with me and encouraging me to take stock and decide where to go from there. Another guy from the bank lost his wife and went through something similar. Both of those guys helped me to see that you can't change the past, but you can change direction. That's when I realized I didn't like what I was doing, even though it paid well. My idea of success changed. After reading books on sustainable farming, I decided I could farm in a different way than Dad. Build on what he started and take it another direction."

Annie's back rested comfortably on Jake's chest and she thought about the couple of times she reached out to Jake after his father died. The long distance made her unable to hear what he was truly going through; when Jake said he was doing fine, she had believed him.

"What about you? When did you know you wanted to come home for good?" Jake asked her.

Annie smiled in the darkness.

"It was the day of the fight with Camille," she said. "My attraction to you was getting harder to push down and the way she acted about knowing what was best for you made me want to put Camille in her place. When the gate slammed, Nutmeg spooked, and she fell off that horse, I suddenly got scared she was really hurt. It was so childish," Annie laughed. "When I knew she was okay and she trounced off in her expensive boots, I felt victorious, as if I had defended my territory or something. There was more truth in that moment than I understood at the time. It was when I knew this place belonged to me and I belonged to it."

Annie felt Jake's arm pull her closer into his chest.

"It was a rough two-hour drive to Cincinnati for me after that, but I'm glad you had that moment. It's the day I broke it off with her."

"I thought the opposite—sure I had pushed you together for good. When you left with her, I just knew you were going back to put a ring on her finger."

"I needed perspective," Jake said. "When I saw Camille so uncomfortable in a place so familiar and comfortable for me, it made me pause, and when I did, the whole thing unraveled." Jake kissed her on top of the head.

Off in the far pond, the frogs croaked their evening lullaby. In only a few short weeks, they would be silent for the winter, making their melody tonight even more lonesome than usual.

"My perspective has certainly changed. Last spring I was pushing Grandma to sell the farm, and now I'm the one trying to persuade her to save the old stone house. It makes me sick to think of losing it."

Jake pushed her off his chest and turned her to face him.

"Look, I just sold my house and have cash in the bank, why don't I lend Beulah the money?"

She pulled back.

"No, she would never let you do that."

"Then I'll donate it," he said.

"She will *really* never let you do that," she laughed.

"Then I'll help work on it when the time comes . . . I'm not bad with a hammer."

"You're already so busy with the farm," Annie said.

"It's what I want to do for the one I love," he said, pulling her close again.

"What did you say?"

"I said, I love you," he whispered in her ear.

She wrapped her arms around him and said the words softly back to Jake, her lips close to his ear, and feeling the rough stubble of his cheek on her face. They held each other for a long time. Over his shoulder, the harvest moon hung full and bold in the night sky. The man on the moon was plain to see and she imagined for a moment she saw him wink.

***

The morning light filtered through the kitchen window. Annie studied a grant application while sipping her coffee.

"Booger is out by the back step, so be careful when you go out," Beulah said, coming into the living room with a broom in her hand. "I'd say it won't be long before he goes to hibernating."

"Do snakes hibernate? I thought only bears did that," Annie said, looking up from the pile of papers in front of her. "I could've swept the porch for you," she added.

"I need the exercise."

Beulah carried the broom to the closet where they kept cleaning supplies. "He goes off every winter and finds a hole somewhere. I don't know what it's called, but he won't come around again until spring. Ever since he showed up, I've hardly seen a mouse on the place. Booger does a much better job than the barn cats," Beulah said and scanned the room. "Now where did I leave my coffee?"

"Personally, I prefer cats," Annie said as she left the room. She found Beulah's coffee cup in the kitchen and refilled both of their mugs.

"How you coming along?" Beulah asked.

Annie sat back down at the table.

"Right now, I'm narrowing down the grants we might apply for. Then, I need to do all the research so I can complete applications. Tom said there are tax credits, which help. Anyway, I'm working on pulling all this together so we can talk about it once I have all the facts."

Beulah nodded, her expression stoic.

"Speaking of facts, I did get an estimate from the architectural salvage company," she said. "Funny thing is, it came to Evelyn's address but she brought it over to me."

"How much was it?"

"Nearly as much as the insurance check," Beulah said. "That makes a nice sum to bank for a rainy day."

***

Jake was bent over the engine of a tractor when she found him in his barn lot.

"Hey you," she said. He looked up and smiled when he saw her, then reached for a towel. "I was just thinking about you," he said, wiping the grease off his hands.

"What were you thinking?" she asked, leaning against the John Deer tractor.

"Kind of a loaded question."

"I'm listening," she said, and took a step closer.

"I want to help with the house," Jake said. "I could make a loan with low interest so she doesn't feel like I'm giving her anything. Let's talk to her and find out what she is comfortable with doing."

"It may be a moot point," Annie sighed. "Grandma got the architectural salvage estimate and it was nearly the same amount as the insurance company."

Annie pulled a folded paper from her jeans pocket.

"Is that it?" Jake pointed to the paper.

"This is Jerry's bid for the renovations," she said, and handed him the paper.

Jake took it and unfolded the sheet, scanned it and looked up.

"This is reasonable. The insurance money will put it in the dry and the rest can be done a little at a time."

"If I can convince Grandma. That darn Betty Gibson just made it a whole lot harder," she said, and stuffed the bid in her back pocket. "I thought you were taking up hay?"

; down. Hopefully tomorrow if I can get it running

holds off."

like we're both hoping for dry weather," she said.

***

Annie drove Beulah's Marquis an hour to Frankfort the following morning and found the stately Kentucky History Center in the middle of downtown. It was a relief to pull into a parking space rather than parallel park the "tank," as she called Beulah's car. She had hoped Lindy could come with her, but she was tied up with depositions. *A lawyer would be handy,* Annie thought, *since I'm building a case to present to Grandma—sole judge and jury.*

Inside, she was directed to a locker, where she was instructed to leave her satchel, purse and jacket.

"You should keep your wallet if you are planning to make copies," she was told by the attendant. With the key on a band around her wrist, she took her wallet and followed the attendant to another door. The attendant swiped a card, the door clicked, and she was granted access to a large carpeted room.

The high security made her especially curious about what she might find in the inner sanctum. There were anterooms with microreaders of one sort or another. Copy machines, large tables and chairs for studying documents, reference books, and map drawers. An information desk was in the center of the room, and she walked over to it.

"Hi, excuse me," she said. The pale-skinned young woman at the desk looked up and smiled.

"I'm looking for letters written by Joseph Crouch around the late 1700s."

"Do you have a particular year in mind? Unfortunately, the letters are not indexed by topic. They're in chronological order, so it helps a bit since they span more than twenty years. They're all on microfilm, let me show you how to find the rolls."

The young woman demonstrated how to find a microfilm number, and then a cabinet to find the actual film. Then there was how to load the film, move it around, and copy anything of interest. It took a few minutes of practice but soon Annie found a rhythm for the work. After thirty minutes, Annie realized she could not read everything. Instead, she simply made copies to take home for later.

After a short break when Annie ran out for a quick lunch, she was back in the darkened room, making copies of letter after letter until closing time.

With a stuffed satchel, she was surprised at how exhausted she felt driving home, despite the entire day sitting down in a dark room. Before going home, she wanted to make one more stop on the way.

***

This time, Vesta was in her room. The door was open, but she knocked and waited.

"Come in," a loud, clear voice answered.

Vesta was sitting in a chair, the Bible spread over her lap, illuminated by a floor lamp next to the chair. The old woman smiled and waved her hand to an empty chair.

"I hoped I would see you again," Vesta said.

"I promised I'd come back."

"People use words they don't mean. I'm glad you are not one of those people," Vesta said, looking at Annie over her reading glasses. "How can I help you?"

"I went to the History Center today and copied all of the letters. But there's so much more. I'd no idea how much information is stored there."

"Wonderful, isn't it?" she said. "Did you go into the stacks? To be surrounded by all those lovely old rare books is so peaceful."

Annie looked around Vesta's room where books lined tall and short bookshelves and some were even stacked on the floor.

"Most of my time was at the microfilm reader."

"May I see some of the copies?"

"Sure." Annie pulled a two-inch-thick stack of papers out of her satchel. Vesta put her glasses on and paged through the top pages.

"Yes, this will be a good start. Mind if I keep a few to read?"

"Fine, as many as you like," Annie said.

Vesta glowed, as if she had given her a piece of jewelry.

"I would love to keep the whole stack, but my eyes aren't strong enough anymore. I'll take what I can manage. If I should find anything, is there a number where I can reach you?"

She wrote her grandmother's landline and her own cell number on a piece of paper and handed it to Vesta.

"I appreciate the help. Can I ask you something else? The last time I was here, you mentioned an oral tradition. It's why you believe the stone house to be first in Kentucky. How do you know the story?"

Vesta smiled and took off her glasses.

"It was a story told in my own family. And there was much talk about it being the first one of its kind west of the Cumberland Gap."

"Your family passed this story down? Why?"

"They helped build it," Vesta said, an amused look on her face.

"They were slaves?"

"Of course. The Douglases owned them—not your family. The Mays came from Scotland and brought with them the skill of laying stone. But they needed help digging out limestone. It was hard work, as you can imagine, and while the May family paid for the labor, the money went to the Douglases since they owned my people."

Annie was silent for a moment, taking in the magnitude of Vesta's words.

"I'm sure it's fairly insignificant to say this now, but I am sorry."

Vesta's eyes were soft under raised eyebrows.

"Words of reconciliation are never insignificant."

***

Beulah was in the living room watching the nightly news when Annie got home. Her grandmother reached for the remote and turned off the television as Annie plopped down on her grandfather's recliner.

"I didn't know what happened to you," Beulah said. "Are you hungry?"

"Did you know the Mays were Scottish?"

"My father told me. I think we're a mix of other things through our different lines."

She told her grandmother about gathering the information in Frankfort and the visit with Vesta.

"The Givens are an old Somerville family. I suppose we are all more intertwined than we realize."

"I would love for you to go with me sometime to see her," Annie said, gathering up her bag.

Beulah nodded. "I'll take her some vegetable soup. Have you had supper?"

"I'll find something while I put on coffee, the real stuff, not decaf. I've a lot of work ahead tonight."

"Don't wear yourself out over all this. You need your rest," Beulah called out.

Rest was not on her mind now. The visit with Vesta had motivated her to find answers. While rich coffee brewed, she began the task of reading handwritten letters from the late 1700s.

Chapter Six

BEULAH FACED A stack of mending that piled up over the summer while she was laid up with her knee operation. If she was going to hem tablecloths for Mary Beth's reception, she needed to get caught up. And as the old green Singer sewing machine whirred away, she had plenty of time to think.

Beulah regretted always being so hard on her granddaughter. It was a thing she had struggled with from day one, being too hard on her own child, Jo Anne. All it had done was drive Jo Anne straight into the arms of slick-talking Eddie Taylor and running off to Jellico for a quick marriage. There had to be boundaries, and *didn't boundaries mean love?* It was how she had been raised, and how she had tried to raise Jo Anne and Annie.

Annie was taking the two-week deadline seriously and had the blurry eyes and dark circles this morning to show for it. If her granddaughter was committed to finding a way to save the old house, well, it suited her just fine. Tearing it down was a last resort; but the value of the architectural salvage was tempting. Big business, apparently, with folks wanting a piece of history in their homes, so much so they spend hard-earned money.

Growing up in the aftermath of the Depression made Beulah frugal. It was a hard habit to break, and one she wasn't sure should be broken. Money was hard to come by and it could be gone in a flash. Those hard times marked her, even though their family had it much better than some people.

Back in those days it was common for people to stop at the house and ask for food. Beulah's mother never turned anybody away and sometimes gave folks eggs or garden produce, especially if they had children. Sometimes it was a single traveler. Other times it was a family. Whoever they were, no one went away hungry. Her mother prepared a hot meal and served them on the porch. It was not like out West with the drought and the dust bowl, but they were hard times. To this day, Beulah could still see the face of a little girl her own age in a torn dress, barefoot, with large brown eyes looking with wonder at their abundant garden. They went right into World War II when gas and tires were rationed along with groceries.

But could money be valued too much? Over a relationship or family heritage?

The house was all she had left of a mother, father, and brother long in their graves. And Annie was right about one thing: once it was gone, it could never be brought back.

There were the steers Joe was just about to sell for her. With beef prices so good now, it would likely be a much larger check than she had anticipated. Beulah prayed for wisdom while she pulled the hem out of an old dress. She most wanted to be a faithful steward.

***

After the supper dishes were cleared away, Annie brought out her papers and placed them carefully on the table.

"I'd like to show you what I've found so far and present a proposal for your consideration."

"Sounds quite formal," Beulah said, her hands folded on the table. "I'm ready."

"If we restore the house according to certain criteria, which Jerry Baker knows and has included in his bid, then you'll receive approximately this much in credits on your taxes."

Annie pointed to a number on a piece of paper she turned toward Beulah. "Of course, the exact number depends on whether it's federal or state, when we get the paperwork submitted, and how much they allow us. This is a conservative estimate."

Annie pulled out another sheet of paper. "Here's Jerry's bid. It's lower than the others and I had him break it down into phases. Phase one includes everything needed to close the house up: roof, glass repair, new windows, and stonework. The insurance money more than covers these things, with some extra to help repair the interior woodwork."

Beulah had made her decision and waited patiently for Annie to explain her idea.

"What's not known are the grant possibilities. There're organizations that might consider us if we can prove certain things of historical significance about the house. Unfortunately, we won't know about that until after the first of the year. Since we can't count on something that is unknown, my proposal is to take the insurance money and do all the repairs we can do now. I'll continue to work on the grants. Jake and I will contribute our labor to cut costs wherever we can. I'll start paying rent here this month. Hopefully, I'll have a job soon anyway. That money will offset some of the rental income you were getting from the house."

"You're already buying groceries," Beulah protested. "When you get a job, you can start paying rent."

"Fair enough. Wait! You agree with everything?"

"Agreed."

Annie nearly came across the table to hug her, making her eyes fill with tears. Annie held onto her a long time and Beulah was glad she had time enough to blink back the moisture. It wouldn't do for Annie to see her soften too much.

Chapter Seven

"THANKS FOR COMING," Lindy said, shutting her office door. "Have a seat."

"You okay?" Annie said and put her purse down on an empty chair.

"Same old thing. Rob's gone again. Every time, I think this visit will be different. He'll realize I'm the only one for him and want to settle down. I'm still in love with him," Lindy slumped over her desk, her face in her hands. "There's a trial coming up. I'm not sleeping but I have to get my work done."

"Did he say when he'll be back?"

"He never says." Lindy seemed on the verge of tears. She was about to offer more words of comfort but Lindy shook her head as if shaking off the emotion. "Anyway, it's not why I called you. This is good news."

She picked up a document and handed it to her.

"Dad was at a meeting yesterday with the Stone Conservancy. He mentioned the stone house to them and they were really interested. They have a program where they offer free labor as part of their training to new stonemasons if the structure is over one hundred years old. We know the house qualifies. If you can fill out this information and send it to them, they will come out and do the repairs."

"Oh, Lindy, thank you so much. We can have Jerry do more work if we don't have to pay for the stonework."

"So Beulah agreed?"

"For the initial work, and that's enough to save it," Annie said. "We still have a long road to finish, but it's a start."

"Dad will be happy to hear it."

While Annie was in Somerville she stopped by the bank, an insurance office, and an accountant's office to follow up on the résumés she had dropped off earlier in the month. Everyone was pleasant and encouraging, but there were no job openings. She had applied with the school system as well, but those jobs were snapped up in early summer. After Janice's visit in October, she would branch out to Rutherford, and then to Lexington if necessary, but she hoped desperately for something close to home.

Her thoughts were on Jake as she drove May Hollow Road in the farm truck. Her heart warmed at the memory of him saying "I love you." They had decided to take things slowly when they began dating. Some might call it old-fashioned, but they wanted to be sure.

Annie also realized there was much more she and Jake needed to learn about each other. Ten years apart was a long time. They needed time to get to know one another again and build a solid foundation for a strong future, despite Betty Gibson's desire to rush them to the alter. It hurt her to think how absent she had been when Jake was dealing with the loss of his father. Her life was going in a completely different direction back then.

Beulah's car was gone when Annie bumped over the potholes and pulled next to the house to unload the groceries. When everything was put away, she sat down at the kitchen table and began filling out the information for the Stone Conservancy while it was fresh in her mind. Once she completed the application, she folded it into an envelope and put a stamp on it. There was still a stack of papers to read from Joseph Crouch's letters, but she stood and stretched, needing to do something with her hands. She knew exactly where to direct her energy.

***

The fire had not reached the downstairs of the old stone house, but water used to extinguish the flames had done its own damage. The odds-and-ends furniture had been abandoned by a previous renter, so at least they were saved the sadness of losing family heirlooms.

There was little to do in the upstairs room where the fire started. The roof opened to the sky and Jake warned her the floorboards could collapse under foot. Across the hall, the other bedroom was spared the most water and fire damage. Still, the stench was strong as Annie swept the floor. She worked around the ragged blue and yellow braided rug in the center of the room until she had a neat pile of trash in the corner. Then she turned her attention to the old bed frame and stained mattress atop the faded rug. There were no box springs, only a mattress on planks, and Annie pitied the person who had called this bed their own. She lifted the mattress and quickly realized it was heavier than she thought. This time she bent her knees and grabbed it with both hands, using her body against it for balance, and then heaved it upwards until it flopped onto the floor like a great fish. After a deep breath, she bent down and lifted again, again using her body to leverage it up and onto its side. Bit by bit, she pushed it into the hallway. At the top of the steps, she leaned it against the wall and considered her next move.

A shadow moved in the corner of her eye and she turned to look. A dark brown rat skittered across the landing to the burned-out room. She screamed and lunged forward, plunging headfirst down the stairs and wedging herself between the mattress and the wall. Wood groaned and creaked as the handrail gave way and the mattress slid down the steps before lodging itself against the newel post at the bottom of the stairs. Annie had covered her head on the slide down and waited, breathless, until the ride ended. When she rolled off and looked back, she was dismayed at the sight. The handrail hung off the side of the stairs like teeth knocked loose but holding on by threads.

"Another expense," she said, and kicked a piece of plaster in frustration. Once she maneuvered the mattress out the front door, she leaned it against the truck and went back up for the bed frame. After taking it apart and carrying it outside, she rolled up the braided rug, sneezing twice as dust swirled, and then carried it outside. On the front stoop, she stopped for rest and looked through the open doorway at the splintered handrail. Tears welled up in her eyes. If she had just waited, Jake said he would help her with anything she couldn't manage. Why was it so darn hard for her to admit she needed help?

After a few moments of rest, she went back upstairs to finish sweeping the empty room before going home. Her eyes darted, watching for a long brown tail and quick movements.

Thick dust covered the area where the rug had been. Broom and dustpan in hand, she started at one end of the room and worked her way across. In the middle of the room, the edge of the dustpan bumped against an uneven board. Annie squatted and noticed two matching vertical cuts against the natural horizontal lines of the wood floor, about a foot apart. The cuts in the wood were aged and had been made a long time ago. With her fingers, she tried to pry the boards but nothing happened. She left it alone and kept working until the entire room was swept clean.

Tired and hungry, she was ready for a soaking bath and some of her grandmother's vegetable soup. Leaning against the broom, she surveyed the room again, pleased to have completed one job, but disappointed in the mishap on the stairs. In an effort to save money she had now cost them more in repairs on the handrail.

Her eyes went to the cuts in the wood. Curious, she examined it again and found the wood moved just a bit when she pushed on the corner. With a table knife scavenged from a kitchen drawer, she lifted the wood a little bit. Another spot and it moved again, then again, until the wide board clattered onto the floor.

She jumped back and waited for a rat to jump out. When nothing happened, she peered into a small dark hole between the downstairs ceiling and the floor and saw the glint of metal just below the surface. She reached in and grabbed a metal handle and pulled a small, dust-covered box into the light. With the tail of her shirt, she wiped the dust off and saw it was dark brown painted on metal.

When she tried to open it, it appeared to be locked. She fished a paper clip from the trash bag and inserted the end into the lock and jiggled it until she heard a click.

Inside were brown envelopes with old-fashioned handwriting. She picked up a letter and held it gently in her hand. It was addressed to Lilah and William May, her great-grandparents and Beulah's parents. The return address said: War and Navy Departments, V-Mail Service, Official Business.

Annie excitedly flipped through the envelopes and saw that each envelope was addressed to her great-grandparents with postmarks beginning in April 1942 and ending in January 1944.

These must be from Great-Uncle Ephraim, she thought.

Opening one of the envelopes, her suspicion was confirmed. It was signed by her great-uncle, the family's hero, the one who gave his life for his country, and was now buried just up the hill from the old stone house in the May Family Cemetery.

All these years, precious letters were hidden away in a metal box under the floor of a house that nearly burned down and then faced near destruction a second time.

She read, first one letter and then another, as she went back to the 1940s and heard the voice of a great-uncle she never knew. Her grandmother spoke of her brother Ephraim as a saint and a brave man who willingly gave it all for his country. The voice she now heard from the letters was a country boy, barely out of his teenage years, who longed to be back among the green pastures and rolling hills of home. A boy used to hard work and handling guns in order to provide food for his family—not to take another's life. A boy who was committed to serving his country at all costs, but like any normal human, preferred peace over war.

"Annie?" There was a note of alarm in Jake's voice and she could hear him taking the stairs two at a time.

"Here," she called.

"Are you okay?" he said, his eyes scanning her even as he spoke. "What happened?"

"Nothing, why?" she asked, taking Jake's outstretched hand as he helped her up from the floor.

"Beulah called when you didn't come home for supper. I got worried you fell or something."

"I did fall back in time, reading these letters. But I had no idea it was so late. Look at this, Jake. These letters were in a metal box, hidden under the floor," she handed one of the letters to Jake. "They're all from my great-uncle Ephraim during World War II."

"Where were they?" Jake asked.

"There," Annie pointed to the hiding place in the floor. Jake got down on his knees. He reached in and felt around.

"Nothing else here," he said. "What happened on the stairs?"

Annie sighed and rolled her eyes then told him about the rat.

He laughed then pulled her to him.

"I'm glad you're okay," he said. "But call me next time and let me help."

Annie gathered up the letters and put them back in the metal box.

"Are you finished with the hay?"

"Almost. Joe and I are putting the last load in the barn. I took a water break and saw a missed call from Beulah," Jake said, as they walked down the stairs together. "You did a number on this."

"Hard to fix?" she said.

"Not compared to the rest of the house. Don't worry, it'll be fine."

Outside, he lifted the mattress into the bed of the pick-up.

"You make it look so easy," she said.

"Just trying to impress you," he grinned.

***

"Thank heavens you're okay," Beulah said when Annie walked in the back door. "I thought you'd fallen through the floor."

"You're not going to believe what I found."

Beulah sat down at the kitchen table and she placed the metal box in front of her.

"Have you ever seen this box?"

Her grandmother put her hands on it as if feeling it would bring back the remembrance.

"I can't say I have."

"Open it."

Beulah opened the box and stared at the letters in front of her. "What in tarnation? These look like the letters Ephraim sent me when he was in service. But mine are upstairs in the drawer by my bed."

"These letters went to your parents."

"Mama and Daddy?" she watched Beulah pick them up, one by one. "I never knew what happened to those letters," Beulah said. "Where'd you find them?"

She told her about the secret hiding place.

"Mama and Daddy's bedroom," Beulah said, fingering each letter. "You mean they cut out part of the floor and hid it there, under the rug?"

"I'll show it to you whenever you want. Do you know why they hid the letters?"

"It's a mystery to me," Beulah said.

Chapter Eight

BEULAH SAT AT the kitchen table and stared at the letters scribed when she was just a girl. Memories of a time that seemed ancient surfaced like bubbles floating to the top of water, as if they had been waiting for some signal.

When her brother had signed up after the horrible attack on Pearl Harbor, he was off to training and then was eventually shipped overseas. They didn't know where until the day when she was the first to get a letter from him. The mail took a long time back then; and they didn't always arrive in the order of when they were written. And so she had received the first communication from the faraway land.

***

It was a warm afternoon in late April, the trees sprouting leaves, the grass growing enough so the livestock didn't need hay any longer, and she was barefoot in the garden helping her mother plant corn.

Her father puttered in from town in the dark green Chevy truck and pulled up next to the old stone house. She sensed the excitement in his voice when he called, "Beuly, come get your letter from Eph." Her mother dropped the sack of corn and they all ran to meet her father. With grave care, her father handed the letter to her and she held it in her little hands as if it were a bar of gold from Fort Knox.

They had waited to find out where he was sent since Ephraim couldn't say anything before he left. If he did, the censor would mark it out or maybe even not let the letter go. So the boys had learned to be careful about what they told. She thought of a slogan from those times on posters everywhere: "Loose lips sink ships."

While her parents waited, Beulah opened the letter carefully. At the top, next to the date, it had said *North Africa*.

"He's in North Africa," she said.

Her parents looked at each other with a strange expression she was too young to understand and too scared to ask the meaning. She read the letter to them, which told her how much he missed her and asking what she had been doing. He told her very little about his own life in the service, but was eager to know what was going on at home.

Ephraim wrote many more letters to her. All those letters were safely stored in her room. But she had never laid eyes on the letters now placed in front of her by her granddaughter. Oh, she reckoned her parents had read them, or parts of them to her when they were received. To now hold them and read them as an adult, well, it was like finding a buried treasure.

The first few letters were from training camp. Beulah skipped those and went straight to the first one from overseas.

> *North Africa*
> *April 21, 1943*
>
> *Dearest Mother and Dad,*
> *How is everyone by this time? Dad, I was wondering if you got the field broke? I sure wish I could be there to help you. It's a lot for you all by yourself. How many new calves do you have by now? I would like to see them. That new bull was fine stock and I am anxious to know what kind of cows he puts on the ground.*
>
> *It's not too bad here. I have made some buddies. One is from Boston and he never handled a gun until he*

joined up. He would tickle you to death the way he talks but he laughs at me, too. His name is Charlie Fitzgerald and he is Catholic. There is another fella called Rooster and you can imagine why.

And then my best friend is Arnie Mason from Texas. We were raised up the same way and he likes to talk about farming as much as I do. Except they call them ranches out there. He talks of cows with horns as long as a bale of hay. Can you imagine it? I have seen them in movies but I would like to see for myself. He has invited me to visit him after the war, and I think I would like to see Texas someday.

We have been awful busy, and I am glad. It is good to pass the time so we aren't left to think of home too often. The food is okay, but I sure do miss Mother's cooking. And Mother, I'm fine and dandy, so please don't worry about me. I will write more when I have time. Give Beulah my love.

Love,
Ephraim

Beulah heard his voice through the words, always upbeat, always cheerful. Even to a little sister ten years his junior, he had treated her with such love and care. He had taken her on dates to the movies with his sweetheart, Bessie Sprinkle. Looking back now, Beulah knew her parents had probably sent her as a chaperone. Still, he seemed glad to have her along and she never knew the fighting or resentments siblings closer in age experienced.

Placing the letter back in the box, she made a decision. She would not devour these all at once. Instead, she would parcel them out, starting at the beginning, and enjoy them one by one. They had waited in silence for nearly sixty years. It seemed disrespectful to read them too fast. She took the box upstairs and placed it by her bedside table. Tonight she would read another one—or maybe two.

On her way back down the steps, she thought about Bessie Sprinkle, Ephraim's old girlfriend. She had died twenty years ago of breast cancer, after raising three kids with the man she married before the war was even over. If she remembered right, Bessie's husband was from another county, discharged for medical reasons. For a while, Bessie was like a big sister to Beulah when she and Ephraim were courting. She even came over for visits after Ephraim enlisted, but those had tapered off and Bessie had gone on to other things, even before Ephraim was killed. Truth be told, she had resented Bessie all these years, her dropping her brother while he was serving his country. Even as a little girl, she had wondered if it had broken Ephraim's heart to lose his girl while being so far away from home. It had troubled her to think he might have died with a broken heart.

Bessie had lived a whole life beyond Ephraim, just as Beulah had. It seemed strange how one person's life was cut so short and others lived to ripe old ages. It was a mystery and one she would ask the good Lord about when she got to heaven. His ways were higher.

***

With much to ponder, she felt drawn to the kitchen to sort it all out. The letters had stirred up deep feelings and cooking helped her think clearly.

The iron skillet was just heating up for pork chops when the harvest-gold wall phone rang out. When she answered, Betty Gibson launched into talking as soon as Beulah said hello.

"I'll tell you one thing, Woody Patterson sure didn't go to Chicago to buy a horse. I saw him drive by the Snip and Curl this afternoon and he wasn't even pulling his trailer."

"How do you know he just got back? Maybe he unloaded it and came back into town," Beulah said.

"Because he goes to the nursing home every Thursday morning to see his mother. You know Shirley Updike? She's in the DAR with me and she works at the nursing home. I called her and asked if Woody had been in this morning and she said no. Woody never misses seeing his mama on Thursday morning, although heavens knows there's not much left to see. She's done wasted away with a brain injury, but he goes every Thursday morning come hail or high water."

She looked at the iron skillet, longing to be off the phone and slopping batter on the pork chops.

"So what do you think, Beulah? Why is he going off to Chicago under the pretense of buying a horse with no horse trailer in sight?"

"Well, Betty, sometimes a man uses sayings to politely hide what he really means."

"So what are you sayin'?" Betty asked, frustrated she wasn't jumping on her bandwagon.

"Your own Joe says all the time he needs to 'see a man about a horse,' and we all know it's a warning that he's going off behind the barn to relieve himself."

There was silence on the other end of the line and Beulah grinned to herself. It was so easy to get Betty's goat. No wonder Joe did it all the time.

"So, are you saying Woody Patterson went all the way to Chicago to urinate?"

***

Saturday night was Evelyn's dinner party and Jake insisted on picking them up, even though she and Annie were fully capable of driving the mile from her farm to Evelyn's. It was a nice gesture just the same. He helped her to the SUV and into the back seat. Thank goodness for those running boards. Who in the world could mount one of those high vehicles without them? It was nearly like climbing up on a horse, an activity she had given up years ago.

Annie, looking so pretty in that perfect shade of red, slid into the front seat and off they went. Evelyn had been consumed with the party planning all week and Beulah hoped she wasn't worn to a frazzle now it was time for the dinner. They were celebrating Jake's official return from Cincinnati and the guest list included the usuals at their after-church Sunday dinner for the single folks with the addition of Betty and Joe Gibson, who normally made a practice of eating at Long John Silver's after church.

The only addition to the dinner party out of their normal circle was Tom Childress, Lindy's father. Jake had been drawn to him as a mentor of sorts after he decided to move back and he was certainly a fine man. He had a stellar reputation and was looked up to in the community as a leader. Jake had picked a good mentor, and Evelyn's invitation for dinner was a nice gesture.

They arrived and Jake helped her out and up the front steps, Annie on his other side. They were back door friends with the Wilders, but she knew Evelyn wanted everyone to come to the front door on a night such as this. They were the first to arrive, which was just as well, since she could offer her help.

"Oh good," Evelyn said, her apron still on when she opened the door. "Annie, can you put ice in the glasses? Beulah, I need you to see to this meringue. It does not want to stand up for me. Jake, can you turn on some music?"

Meringue was her specialty and Beulah was glad to be assigned a job she could do.

"Do you have some cream of tartar?" she asked. Evelyn produced it and she added just the right amount. The meringue was stiff as a board in just a few minutes. And without even asking Evelyn, who seemed quite preoccupied, she put it on the pies, giving the tops some nice curls to brown just so in the oven.

Actually, Evelyn seemed nervous, which was odd for a woman who was no stranger to entertaining. It wasn't like her to be this behind in preparations, but she must have spent her time on getting dressed, because Evelyn was quite a vision in a baby blue knit suit that accented her slim hips and her blue eyes. One of those St. Somebody brands. Evelyn's mind was not on pies this evening, so Beulah decided to take over the desserts and slid them in the oven for browning.

Woody Patterson came in through the back door, his reddish brown hair slicked back off his freckled face, making him look younger than his forty-odd years. He wasn't a bad-looking fellow when he cleaned up, except for the unruly upper plate that flapped about when he talked too fast.

"Beulah!" he said, his voice bouncing off the kitchen walls. And then he eyed the pan lying in the sink and swished his finger around it, gathering up leftover pie custard.

She started to fuss at him for coming in the back door and for slopping around in Evelyn's dirty dishes, but poor Woody was raised up rough and probably didn't know any better. Instead, she decided to help him.

"Go back out and come in the front door," she whispered. "Evelyn wants everyone to come in the front door tonight so she can greet you."

"Huh?" he said, leaning over so he could hear. Again, she said, "Go out and come in the front door," louder this time, and taking care to enunciate each word.

"Go out the front door?" he asked, a look of total confusion on his face.

She gave up. Woody was hopeless, bless his heart.

"Everybody's in the front room," she said in a normal voice and bent over to check on the pies. Just a bit more time for browning the meringue. Woody had gone into the front room when she rose from peering in the oven door. She recognized voices as Betty and Joe Gibson came in and then Scott and Mary Beth, who were without her two children this weekend. Next she heard Lindy and then Tom's mellifluous voice, which made a body feel like all would be well no matter how twisted the problem.

With the hot pads, she slid the pies out of the oven and placed them to cool on trivets. Coconut cream and chocolate, her favorites. Even better, they would still be warm in time for dessert. Her job was finished, so she wiped her hands, and joined the others in the front room where Evelyn had prepared wine punch and sparkling grape juice to go with the appetizers. This was a fancy party, not like their normal sit-right-down-at-the-table functions. Beulah noticed Evelyn still had on her apron. She eased in front of her friend and nodded down when she passed Evelyn, hoping she would get the hint.

Evelyn caught the nod, looked down, and blushed red. She did an about-face and reappeared seconds later without the apron.

She accepted a glass of sparkling grape juice from Jake. It was well enough for Evelyn to serve wine punch, but she would never be caught serving alcohol in her own house. Evelyn was a Presbyterian and they had different views from the Baptists on whether or not the wine was fermented at the Cana wedding.

Evelyn was talking with Tom Childress and seemed a bit calmer now. Sometimes the anticipation of a thing was more nerve-wracking than the thing itself. Betty and Joe were talking with Scott, the young preacher at the new community church, and Mary Beth, the elementary school teacher, about marriage. Actually, Betty was giving marital advice and Joe was listening. Beulah hoped Scott and Mary Beth would take a grain of salt with whatever wisdom Betty was imparting.

The appetizers looked tasty and she took some bread with green sauce on it and popped it in her mouth. *Oh no. Garlic.* The one spice she could not tolerate. One more of those and she would be up all night with the indigestion.

"How did you like it?" Annie asked, leaving Jake with Lindy and Woody. "I helped Evelyn make the pesto and she taught me how to cut and toast the bread, then put the sauce on at the end."

Beulah needed to strike a balance. She did not want to discourage Annie from cooking. Her granddaughter needed to learn a few things if she was ever to set up housekeeping. The key was to be agreeable, but not gush, or else Annie would be fixing pesto regularly.

"Right tasty," Beulah said. And it was tasty, just not to her liking.

"Try this," Annie said. "It's bruschetta, same concept except it has tomato sauce."

Garlic again, she thought. Beulah managed to nod her head while she was eating it. She needed to get away from Annie before being asked to try something else.

"I better see if Evelyn needs anything," she said while easing away.

When Tom saw her coming toward them, he greeted her warmly.

"Beulah, I was just telling Evelyn how much I appreciate what you two do for these young folks. Lindy loves having lunch on Sundays with you all. It's helped her transition back to small-town life after years at the university in Lexington."

"It gives us a great deal of pleasure to do it. They keep us young. It was an added bonus to see Scott and Mary Beth develop a relationship after being at our table," she added, and looked to Evelyn for agreement. But just then, a look of panic swept over Evelyn's face and she excused herself and headed to the kitchen. Beulah followed, as fast as her recently operated-on knee would allow.

Evelyn stood for a minute at the counter and looked at the finished pies. She turned to her, relief washing over face.

"Thank you, Beulah. I don't know what's wrong with me today. I'm a scatterbrain!"

"You had too much on your mind. It's a nice party, it's obvious you put a lot of work into it."

"Do you think so?" Evelyn asked. For a moment, her expression took Beulah back thirty years to the young bride Charlie Wilder brought home with him down from Lexington. Evelyn was raised up with fine things and good schooling; farm life was new to her. Beulah had taught and coached her because Evelyn wanted to learn and to make a life, as hard as the change was.

"Yes," she said with all the confidence she could put into one word. "It's wonderful! And everybody is enjoying themselves. You need to relax and enjoy it yourself."

"You're right! I do. This is a celebration, after all."

They all moved into the dining room and feasted on pork loin with mashed potatoes, green beans, glazed carrots, and a frozen salad. The conversation flowed like warm butter.

They were nearing the end of the dinner when Betty looked down the table at Woody.

"Woody, Joe said you went up to Chicago to buy a new horse. What kind did you get?" she asked with a devilish glint in her eye.

Woody leaned back in his chair.

"I spotted several I like. I'm going back next weekend to pick 'em up. This was just a scouting trip," he said and scooped up a huge forkful of mashed potatoes.

Aha. Beulah looked at Betty to see how she was taking that little tidbit. Betty's eyes glinted in satisfaction.

"Stella Hawkins lives in Chicago, doesn't she?" Betty asked and then jumped like she had been kicked under the table. She cut her eyes at Joe.

"Chicago?" Woody said. "Big place. Ever been there, Tom?"

He might not be too smooth on the outside, but Woody Patterson was wily as a fox.

***

After the dinner party, Jake helped Beulah into the house and she went on up to her bedroom and let Jake and Annie have the downstairs to themselves. She was eager to read another letter from her brother, Ephraim. It was as if she was going to have a visit from him, even if it was only a short one.

After getting her nightgown on, she slid under the cotton quilt made by her mother and pulled out another brown envelope.

North Africa
May 17, 1943

Dear Mother,
I am sending you some money and I want you to use it for anything you want. I can't be there to help on the farm, so at least I can do this.

How is everyone by this time? I'm fine, the only thing is, I'm about to burn up during the day. It is hotter than any Kentucky summer except it is a dry heat, not like our humid and hazy afternoons. At night, it cools down like October at home.

How is everyone to-nite? I'm feeling fine and staying busy.

You asked me if I have heard from Bessie Sprinkle. Yes, she has written me but I have not written back. I don't know what to say to her. She is a good girl and I like her. I am just not sure how to write her or if I should, not knowing how long we will be over here.

Has Dad put out any tobacco yet? How much corn did he plant? I will be there next spring to help, I hope. Farming and more farming is what I want when I get home.

I hope you are both not working too hard. Mother, don't worry about me for I will be okay. Tell everyone hello for me and I'll be home soon.

Love,
Ephraim

Beulah sighed deeply. Ephraim wasn't home the following spring—or any of the following springs. He was headed to a date with death, just months later. But instead of sadness, the pleasure of his love flowed from the letter to her soul.

She took off her glasses and turned off the bedside lamp. In the dark, she imagined herself as a young girl, safe in the upstairs room of the old stone house. Her parents were sleeping in their bed across the room. Her brother was asleep in the other bedroom. In that sweet memory, they were all alive and happy, living under one roof.

Chapter Nine

FROM THE WILDER'S STOCK barn, Annie crossed her arms and wished she had worn a sweater while she watched a dump truck scatter lime in the field beyond. Jake dug around in a toolbox and handed her a pair of work gloves.

"You'll need these," he said. He carried the toolbox to the bed of the side-by-side utility vehicle. "Ready?"

"I hope you know what you're getting into," she said, climbing on the seat next to him. "I'm better known for breaking things than fixing them."

"I know what I'm getting into," he grinned, his eyes focused on what was ahead.

Annie smiled back at him, taking in his dark hair and light blue eyes. There was a tiny scar just above his left eyebrow from sliding into home base when he played high school baseball. These features she knew as well as her own and the warmth of love spread all over her heart once again.

They bumped over rough ground and the openness of the farm made her worries seem far away. It was a beautiful day, the sun bright against the deep blue sky, the air clean and crisp with all the haze of summer gone. Days like these were precious and few with colder weather right on their heels.

The old plank fence on the perimeter of the farm was in bad shape, sagging in places and missing planks, and the paint faded from white to the gray, aged wood. Annie saw where Jake had repaired parts of the fence, but there was much to be done. He stopped the utility vehicle next to a pile of new wooden planks.

"I thought you're doing mostly electric fence." She met him at the back of the vehicle.

"I am . . . inside the farm. Electric fence gives me the ability to move the herd around for intensive grazing. If it were up to me, I wouldn't use plank anywhere, except around the house. It's a trade-off with Mom since she's given me free rein with the rest of the farm."

Jake smiled at her and grabbed the toolbox. Annie followed him to the fence.

"If you'll hold the plank, I'll nail this side." The new unpainted boards were rough and splintery.

"I've been reading all these pioneer letters and it makes me think about how it must have been back then," Annie said, looking around. "Imagine us out here with Cherokee on the prowl. There's nowhere to hide."

"I imagine the Indians felt pretty vulnerable, too, with everybody moving in here and settling down in their territory." Jake dropped some nails inside the pocket of his khaki work shirt. "Any luck so far?"

"It's slow going. The script is hard to read and some of the words are misspelled, so I have to interpret what he means. If I don't find anything in his letters, there are more letters from other pioneers, even diaries. The frustrating thing is not knowing if there's anything about the house. It could be a wild-goose chase."

"The house isn't going to be torn down now, so you don't have to keep looking," Jake said, taking her end of the board, and squatting down to position the bottom plank.

"I know, but getting one of those grants would help so much. And I would like to know for sure if it's the oldest stone house in the state—for us and for Vesta. Her family had as much to do with building the house as mine did. If there's a way to honor the work of both families, I would like to do it, especially while she is living."

Jake handed her another plank and she held it up.

"You've really taken to Vesta," he said, smiling.

"It's strange, like I've known her all my life. I want you to meet her."

Jake nodded and pounded a nail, the metal on wood echoing off the hill behind the pasture.

"Maybe you can find a way to honor the work even if it's not the first stone house," Jake said.

Annie steadied her end of the plank while Jake nailed.

"Like what?" she asked.

"I don't know, but there's bound to be something. Talk to Beulah and see what she thinks."

"Right now we can hardly communicate. She's in the 1940s and I'm in the 1700s," Annie said.

"I wish I had letters to blame for the way Mom's acting," Jake said.

"What do you mean?"

"I found her portable phone in the mailbox yesterday. I brought it to her and she got embarrassed and said she was talking on the phone and must have laid it there when she picked up the mail."

Annie shrugged. "That could happen, especially if she's distracted."

"I came in to do my laundry the other day and found her sitting at the kitchen table and staring at the wall."

Jake reached for a nail, placed it on the wood and hammered.

"Did you ask her if anything's wrong?"

"As soon as I said something, she stood up and acted a little flustered."

"I'll ask Grandma. She'd know if something was wrong."

***

Annie's grandmother leaned over a simmering pot of soup and stirred.

"Anything you want me to do in the garden?" Annie asked as she poured a glass of iced tea.

Beulah laid the wooden spoon on the spoon rest and turned to face her. "You can pull up the green beans now. Make sure you get any beans still on the vine, and you can cut me some greens while you're out there."

Annie reached for a large metal bowl and the kitchen scissors.

"Grandma, have you noticed anything wrong with Evelyn? I mean, does she seem okay to you . . . mentally?"

There was a slight hesitation before her grandmother responded.

"No, she's fine. Why?"

"Nothing really, just a couple of things Jake noticed."

Before Beulah could prod her further, Annie went out to the garden.

Situated at the end of a row, she searched for beans as she pulled plants and thought how familiar the garden was to her now and how foreign it had seemed earlier in the summer. At first, she had hated losing her life in New York for a small town rural life she had left long ago. What had seemed the end of the world became a beginning. Since then, she had learned so much: gardening, preserving and canning food, repairing fences, painting. She had even learned to cook a little and the art to making good sweet tea.

It was all about how you dissolved the sugar and how the tea steeped.

Back then, she remembered thinking it was too quiet. But once her ears tuned to the sounds of nature, she was amazed to find it could be downright noisy at times. Squawking birds, croaking frogs, mooing cows, and a breeze moving tree limbs and bushes. Rain and hail on a tin roof along with thunderstorms that turned gurgling creeks into rushing streams.

There were still so many things she didn't know, and hardly a day went by that wasn't marked by a new discovery. Just last week she had cut a pan of greens, thinking it would be enough for both her and her grandmother. Beulah had laughed and sent her back to the garden for more, and even then it cooked up so much it barely made a hearty serving for each of them.

As a teenager, her mind was on other things, and she never considered all her grandparents did to run the farm. There were the chickens, of course. That was her main responsibility as a teenager. Now the chicken house was empty.

Inside, she let her eyes adjust to the dark. It was quiet now, a few dust mites swirling in the light from the window. A double row of nesting boxes clung to the back wall. Roosting rails were suspended near the window. Nutmeg, the horse Woody loaned her for the summer, had gone back home, leaving cows as the only living things on the farm.

It would be nice to have more life on the farm.

***

Annie put the pan, mounded up with greens, on the kitchen counter.

"Thank you," Beulah said, and turned two grilled cheese sandwiches over on an iron skillet. "Add some salt water, please, so we get all the worms off."

"Sounds tasty," she said, as she set the table for lunch.

"It's a fact," Beulah said. "Food was never meant to look like it came from Disney World. Everything's so sterilized and pretty these days with no taste at all."

"You've been talking to Jake."

"He talks sense. It's how I was raised. Somehow, we got off track."

They sat at the table and Beulah offered grace.

"I was thinking about getting a few chickens," Annie said.

"Sounds like a real good idea," Beulah said. "I always loved country eggs. These pale, anemic eggs from the grocery don't have the same taste."

"I'll need feed. I remember something about oyster shells."

"They're mixed in so the chickens get enough calcium. Pine wood shavings are good for the nesting boxes," Beulah added, wiping her mouth.

"Where do I get chickens?"

"There are mail-order hatcheries who ship. Be several months before you'd be able to start collecting full-sized eggs. You might want pullets or young hens," Beulah said.

"I'll check with Jake. He's getting a bunch next spring, so he probably knows a source," she took her dishes to the sink.

"Where are you off to?" Beulah asked.

"Back to the stone house."

"Well don't go diving down the stairs again, please."

**

Annie had just parked the truck next to the house when she realized she had gone off without her phone. She was expecting a call from Jerry about when they would start work. Instead of driving the truck back, she jogged on the farm lane back to her grandmother's house and saw Betty Gibson's Cadillac parked in the driveway. *Again.*

She didn't want to get caught up in Betty's nosy questions. If she slipped in the front door, she could go up the steps and to her room without being seen. She was just inside about to quietly take the stairs when she heard her name mentioned. She hesitated at the base of the stairs.

"Beulah, it's in her blood, and blood runs thick when it comes to things like this. None of those Taylors can handle a long-term relationship, let alone marriage. You name one Taylor who has married and stayed married? Most don't even make it to the altar," Betty said.

Annie stood, unable to move a muscle.

"Now Betty," Beulah said, her voice chided.

"You saw it yourself. Eddie Taylor left Jo Anne when Annie was a baby and didn't even come home when Jo Anne got sick and died. He wanders the world and lives in some foreign place nobody here can pronounce. I know you don't like to hear it, but Annie's just like him. Look at the past ten years. She's been everywhere but here. Mark my words; she'll leave Jake Wilder high and dry sooner than later. Nobody in town believes she'll stay here. Why do you think no one's offered her a job?"

"Betty Gibson, that's enough now!"

Annie stepped back, edging away from her grandmother's raised voice. Outside, her breathing came hard as she ran, from the back yard to the farm lane, until she finally reached the front door of the old stone house. She folded down onto the stone steps and rocked back and forth with her knees to her chest.

Father, again.

The tightness in her chest edged upward to her throat and she felt as if she might suffocate. Her breathing came fast and shallow and the bright fall colors dimmed into a blurring whir of dizziness.

He left, and her mother died. The two events were years apart, yet inextricable. Her mother's death certificate read "Hodgkin's disease," but what coroner would be brave enough to list the words "Broken Heart." Her father wrecked her childhood and now his legacy threatened to wreck her future.

How dare Betty Gibson accuse me of being like that man. Despite her indignation, the caustic words settled onto a tender part of her exposed soul.

Chapter Ten

BEULAH HAD MADE a study of people for most of her life. It wasn't hard, really. If a body simply listened and watched, there was much to be learned about other humans. An extra dose of intuition helped. For her examinations, she had been rewarded, or maybe cursed, with a refined sense of what lay beyond simple words, expressions, and actions. Fred had called it *radar*.

Tilting her face up to the warm September sun, she shifted in the metal chair and stretched out her legs. She had her suspicions as to what was wrong with Evelyn. Even if she did guess right, it wasn't her news to share. No, it was Evelyn's hand to play when she felt the time was right.

Then there was Annie. Her granddaughter came home from the stone house last night dragging and going to bed without her supper. When she found Annie's phone in the upstairs bathroom, she couldn't help but see Jake had called. Later, Jake came to the door looking for her granddaughter. What was Beulah to say? That Annie had gone to bed? After all, her bedroom door was shut and the room was dark.

Jake had frowned when she told him and seemed perplexed before thanking her and leaving. It didn't appear to be a lover's quarrel. Maybe Annie was sick, what with running herself down and burning the candle at both ends. A thought struck her and made her feel like she had been punched in the chest. Could Annie have Hodgkin's disease, just like her mother?

No, no. Beulah could not let her mind go down the old worry road. Beulah pushed herself up and went into the house where she pulled a chair to the refrigerator. With the door open, she pulled out condiment jars and wiped off shelves.

Beulah prayed while she combined two open mustards, which gave her plenty of time since the especially tedious process involved a knife, a small spoon, and ultimately a tiny spatula. When she finished she felt calmer; there was only one mustard container in the refrigerator and the shelves were sparkling clean.

***

"Just checking to see if you needed anything," Evelyn said, taking off her cardigan and settling into a chair. "I'm on my way for groceries."

Beulah sensed the visit was about more than groceries. After all, her house was in the opposite direction from town, not to mention a quarter mile off the road.

"Well, I could use another gallon of whole milk. I had a mind to make some potato soup later," she said. "Fall gets me in the mood for soup. Coffee?"

"Yes, I will, if you have some left," Evelyn said.

"Annie's off so early these days, she's not drinking nearly as much. I reckon she and Jake will have the farm whipped into shape the way they are going at it," Beulah said, putting a mug in front of Evelyn, and then sitting.

"They are working hard," Evelyn smiled. "It's so good to have them both home. And together."

"Yes," she said, and waited. Evelyn looked deep into the coffee mug, as if it had a secret.

"Beulah," Evelyn said. "I don't know what's wrong with me, but I'm all out of sorts these days."

"Having Jake back and running the farm is an adjustment. Even with him living in the cottage. And you've taken on this wedding, which is no small thing," she said, thinking a wedding alone would put anybody out of sorts.

"True," Evelyn said. "I suppose we never realize quite how much a thing might take from us until we are in the thick of it. Maybe it's a combination of those things. And you're right about Jake. Having him here is wonderful, but seeing so much of Charlie's work with the dairy changing over to Jake's dream of raising beef cows, chickens, pigs, goats, sheep and who knows what else before it's all over with." Evelyn chuckled. "It seems like he's biting off an awful lot. I don't know what Charlie would say about all this." Evelyn was quiet a moment. "I suppose maybe it's a little bit of grief. Somehow I think if everything stays the way Charlie left it, maybe he'll come back. Strange?"

"Normal," Beulah said. "Every single time I come in the back door and see Fred's boots sitting there, it makes me think he's inside waiting on me. Of course, it's why I leave them there, so if anyone has the intention of breaking in, they will think the same thing."

"Maybe so," Evelyn said, pushing her chair back and reaching for her cardigan. "Thank you, Beulah."

"Is that all?"

"Hearing I'm not crazy is salve," Evelyn said, looking back at her from the door.

Beulah watched her friend walk out and it finally dawned on her. *Evelyn doesn't realize what's happening. Well, I would not be the first to tell.*

***

For all her self-promises not to gobble up the letters, Beulah had read all the correspondence from Ephraim's boot camp and training time in a matter of days. She was back in North Africa and could hardly wait for bedtime when she was alone with her big brother through his words. Bedtime had grown to be her favorite time of day and she found herself edging it earlier and earlier until she was now going up by eight in the evening. It was nearly dark at least, with the days growing shorter.

She pulled the metal box onto her lap and opened it. A ribbon marked her place and she pulled out the next brown V-mail envelope.

Sicily
August 21, 1943

Dearest Mother and All,
I don't know what news you get at home but I am fine.
We _____ _____ _____ _____.
Please don't worry and know I am looking forward
to being home as soon as we get the job done here.
How is the corn crop? Is it any better than last year?
I sure hope I'm there to help with the crop next spring.
Do you have a good garden this time? How are the
cows doing? I guess you are busy canning beans and
tomatoes. Well Mom, I could ask a million questions.
Don't worry about me.

Love,
Ephraim

Black lines marked out several of the words the censor didn't like. The censors did not want much detail traveling home for fear it could be used against them.

Those times were tough, she remembered well. She was only a little girl, but the hardship of losing Ephraim—to the war, first, and then to death—had marked their family on so many different levels. Ephraim had been her father's help and partner on the farm. Ephraim loved the farm and would have taken it over when her father passed.

If Ephraim had lived, she probably would not be on the family farm. When she married Fred Campbell, she might have left the May farm and moved with him over to Gravel Switch in Boyle County, where he was from. But as it was, her father needed Fred's help, without a son of his own to share the work.

If Beulah followed that line of thinking, her daughter Jo Anne would have not met Annie's father, Eddie Taylor, which meant Annie would not have been Annie. And Beulah and Fred would have had other friends instead of Betty and Joe Gibson and Evelyn and Charlie Wilder. Which meant there would be no Annie and Jake. *How strange to ponder,* she thought, *how one life affected so many others.*

Feeling a chill, she pulled the quilt over her legs. If Ephraim had lived, he would have married Bessie Sprinkle and then Bessie's life and children would be different. Ephraim might have had sons to carry on the May name. Would her parents have lived longer if Ephraim had survived the war?

A heartbreak takes its toll on the body and both her parents seemed to age faster after the telegram was delivered. Beulah remembered her mother's dark hair had turned white within months of hearing about Ephraim's death. She had heard some old-timers talk about hair turning white sometimes even overnight after such a shock. Hair was simply an outward sign of what might be going on inside the body. There was no telling what went on inside, but she felt sure it had contributed to the illnesses that eventually took her parents.

A scripture from Job came to mind: "A man's days are numbered. You know the number of his months. He cannot live longer than the time you have set." In that case, it was no surprise to God Ephraim was born in Kentucky and died in Italy. It was as it was supposed to be.

She lay back on her pillow and felt a tear slip down her cheek. A body didn't realize how much they missed someone until they let themselves go to the secret heart places where memories were stored. And then the pain of the separation was as fresh and new as it had been back then. Even worse, now she knew what all Ephraim missed.

After a few moments, she sat up in bed and looked at the metal box. One more letter. After all, that had been a short one. Inside the box she found the place where she stopped and pulled out the next brown letter.

Naples, Italy
November 1, 1943

Dear Mother,
I am sorry it has been so long since I wrote last. We have been on the move and are now in Naples, waiting and training, but it is the nicest place we have been. It's raining tonight, so we are all sitting in our bunks writing letters home, smoking and reading.

I am sending you a lace pillow cover for your birthday. No, I did not pick it out myself, so if you like it, you must give the credit to the shopkeeper's daughter. She doesn't speak any English, except for a few words, but when I said it was for my mother, she picked this one out for you.

The Italians are having a rough time here but they are grateful to us, and the troops around Naples right now are giving the city a boon. I watched a farmer tending his sheep the other day and I realized we are all just the same, even though he lives here and I live across the sea. He cares about his animals and his land. He wants a better life, a quiet life, filled with work, rest, love, children, and he wants the freedom that makes those things possible. But this war has changed all of us.

How are the neighbors? Have you heard from any of the other boys who signed up? My old teacher, Mr. Ellis, has been good to write me often and tell me about the others when he gets word. He told me about Eddie White. I was sorry to hear he was killed. I know you must not be telling me everything you hear, and I understand. But I don't want you to worry.

Bessie Sprinkle sent me a letter and I did write her back. Mother, you might not like to hear this, but I told her not to wait for me. It isn't fair to her and who knows how long this war might go on? I don't feel for Bessie as a man should feel for a woman. I don't know how all this will turn out, but when all this is over, I will trust God for who I should marry.

How is Dad doing with all the farm work? I sure hate I can't be there to help. Please don't worry about me, Mother. I will be okay no matter what happens. I hope to be home and working in the fields come spring.

All my love,
Ephraim

Beulah took off her reading glasses. Ephraim had broken off with Bessie Sprinkle while he was overseas. Bessie stopped coming to see them and quickly married someone else because Ephraim had broken it off with her. Her parents had known this, but they never explained. Back then, they were all too busy surviving to explain much of anything. With a red ribbon, she marked her place.

Fingering the remaining letters, Beulah's mind reset past events in light of this new information. All these years, she had held hard feelings against Bessie Sprinkle for going on to someone else and living a nice life, leaving Ephraim just when he needed the comfort of a girl back home. Just when he was about to die, Ephraim called it off and may have broken Bessie Sprinkle's heart. She shook her head in wonderment at the truth. *How easy it is to make judgments without all the information.*

Mindlessly, she pulled all the letters forward in the box and when she did, she noticed a felt tab in the bottom of the box just behind the last letter. Beulah put her glasses back on and carefully lifted the letters out, placing them in order on the quilt. Then she pulled on the short tab ever so gently. The bottom of the box moved in response. Pulling harder, the brown felt bottom lifted. Underneath were two more letters in the same aged ivory, along with a photograph.

She squinted and saw an exotic young woman in sepia tones, modestly dressed.

It was certainly not Bessie Sprinkle.

Chapter Eleven

ANNIE DIDN'T TRUST herself to speak to anyone after she came back from the old stone house, especially to her grandmother, who always had the ability to look straight through her. She went to bed early, hoping for sleep to take away the pain. Betty's words pricked some fragile bubble inside her, spilling out darkness in her soul. When she awoke, it was as if all the colors were a few shades darker.

When Jake called that morning, it was easy enough to blame her early bedtime on exhaustion. And when they went in search of hens for the chicken house, Annie was determined to suppress her emotions until she had time to sort through the implications later. As an airline stewardess she was skilled at smiling—no matter what was going on in her private life.

When they pulled in the driveway with a cage full of squawking chickens in the back, Jake was distracted by a phone call. When he hung up, she was already putting the tailgate down.

"I need to help Joe with a cow," he said. "Think you can take it from here?"

"Sure, just put them in the coop, right?"

"I'll carry the cage inside, just be sure to close them up

and leave them inside for a day or two so they know it's their new home."

"Easy," she said. "Thanks."

Annie watched him drive away and envied his excitement for a moment. Jake had found his passion. She, on the other hand, was unemployed in a town that didn't trust her to stick around long enough to give her a chance at something. She missed her old job; not the flying so much as the routine work of serving people.

She closed the door of the chicken coop and then opened the cage. Rhode Island Reds and Black Australorps tentatively stepped out into their new environment. Beady eyes darted back and forth and heads bobbed.

"Believe me, I know how you feel, walking into a new place," she said, and poured feed into the container. They rushed for it with happy clucking sounds. While they pecked, she poured oyster shells into another container.

"Be back with your water," she said.

In the lawn mower shed, she found an empty five-gallon bucket and filled it from the water spigot nearby. The bucket was heavy and she walked slowly, sloshing water onto her tennis shoes. When she rounded the corner, a line of chickens fled the coop and headed toward the garden.

"No!" she yelled, dropping the bucket to the ground. She raced after them, which only set them spreading their wings and doing a half-run, half-fly step. They scattered in all directions. She circled around them and tried herding them back to the chicken coop.

"C'mon chickies," she said, bending down with her arms outstretched. She was within three feet of one bird but as she grabbed for it, up it went, feathers flying.

"May as well let 'em be," Beulah said, smiling as she approached the mayhem.

"I went for water and forgot to shut the door," Annie said, raising her arms in the air and then dropping them to her sides in frustration.

"They might come back," she said. "Chasing them will only make it worse."

"I don't know how things could get much worse," she said.

"Something wrong?" Beulah said.

"Nothing. Since I can't do anything else here, I think I'll go over to the old stone house and see what else I can wreck."

**

After an afternoon of frenetic scraping, sweeping and filling trash bags in the dusty house, Annie's irritability had grown. She almost forgot about an earlier promise to have dinner with Lindy until her friend called to confirm the time.

A bath helped lift her mood. She looked forward to a dinner with Lindy and eating something other than her grandmother's soup, as much as she liked it.

Annie drove to Maple Avenue and pulled into the drive of a stately old Greek revival. The street was lined with old maples and oaks that stood like guards between the sidewalk and the road.

Inside the grand hallway, she waited while Lindy grabbed a light jacket and her purse.

"Lindy, the crown molding is amazing, and that medallion is beautiful," she said and pointed to the chandelier hanging from the center of the plasterwork.

"How do you know so much about architecture?" Lindy said. "Did you study it in school?"

"I studied art, but I was always drawn to buildings. European travel as a flight attendant fed my interest," she said. "This has been restored so well."

"My mom fell in love with it," Lindy said. "But she only got to live here for about five years before she died. Dad got it for a song but they put a lot of work in it. I'll show you around when we get back. Our reservations are at seven, so we better go."

She ran her hand along the ornate woodwork on the stairway. "I want to see every inch," she said.

When they reached the restaurant Lindy chose, Annie was reminded of the New York restaurants she used to frequent with her old boyfriend Stuart. Just the right lighting, cozy leather booths, an attentive staff, and good Italian food.

Lindy ordered a Merlot and she selected a Chardonnay. The waiter brought their drinks, took their dinner order and removed the menus.

"So, how are you doing?" she asked.

Lindy sighed deeply. "Honestly, I'm tired," Lindy said. "Tired of being single. Tired of loving someone who doesn't love me back the way I want. Tired of being here when he comes and still being here when he goes."

"Have you talked to him about how you feel?"

"I don't know what else to say. If he wanted to be here, wouldn't he move back?"

"You're both from Somerville?"

"He's from Rutherford, so we didn't really meet until college. It was our senior year before we dated. Rob always talked about traveling and seeing the world and I planned to go with him. When my mom died suddenly, it changed everything and I decided on law school so I could come home and practice with Dad. I thought Dad needed me and I didn't want to take him for granted. Rob went to Namibia with the Peace Corps." Lindy took a sip of her wine.

"West Africa?"

"Southern Africa. It was supposed to be temporary so he could get it out of his system. We dated the whole time he served in the Peace Corps—if you can call it dating. Long e-mails and even handwritten letters for nostalgia's sake. I couldn't wait until he came home and we could be together. When he finally got here, it was only a couple of days before he took off for South Africa to rock climb and backpack. I thought the two years in Namibia would be enough for him, but it was only the start. We had a big fight, I cried a lot, and we decided to take separate paths for a while."

"An ambiguous ending," Annie said.

Lindy nodded. "I finished law school and moved home to practice. Rob returned from South Africa and spent all his time with me, even though we never talked about officially dating again. Then he left for New Zealand. A few emails here and there, and then he comes in this last time. Same thing. And now he's off to California."

"You don't have any resolution."

"Exactly," Lindy said, and leaned forward in her seat. "I've been waiting around on him to decide he's ready to stay home. I need resolution. Does he simply need time to get the traveling out of his system? Or should I move on?"

The waiter brought their salads with herbed vinaigrette.

"Have you tried asking him?"

"Sure, you know me."

"And?"

"He says something like, 'Lin, it's all good, let's just roll with it for a while and see what happens.'"

Annie started to speak and then paused. It was important to tread carefully in this tender place. She remembered her own situation only months before when she was in need of hard advice she was not quite ready to hear. "Do you really want to go on living in this ambiguity?"

Lindy put her fork down and looked at her as if she had revealed a secret.

"I do have a choice, don't I? What is wrong with me? I've turned into one of those victims they teach you about in law school."

Annie took another bite of her salad, savoring the salty sweetness and then waited before responding.

"You both seem to want different things. Emotions, or even physical attraction, are not enough to make a life together. Believe me, I've learned the hard way."

"I've let my emotions run over my brain. I'll call him and lay it all out. If he wants to be here, then we can have a life together. If he doesn't, he can't keep coming around me. End of story," Lindy said with a resoluteness Annie wasn't quite sure her friend felt just yet.

"If you want a guy's point of view, ask Jake. Or even your father."

"Dad's already told me. He likes Rob well enough, but doesn't like the effects of his visits. He thinks I need to go out and meet other guys, but there's nobody else to go out with. Scott and Jake were the only two single guys around, and they are both taken," she teased.

"Well, there's always Woody," Annie said. Lindy gave her a scathing look. "But you don't need another guy to give you the strength to do this."

"No, I don't. I'll call him this week." Lindy said, putting her salad fork down and leaning back in the booth as the waiter removed her plate. "Now how about you? I have to admit, I'm jealous of you and Jake finding your way back to each other. You're so lucky. Jake's handsome, but he's a real man, not some pretty boy who is afraid to get his hands dirty. Everybody in town admires him for coming back and taking over the farm."

"People talk about Jake in town?"

"Dad says the bank wants him to consult for them while he's getting all the farming stuff going. He's well respected."

Annie decided to plunge in with a question she would have never thought to ask before hearing Betty Gibson's comments.

"Lindy, what do people say about me?"

Lindy hesitated. "People are impressed with the exciting life you've had, traveling all over the world."

"And they don't think I'll stay."

"Well, you have to prove yourself in these small towns. Jake's been around more regularly over the years, especially since he lived in Cincinnati. He's kept relationships with the locals."

Lindy reached across the table and placed her hand over Annie's.

"Don't sweat it. You're different from what people think."

The waiter brought their pastas. It looked and smelled delicious, but somehow she had lost her appetite.

***

Her grandmother's bedroom light was still on when Annie came up the stairs. Before going into her room, she knocked, and cracked the door open.

"Just checking on you," she said. Beulah was sitting up in bed, holding the metal box of letters found in the old stone house.

Annie couldn't read the look on her grandmother's face; it seemed part anguish and part joy.

"Everything okay?" she said, coming into the room and sitting on the edge of the bed.

"Fine," Beulah said, in a husky voice.

"What is it?"

Her grandmother handed her one of the letters. It was not a military letter, but instead an old-fashioned script in a feminine hand addressed to Ephraim May on Gibson's Creek Road. The postmark was dated January 17, 1946. Annie opened the envelope and pulled out the ivory paper. The letter was written in Italian. Beulah handed her a picture in muted tones of a beautiful, dark-haired young woman, erect and serious in front of the camera.

"I think the letter might be from her," Beulah said.

"A love interest?"

"It's the first I've heard of it," Beulah said. "I never knew anything but Bessie Sprinkle."

"I didn't see it in the box."

"There was a false bottom," Beulah said. "I noticed a felt tab when I was going through the letters and when I pulled it, there was this picture, this letter, and also this one," she handed another letter to Annie.

"At least this one's in English," she said. "Have you read it?"

"Oh yes," Beulah said. "And I want you to read it, too. Out loud, so I can hear it again."

Chapter Twelve

ANNIE READ THE return address out loud: "Arnie Mason, Fort Worth, Texas."

"I remember a guy from Texas in one of his letters," Annie said as Beulah nodded. Annie picked up the letter and read it aloud.

January 15, 1946

Dear Mr. And Mrs. May,

My name is Arnie Mason and I was in the same company as your son, Ephraim May. In fact, we became good pals. We were both sent to North Africa for training, then to Sicily, and on to Salerno and what is now known as the Italian campaign. Although I can tell you we called it many other things.

We had much in common. I lived on a cattle ranch and we both knew cows. Both of us grew up hunting and handling guns. I trusted Ephraim and he backed me up many a time as I did him.

This trust served us well as we began in Sicily with several skirmishes there before getting into the real stuff on the mainland of Italy. We landed at Salerno and made our way on foot north, headed for Rome. You will have heard all about this now and know what a disaster it was at Monte Cassino, although we were not in the battle. Our company was charged with taking the Volturno River and that was where Ephraim saved my life.

We were in a valley approaching the river and the Germans were placed in better positions on the cliffs above us. They had all the advantage, but we were there to draw them out and distract them while our troops were building a bridge upstream. We were advancing to the river when two Germans came up from a hiding place as I moved positions. In a flash Ephraim took out both of them before they could raise their guns. If he had not been there, I would not be here today.

We did take the Volturno but at a great cost. With our troops bogged down in the Italian mountains, a new plan for taking Rome was developed and we were sent to Naples for training. We didn't know for what or where back then, but we had our own ideas.

We were in Naples for nearly three months. During that time, Ephraim got to know a shopkeeper and his family. I went with him many times and shared a meal with them in their home. There was little English spoken, so we had to learn some Italian and do the best we could in both languages, but they were fine people and took great care of us. In turn, we shared cigarettes and tins of meat they could sell. Times were hard then for the people of Naples. They were caught under the rule of an ambitious dictator, but the people wanted freedom and they caught hope when the American troops arrived.

While we were in Naples, Ephraim came down with malaria. He never told you of this, I am sure, since his main concern was to keep you both from worrying about him. He spent a week in the hospital and the shopkeeper's daughter, Elena, often visited him and was better for him than the medicine.

The picture I am enclosing is of Elena. I took this picture out of his pocket after he was killed. I was determined to send it to you myself. We have heard all the personal effects don't always reach the family in order to "protect" them. He told me too much about you all and I know you don't need protecting from knowing how happy he was the last few months.

After battling through Sicily, Salerno and the Volturno, our time in Naples had been a good break for us, even with the rigorous training. And what was ahead, we did not know, although rumors abounded. Some thought we were on our way to take southern France. Others thought we were headed straight to Rome. Training in full battle gear and wading through seawater made many of us believe we were headed for a beachhead assault.

In mid-January, the training stops. We are confined to the company area and given a day to rest other than the inspection of our equipment. We understand what is unspoken. Church services are held, chaplains are called in, and letters are written home.

The next morning, we left for what we now know as the battle of Anzio. We loaded onto ships down at the port and sailed up the coast of Italy, landing at the beachhead off Anzio, with Rome as the ultimate prize. Rome meant we had Italy.

When going over the mountains failed with Monte Cassino, they decided we needed to attack from the closest beach to Rome. It is strange how these decisions are made in strategy rooms. A sleepy town is selected for its geographic and logistical connections and then its name becomes infamous ever after. That's what happened to Anzio.

We were supposed to attack and go inland for Rome, but it didn't work out. We took the beachhead easily enough, but in the week we stayed to organize our forces, the surprise we had on the Germans diminished and they responded with a vengeance. The Germans fought hard to keep what they had left of Italy and the history books will record these months as some of the worst fighting in the war's history. Slowly, we edged our way inland, pushing towards Cisterna. On February 1, we were still a mile outside the village under heavy attack.

Ephraim was lying next to a haystack. I was under the cover of an old wagon. Strange thing is, he loved those haystacks. He said they reminded him of home. The bullets came in fast and hard and out of the corner of my eye, I saw him drop his gun. I ran to him, yelling for a medic. When I got there he was already gone. You should know he didn't suffer. There was no time for it.

For the first time in the war, I was in shock. It was all wrong since Ephraim and I were in this together and I could not believe he was gone when just a minute before we were joking about who owed who a cigarette. My captain came by and told me to leave him and move on, but I couldn't go until I took the picture from him. I guess one thing I could do for him, is to save the picture of the girl he loved. I know this must be painful for you to hear, it is painful for me to write. I debated telling you these details, but my parents encouraged me, saying they would want the same from Ephraim if it had been me.

We took Rome, but it was three more months of fighting. Afterward, I was sent to France. When VE day came, I was discharged and sent to a hospital to recover from some constant health issues not for polite mentioning. I just got home a month ago, in time for Christmas. I wanted to write as soon as I could, as hard as it was for me to tell this story.

I don't talk much about what happened. They are lost years and a time to put away. I am one of the lucky ones. I am alive and home.

I write all this because I want you to know, your son was my best pal, and I will never forget him nor that he saved my life. I hope my life will honor his memory.

With all due respect,
Arnie Mason

Annie wiped her eyes and dropped the letter to her lap. Her grandmother was looking past her, staring into a dimension of time Annie had not experienced and could never know.

There was a long moment before either of them spoke and Annie did not want to be the first to break it. It was as if she were a guest witnessing an intimate moment with her grandmother's immediate family.

Beulah shook her head.

"I never knew all this, but I guess they thought I was too young to hear it," she said. "When I was old enough, it was too painful for them to bear it all over again. They hid it away in a secret bottom under the rest of the letters and then they hid the box under the floor of their bedroom."

"Like Arnie said, lost years to be put away," Annie mused. "I always thought the room where I found the letters was your room?"

Beulah fingered the fold in her nightgown.

"I slept in the same room with them until Ephraim went off to war. We only had two bedrooms. After he left, I moved into Ephraim's room since I was getting older and it was time I had a room to myself." Beulah leaned back and closed her eyes; her cheek was still wet from the tears.

"The night we got word was the worst of all. Mama cried so loud. No, it was more like a howl. Like some awful sound from a dying animal. I never knew such a noise could come from a human being, let alone my mama. Daddy held her and tried to console her. Finally, the doctor came and gave her something to help her sleep. By then, word had got out around the community and people were paying respects. Eunice Gibson, Joe's mother, was one of my mother's best friends. She came over and took charge of the kitchen and me. We had a wake of sorts for several days, but there was no body, and no funeral to give us closure. After the war, they had a place for Ephraim at the American cemetery in Anzio along with thousands of other boys. But Daddy wanted him back here in our family cemetery, resting with our kin. So we waited.

"It was in March of 1948 before we got him home, a long spell to wait for a funeral. Apparently, there is much to sort out at the end of a world war. When we finally did have the funeral, the entire town of Somerville turned out for it. The color guard escorted his body down Main Street with flags on the car while the mayor arranged for a band to play taps when the hearse stopped in front of the courthouse. We followed in a fancy black car with leather seats. I had never seen anything like it. People lined the street so thick they were three and four deep. Farmers who should have been in the fields were dressed in their best clothes. School had let out and the teachers stood with the classes. There were housewives with small children, all with sad faces, and all grieving with us. Out of the seven boys killed from our town, Ephraim was the only one brought home. I don't know why he was the only one, but Ephraim ended up representing all the boys we lost."

Annie was transported by the story, seeing in her mind the parade of cars going down Main Street, headed for the cemetery on Gibson's Creek Road.

"I was young enough to think once we buried Ephraim, our grief would end. It didn't," Beulah sighed. "Survival demanded we move on. No one had the luxury of wallowing in misery back then."

Annie waited and hoped her grandmother would continue. After a moment, she did.

"It was an economic hardship as well. Daddy depended on Ephraim to help with the farm. They were partners in it and Ephraim was the future of it. There was no one else to do the work, so we put our heads down and did what had to be done. After the war, Daddy hired on Fred and his brother Pete to help with our tobacco. If Ephraim had lived, Daddy wouldn't have needed them."

Annie sat in the silence of the memories, hardly daring to move, as if paying respect to what her family had suffered. After a few moments, she put the letter back in the box.

"What a treasure to have this letter. I wonder if your parents ever wrote him back?"

"Surely they did, if nothing else, to thank him."

"And what about this letter, the one written in Italian?" Annie picked up the letter and studied the handwriting.

"I can't imagine how they would've managed."

"Do you think it's from the shopkeeper's daughter?" she asked, opening it up and scanning the two pages in beautiful script.

"I wouldn't venture to say, although it seems possible with what the other letter says about how Ephraim fell in love with her."

"Janice could translate it, if you want her to," Annie offered.

Beulah was quiet.

"Let me think about it. Sometimes it's better to let sleeping dogs lie."

Chapter Thirteen

BEULAH WENT TO bed feeling unsettled, and knowing sleep would not come easy. It was like stirring up some dark matter long ago settled to the bottom of her soul. And when she did sleep, her dreams were anxious. In one, she was a little girl and it was her birthday. One present looked like an envelope, which then turned into a gift. Try as she might, she could not open it. In another dream, she was with her mother in the garden with a shovel, digging one hole; and then in another she was looking for something but never found it.

It was a relief to finally wake up even with the fuzzyheaded feeling that comes after such a night. Swinging her legs slowly over the side of the bed, she sat a minute, before pulling her favorite work dress off the hanger. It had cotton soft as lamb's ear and felt good on her skin.

Light shone from under Annie's door and she heartened at the thought of coffee, already brewed. The rich smell greeted her when she entered the kitchen and she filled her cup and sat at the table. Her morning devotional, her Bible, and her Sunday school book lay on the table, but she wasn't ready to read just yet. She wanted empty mind time to think about what she found in the secret compartment in the bottom of the old metal box.

The letter from Texas was straightforward enough. But what to do about the letter from Italy? Had it ever been read by her parents? In the 1940s, there were no Italians living in Somerville, at least none Beulah knew about. The Somerville library was just a small office off Main Street with a small collection of books donated by a local teacher until the 1950s when a real library was built and the collection had grown. The University of Kentucky or maybe even the Lexington library could have helped, but trips to Lexington were few and far between, and she could not imagine her parents trying to navigate the university campus.

Beulah smiled, remembering an incident when she was eighteen. She had driven her mother to Lexington so they could go to one of the big department stores down on Main Street near the old Phoenix Hotel. While in a crowded elevator, someone had stolen Beulah's purse. Distraught, they returned home to tell her father the story. He shook his head and said, "You've got no business up in Lexington." A trip to Lexington to search out an Italian dictionary was most unlikely.

And if her own parents didn't see the matter through, then why was it her responsibility? Or was it even more her responsibility because now she had the means to translate it?

There was a niggling fear about knowing the contents of the letter. Ephraim died a hero, not only to her, but also to the community. His name was engraved on a monument that memorialized all the World War II dead on the courthouse square. Beulah had simply idolized him. If she were honest, part of what drew her to Fred was the qualities similar to Ephraim.

And there was the heart of it: What if there was something in the letter that would destroy her view of him? What if Beulah saw a side of Ephraim in the letter not consistent with her view of him as the perfect older brother? No one was perfect, no not one. But the idea of Ephraim was all she had left of him. If she lost that, he might be lost to her forever.

***

The screen door squeaked open and Annie kicked off her muck boots before coming inside.

"The hens came in the coop to eat, so I shut the door on them. They are impossible to herd. Food was the only thing that got them inside the coop this morning, and that was after I hid behind the smokehouse and waited for thirty minutes," Annie said, and filled a bowl with cereal and milk. "How'd you sleep?"

"Not too good, but I'm sure tonight will be better."

"Me neither," Annie said.

"What're you doing today?"

"More of the same, reading the old letters and lots of work still to do at the old stone house."

"Busy day," Beulah said, envious of Annie's youth and energy. She remembered well her own ability to work circles around most people. With the onset of age, her energy had declined, and the recent knee surgery had slowed her down even more.

"What about you?"

"I'd like to do a little more work in the garden. Then I want to make up some more vegetable soup. I've never seen the like of sick people in the congregation. Seems like every time you turn around, somebody's getting a bad report from the doctor. It does make a body wonder if it's not in our food system, like Jake says. Something's not right."

"Your home canned, organic vegetable soup is just the thing," Annie said.

"At least we know what's in it."

***

Beulah popped open the sealed lid of a Ball jar, drained off the canning water, then dumped the squash into the pot. A problem like this made losing Fred even more grievous. He would pray with her about a troublesome situation and they would nearly always come to the same answer. It was confirmation they were making the right decision.

The simmering soup smelled good and she stirred spices into the mixture. There was never a recipe for soup, just whatever she decided to add to the mix. This time she had yellow squash, tomatoes, onion, potatoes, corn, green beans, and carrots in it, all from her garden. Now all it needed was time to blend all the flavors together. Later, she would dole out the soup in quart jars for the singles and half-gallon jars for families.

There was an old movie that won a big Hollywood award

years ago. One of the characters said when he ran, he "felt God's pleasure." Beulah knew exactly what he meant when she cooked.

After a while, she went upstairs for one more of Ephraim's letters. After the one from his best friend, Beulah wanted to hear from Ephraim. Especially now with this dilemma of what to do about the letter from Italy. Settling into a kitchen chair, she opened the envelope.

> *Naples, Italy*
> *November 24, 1943*
>
> *Dear Mother and Dad,*
> *We are still waiting around, which is just fine with me. Naples is a nice place, but there are a lot of street kids who beg and steal sometimes. They are tricky little fellows and if you don't watch, they'll take your wallet right out of your pocket. But I can say I don't blame them. Everyone has suffered for this war, but them maybe the most. Naples is called Napoli by the Italians and I am even picking up a few words. They speak little English, but somehow we can talk through hand motions.*
> *I have become friends with the shopkeeper's family—the one where I bought Mother's lace pillow cover—and they try to help the street boys by feeding them. But no one has too much to share. I have had supper with them several times. My pal Arnie comes with me and we give them cigarettes they can sell for food in exchange for feeding us. They have a daughter called Elena and the whole family has been very kind to me.*
> *We are training while we are here, but I can't say much more. We all hope whatever it is we are going to do when we leave here, it will bring us closer to coming home.*
> *Tomorrow is Thanksgiving and it looks like we are going to have a real turkey dinner. A truckload of birds arrived today and we were happy to see it. I would like to be eating dinner at home with you all and Beuly, but*

it don't do to think about any such things as that.

In a few minutes I have to report for guard duty, so I better sign off. I love you both and look forward to being home soon. Mom, promise you won't worry about me.

Love,
Ephraim

She was startled to hear the back door open and a "Hello" called out since she hadn't heard the crunch of gravel in the driveway. Evelyn walked in carrying a bag from the craft store and then stopped short at the threshold to the kitchen.

"Are you okay, Beulah?"

"Fine as a person can be digging up old bones," she said, and put the letter back in the envelope.

"The letters from Ephraim," Evelyn said, sitting down in a chair next to her. "I thought about them all last night after you told me on the phone. I'd have to know what the letter said, but you've always had more discipline than me."

"Well, I don't think discipline is behind this," she said.

"Fear is not of God. I'm having to remind myself a lot these days," Evelyn said, her face clouding over.

"Something you want to talk about?" Beulah said, seeing worry in Evelyn's face.

"No, no, I'm fine. I do want your opinion on these fabrics."

She laid out a sample of four different color schemes.

"I showed them to Mary Beth, and she likes them all. She told me to pick and just let her know how much she owes me. They're all about the same price, but I kind of lean toward this combination."

Evelyn pointed to burnt orange and golden yellow.

"Since it's a fall wedding, I thought those colors on the table would make it easy to decorate with small pumpkins, winter squash, and branches of bittersweet. But is it too boring?"

Beulah examined all the colors but her eyes were drawn to the burnt orange and gold. "No, I think it's just right. And like you said, it'll help keep everything else simple."

***

She was anxious for bedtime and another of Ephraim's letters, but Joe and Betty Gibson had invited them all over for pie and a game or two of Rook. Truth was, things had been strained with Betty since she made those remarks about Annie. It simply wasn't true, and she had told Betty so, to the point Betty had gotten her feelings hurt and left in a huff. But Beulah saw no sense in sitting there and listening to untruths and gossip about her granddaughter. Betty had to be corrected and there was nothing for Beulah to apologize about.

The invitation was Betty's way of extending an olive branch. In times past, when harsh words were spoken or a disagreement had popped up, they let it go for a few days, but one or the other extended an invitation—a sign that all was forgiven. It was the unspoken path of reconciliation for nigh on forty years.

Even though she didn't feel like it, Beulah had to accept the invitation as a way of forgiveness. Jake brought Annie, although her granddaughter was unusually subdued this evening, and along with Evelyn, they crowded into the small living room of the Gibson house where Joe had set up a card table.

While Evelyn, Jake, Annie and Joe played the card game, Beulah sat next to Betty on the couch.

"Beulah, what about those letters. I couldn't believe Annie found them. Aren't you glad now you didn't tear the house down? I'd dearly love to read them sometime," Betty leaned in, talking quietly.

Beulah brought her hand to her throat.

"I don't think you would enjoy them," she said. "If I come across something interesting, I'll let you know."

Of course the letters were interesting and of course Betty would love to get her hands on them. She would be especially eager to find out about the mysterious Italian woman. In Beulah's mind, it was a private family matter and this mystery was too dear and too precious until it could all be sorted out.

A whoop went up from the card table where Annie and Joe had beat Evelyn and Jake. She hoped that signaled the end of game playing. All she wanted was to get in her nightgown and climb into bed with another of Ephraim's letters.

Something Evelyn said earlier today stayed with her and made her think she had come to a decision. But she wanted to hear from Ephraim again and she wanted to sleep on it one more night, in case the Lord needed to turn her in a different direction.

She was glad when the party broke up a few minutes later and Annie drove her home. Finally, she settled in and took out another ivory envelope.

> *Naples, Italy*
> *December 16, 1943*
>
> *Dear Mother,*
> *I sure do like getting your letters and knowing what's going on with the neighbors and the farm. It makes me feel like I am there, even for a little while.*
> *My buddies and I like to sit around and tell stories. It passes the time and we need to laugh. I've been telling them about some of the characters in our town. They like especially to hear about Peddler Joe who travels around with his pet goat. I have told them every story I can think of, but if you remember more, please tell me. Sometimes it's all we have to do to keep us entertained.*
> *Mr. Caivano and his wife send their greetings to you and Dad. They are the shopkeepers I wrote you about who have been so nice to me. I am teaching Elena English. She can speak a few words, but I haven't taught her how to write much yet. I am just telling her what things are in English. I never thought of myself as being a teacher, but here I am. I eat with them as often as I am allowed. It makes me feel like I am a part of a family, even though their ways are different than what I have known.*
> *Please don't worry. It's hard enough to be here but knowing you worry makes it even harder. I think it must be over soon. We hope our training will help bring about the end of it.*
> *Love,*
> *Ephraim*

Beulah folded the letter up and placed it back in the box with the others.

"Caivano," she said the name out loud, turning it over on her tongue and feeling the strangeness of it. The name on the return address of the letter written in Italian. And the picture had to be Elena. *Elena Caivano,* the girl Ephraim loved.

Yes, she had made a decision, but she would sleep on it one more night. Unless her path was redirected between now and tomorrow morning, she had her answer.

Chapter Fourteen

IN THE KITCHEN, there was a note from her grandmother. It was on top of the letter written in Italian.

Please have Janice translate.

When she called Janice, the message went to voicemail.

"I have a favor to ask; we found a letter written in Italian. Long story, and I'll fill you in later, but I was wondering if you could translate it? I'll scan it and e-mail it to you. See you next week." She hung up and knew it might be another day to wait if Janice was on an overseas flight.

Annie tucked her phone into her jeans pocket and felt confident her grandmother had made the right decision. In the meantime, there was still another day's work or more of cleaning at the old stone house.

After walking back through the farm lane, Annie snugged the work gloves onto her hands and grabbed a flat end shovel. In the room below the burned-out bedroom, she began scooping up pieces of broken glass, charred embers, and chunks of plaster.

The mysterious letter had served as a temporary distraction from the penetrating reminders of her father's abandonment. She had loved her grandfather and he had filled the role she needed. Her biological father was more like an exotic uncle who showed up from time to time bearing gifts, apologies, and outrageous stories. Annie had learned early that with no expectations there were no disappointments.

But now, after all these years, coming home had created an unexpected situation: to be judged in a community not only on her father's behavior, but the entire disreputable Taylor clan. For it seemed that in a small town, a person was never left to stand alone.

Annie was angry at her father, not only for saddling her with this legacy, but the raw reminder of his selfishness by leaving her mother alone with a baby. What if Jake did the same to her? Or worse. What if Betty Gibson was right? What if she did the same to Jake because of some coded DNA?

The sweat dripped down her back as she worked harder and faster, sweeping and shoveling. The relationship with her father had consisted of phone calls and the rare visit until she was older and she made the effort to reach out more. When she was in her twenties, he had paid for her to visit him when he lived in South America and then in Spain. On one of those trips, she had finally gotten the courage up to ask him, after all these years, why had he left her mother?

"I got claustrophobic," he said, and shrugged his shoulders, as if he were explaining why he had walked out of a restaurant. And after her mother, there were countless women, one after the other, as he followed his desires without looking back at the wake of destruction.

Could I become claustrophobic, too? Her shovel hit shiny gunk on the hardwood floor, like hardened glue. She pushed again and it didn't move. Harder this time until finally she dropped her shovel and folded onto the ragged couch. The thought of being without Jake was unbearable now that they had found each other again. At the same time, the fear of hurting Jake was growing and she had no idea how to stop it.

***

The walnut leaves crunched under her feet in the gloaming as she stepped over the old stone fence to the Wilder farm. It was nearly October and the gentle breeze held a promise of cooler weather to come. The door to Jake's cottage was open and she called a "Hello" before stepping inside. A baseball game blared on the television but he wasn't in the living room.

"Hey," Jake said, coming out of his bedroom and putting on a flannel shirt over his T-shirt. Annie went to him and pressed her head to his chest, her arms around him and holding tight as if he might be ripped away from her. Jake wrapped his arms around her and they stood like that for a long and quiet moment.

"Everything okay?" he said. His eyes searched hers until she had to look away.

"A little tired," she said.

He kissed her, and then again. After a few minutes, she pulled away and sat down on the couch.

"I e-mailed a copy of the letter to Janice. It might be a couple of days if she's working," she said, watching Jake as he found the remote and turned off the baseball game.

"Then Beulah wants to know," he said.

"She does. I hope it's nothing too earth-shattering after all these years. How did your meeting go?"

Jake sighed. "Discouraging," he said, sitting down next to her.

"What happened?" she said.

"I met with a bunch of guys who are in the thick of what I'm trying to do. Some of their stories . . . I don't know."

"Like what?" Annie asked.

"Like one guy who sold eggs but ended up making regular trips to the local food pantry because a customer didn't come through on the order. Another guy said he was just about to turn the corner on making a profit on his beef when a late season drought kept his steers from finishing at prime weight. So many things are out of your control: weather, market price, and even seasonal changes. Another guy tried for a year to get this bakery to buy his eggs. They finally committed just before the fall equinox when his egg production dropped from fifty dozen a day, to twenty-three. Eggs, not dozen. I need to give it more thought before I get too invested."

"Wow," she said. "I'm sorry."

"Yeah, well, it's not like I'm a stranger to the farm. I grew up milking cows. And maybe I need to figure a way for the dairy to work for us, incorporating it into what we do, rather than trying to convert it. I know one thing—there's a lot more research I need to do first."

"At least you have the family farm paid for," she said.

Jake nodded. "I have a lot of advantages over most of those guys," he said. "The farm, savings from ten years in the corporate world, good investments. Even so, continuing to pour money into something with little return will be a hard road."

"It's difficult to do something new," she said. "But the beef cows are doing well, right?"

Jake nodded. "Let's take that, for example. I'm realizing how important genetics are to the herd. I need to cull the cows and get some great bulls to bring the quality up. Another big expense and it takes time."

"So the cows will be bigger and produce good meat?"

"Big can be less efficient. I actually want a smaller cow that raises an early maturing calf. The cows should have good maternal traits and milking ability. You want a herd easy to handle."

"So you're saying some of it is personality," she said.

"Temperament is the word, but sure, you breed for it."

She thought for a moment. "If the bull has bad temperament and the cow is good, then how does the baby turn out?"

Jake scratched his head. "It can go either way. But why risk it? If I have a good bull and good cows, the whole herd will be better."

She stood, feeling the color in her face.

"What's wrong?" Jake said.

"Nothing. I got hot all of a sudden," she walked into his small kitchen. "Do you mind if I open a window while we cook?"

***

Jake's discouragement was palpable during dinner, which helped Annie mask her own malaise. He drove her home afterwards, and it was a relief to put on her pajamas and climb into bed. Finally in the dark and quiet room, she let her tears flow before finally taking respite in sleep. When her phone vibrated at an unknown hour, she was disoriented.

"Hello?"

Sniffling came before Lindy's broken voice.

"Annie, can I come talk to you now?"

"Sure . . . What's wrong?"

"I'll tell you when I get there," Lindy said. She was dressed and downstairs by the time Lindy was at the back door.

"Want coffee?" Annie said.

"No, thanks. I don't want anything," Lindy said, her eyes puffy and red. "I'm sorry," she said. "I had to tell somebody."

"What happened?" she asked, leading Lindy into the living room and turning on a lamp.

"I called Rob," her voice broke. "Before I could say my piece, he thanked me for calling and asked how I knew," Lindy said.

"Knew what?" Annie said.

"That he just got engaged," Lindy's voice broke as tears flowed. "He thought I was calling to congratulate him." Annie handed her a wad of clean tissues. "Rob met her in New Zealand. They went to California together."

"Oh, Lindy," she said. "I'm so sorry."

"When he told me, I couldn't even talk. Imagine that?" she said in a half laugh, half cry. "Me, not able to talk. I sat there, trying to comprehend what he was telling me. Then he started saying how he should have told me about her, but couldn't seem to bring it up," Lindy said, and her face crumpled into a sob.

Annie pulled Lindy to her and held her while she cried. She stroked her hair and realized how much this young woman must miss her mother at a time like this. It was a feeling Annie knew well.

"It's okay. You'll be okay," she whispered soothing words to her until Lindy began to breathe deeper and finally pulled away.

"I'm sorry," Lindy said. "I know it's late, but I had to tell somebody. Dad was already in bed and he wouldn't have had quite the same reaction."

"Don't apologize," Annie said. "This is what friends are for. Now, I'm putting the kettle on for some hot tea. I won't let you go home until you've had a cup with lots of sugar."

Lindy gave her a faint smile and wiped her eyes. Annie went to the kitchen and put on the kettle, her heart aching for her friend. When Annie returned with the teapot and the cups on a tray, Lindy was calmly staring at her hands. She handed Lindy a cup and took one herself before sitting.

"Are you in the mood to hear about a mystery?" Annie said.

Lindy looked up from the tea, a glimmer of interest sparked in her green eyes. "A mystery?"

She told her about Beulah finding the secret compartment with the picture and the letters. "Who do you think the letter is from?" Lindy asked.

"It's from someone named Caivano, but the first name is hard to make out. My uncle met a woman when fighting the war in Italy, but it doesn't really look like Elena, which is the name of the girl Ephraim fell in love with. The script is so flowery; it's hard to make out. It could be just someone from the family, writing to offer condolences. Who knows? Janice has the letter—or will have it when she gets home from work—and hopefully she can translate it word for word."

"A mystery from World War II," Lindy said, holding the cup with both hands.

"Do you have any theories?" Annie asked.

"Maybe Ephraim owes the family money."

"I don't think they had any money to lend back then. He says in his letters he was giving them cigarettes to sell."

"If he got close to them, then it's likely an effort to keep in touch after the war. When he didn't respond, they never wrote again. Of course, they had to know writing in Italian would be difficult, but if they couldn't write in English, it might have been the only way they could communicate," Lindy said.

"Hopefully we'll know soon enough."

Lindy put her empty cup on the coffee table. "Thank you," she said.

"I'm sorry," Annie said. She hugged her friend again and watched her get into her car and leave before turning off the back porch light.

Chapter Fifteen

"YOU KNOW WHAT I like about restoration work?" Jerry said. "It's a form of stewardship. Look at this stone," he pointed to one of the stones in the foundation. "These stones were quarried by somebody, backbreaking work, and then laid on one another to make the walls. So instead of tearing this down and destroying the hours of labor already given to the job, we add to the labor already done."

Annie stood outside with Jerry and noticed the indentations in the rock, the weight of Jerry's words settling on her. Vesta's people dug the stones out of a limestone quarry and were never paid a dime for their work. What an even greater insult to their legacy if the house had been torn down.

"The guys will be here to start the stonework next week, so I'll coordinate with them on the roof," he said as they walked inside the house. "You did a good job of preparing the house. That's less for us to do."

Jerry pressed on the plaster in the room. "If I can leave any of the plaster, I will. We'll only take out what's damaged. When we get down to the studs, we can take care of the smell."

"Even if we do catch a whiff of it from time to time, it will remind us the fire was part of its history," she said.

Jerry nodded. "When we get started, it will look worse before it gets better. But it will get better."

***

The letters of Joseph Crouch had yet to back up the oral tradition Vesta had shared. Instead, he wrote about buffalo, bear and deer, Indian attacks on pioneers, hunting parties, trackers and settlers. He mentioned the Kentucky forts like Boonesborough, Harrod and Logan, but nothing about her family or the old stone house.

Annie picked up one of the pages and read:

"There was a remarkable lot of bear meat and buffilow and venson aplenty to eat, but not any salt nor bred. The people in the fort was hospetable to us but there was no fruit and no vegetables. It was a hard winter. Men came in that had been lost for days. It clouded over and that night had fell a deep snow. We had a good fire started the next morning.

There is a surprising quantity of people coming to Kentucky and more are a coming. We need the help with the terrable Indian troubles."

Annie rested her head on her hands; papers spread out on the dining room table this time, and reflected on the importance of the historical account this man had taken the time to document on paper. Letters served the purpose of connection to family and friends, but it also provided a way for daily life to be documented for historical purposes.

They were crucial in the 1700s, and even in the 1940s when Ephraim's writing provided an important connection to his family overseas. Letters were now a part of the history of the old stone house.

Hardly anyone wrote in longhand anymore, and cursive wasn't even taught in the local school. It made her wonder what that meant for the future, if so much information was lost to print for future generations. *How will there be a visual reminder of the past if words were stored in bits and bytes?*

Annie put a piece of paper in the *read* stack and rubbed her eyes when she heard her grandmother's car.

"Where've you been?" She held the door open as her grandmother gingerly stepped inside the house.

"Evelyn brought fabric to me this morning for the reception tablecloths and I realized I was out of the right shade of thread."

"Anything else in the car?" Annie said.

"That's all. Has Janice called?"

"No, but I haven't checked my phone lately. I'll get it."

There was a voicemail from Janice and she played it as she walked back to the kitchen.

Got your message. I just got back from Rome and I'm headed home now. I'll check e-mail and get back with you. Can't wait to see you real soon.

***

"Would you like soup?" she asked her grandmother, preparing to ladle it into bowls.

Beulah nodded, pulling spools of thread out of the shopping bag and examining them.

"Janice gets here the weekend you host Sunday lunch," Annie said, putting the soup on the table and then reaching for crackers. "She would love your fried chicken with the cream gravy and biscuits."

The phone Annie laid on the table vibrated.

"Janice, I was just talking about you."

"Annie," Janice said, her voice was calm and measured. "I translated the letter."

"You did? . . . So?"

"I'd rather you read it so you hear it from the person who wrote it," Janice said. "I typed it all out and emailed it to you."

Annie sat in a chair at the kitchen table and cut a worried glance at her grandmother.

"Is it bad?" she asked.

"Well, no, it's not bad. But it is serious. It's certainly not time-sensitive, after all these years, but Beulah needs to know."

"I'll call you later," she said and hung up.

Beulah frowned. "What is it?"

"She didn't tell me, but she's e-mailing the translation right now. She said it's *serious*."

Beulah's face drained of color.

Annie clarified, "Not bad, just serious . . . Janice said we need to hear it from the person who wrote the letter."

"I can't eat," Beulah said.

"Me either. I'm going over to Evelyn's to print Janice's e-mail out right now. I'll bring it back here and read it to you so we can hear it together."

"I'd go with you, but my knee will slow us down. I'll wait right here," Beulah said.

Chapter Sixteen

IT TOOK ANNIE twenty minutes to get back with the printed e-mail from Janice. Pretty fast time for walking across both farms but it still seemed to be an eternity to Beulah.

Beulah waited the whole time at the kitchen table and fiddled with the soup spoon. Eating was the last thing on her mind.

When Annie finally sat down across from her at the table, she could feel her body tense as if preparing for some blow. There was no going back now.

Annie began to read.

May 29, 1946

Dear Mr. And Mrs. May
I write you out of desperation because we feel the worst must now be true about our dear Ephraim. There has been no word from him since he left us. This is not true to his character. For we found him to be a most honorable and faithful friend to our entire family.

I must tell you how much he became a part of us during the time the American soldiers were training in Napoli. The Americans gave us hope during that time, we who had lost all hope after years of suffering under a man who thought only of himself. We first met Ephraim when he came into our shop looking for a gift for you, Mrs. May. My husband sensed this young man was different than some of the other G.I.'s who had been in and out of our shop door. He was buying a gift for his mother, which certainly endeared him to me. My husband invited him to have dinner that evening in our small apartment above the shop and that began the friendship between us.

It was during these visits that he and my daughter Elena formed an attachment. It became obvious to Pietro and me and we wondered if we should forbid it, knowing it could have no good end when he lived on one side of the world and she on another. But during the middle of a terrible war, if a boy and a girl can find love and hope, who were we to take this gift from them?

Ephraim got sick and stopped coming. He had malaria, we found out later, and he was in the hospital on the American base. His friend, Arnie, got word to us so we would know why they stopped coming. Elena went to see him and a kind nurse allowed her to visit, seeing the healing effect it had on your son. We did our best to chaperone their time together. But we suspect the hospital visits sealed their love for one another.

By mid-January, Ephraim had recovered and was sent back to the base. We saw little of him in the days following until he came one evening with the message that they were to ship out the following day.

We gave Ephraim and Elena time alone that night, the only time we ever allowed that. But we knew he would not be back here during the war, and maybe not ever, so we allowed them privacy to say their goodbyes. When the troops left from the port of Napoli, Elena took to her bed. We worried that she might have malaria as well. She became very ill for many weeks and a doctor was called. We found out it was not malaria. Elena was heartbroken, but she was also pregnant.

At first, Pietro and I were angry. At her, at Ephraim, at the war that threw them together. Soon, we saw the pregnancy gave her great hope that they might someday be reunited. We of course knew this to be unlikely but we knew enough of him to believe that he would not disown this child.

I write you now, still confident of his character, and knowing that since the war is now over and we still have not heard from him, we are sure the worst must be true.

We do not wish to be a burden in any way, but you are the grandparents of this child, and if you have lost your only son, we believe that you might like to know you have a grandson and that Elena is proving herself a very good mother.

If the worst is true, Pietro and I give you our condolences and our deepest respect.

Lilliana Caivano

During the reading, Beulah sat straight up in her chair with her hands clasped tightly together on the table. While Annie folded the letter and put it away, it was as if the air went out of her body, and she slumped onto the kitchen table, her head in her hands.

Ephraim loved an Italian girl named Elena, who bore him a child.

A son.

A tapestry she had long ago sewn and hung on the wall as finished now unraveled, thread-by-thread. Her hands grew hot and wet. Her shoulders shook, and she felt hands on them, comforting, as her mother had done when she was a child.

Time disappeared. All her reserves and all her steel had evaporated like mist. The silent tears came, dripping off her nose and onto the wooden harvest table. She stared down into the pool of tears and remembered how her mother collapsed after the uniformed stranger delivered that hateful piece of paper. " . . . deeply regrets to inform you . . ."

Her father had gathered her mother up in his arms and carried her upstairs to their bedroom. Beulah remembered standing alone in the hall, starring at the telegram on the hall floor, where her mother dropped it. She picked up the telegram and looked at it. It was strange how simple words on paper caused such terrible suffering. The letter in hand, she carried it to the fireplace and dropped it in the fire. After that, she went to the kitchen and cooked a meal. It seemed the only thing to do.

When she finally rose up and rested her chin on her hands, Annie was still behind her with her arms on her shoulders. Evelyn was here now, sitting across from her with a cup of hot tea that she pushed toward Beulah. Where had she gone in the last few minutes that she didn't hear Evelyn come in the door? Or had it been hours?

Neither spoke, and Beulah was glad for the silence. She just shook her head and took the tea. *Dear God*, she prayed. *Help me*. After a few sips of the tea, she spoke.

"I'm sorry. I never knew all that was inside me."

Evelyn's eyes were full of compassion, not pity, and Beulah appreciated that not a little.

"This must be very hard for you after all this time," Evelyn said.

"He had a son," Beulah said. "To find out now, after all these years. He'd be just a decade or so younger than me, if he's still living."

"I can't help but think that is something positive, once you get over the shock of all this," Annie said. "We actually have relatives in Italy."

Beulah was not ready to think about Italian relatives.

"It makes me wonder if my parents suspected anything like this. Did they know and not ever act on it? Or did they go to their graves never knowing what the letter said?"

"Even if they did know, they wouldn't have been able to act on it," Evelyn said. "Back then, no one around here was able to travel overseas like they do now. Even if they could have afforded it, they couldn't have left the farm long enough."

"There was certainly no Skyping or e-mail," Annie said. "Only letters and photographs."

"They may have written in English," Evelyn said.

"Either way, the communication we have stops here," Annie said.

"We'll never know for sure, but whatever happened, they put it away in a secret place and went on with their lives as best they knew how," Beulah said. "I guess that's what we need to do now."

"Are you sure about that?" Annie asked. "I mean, with the Internet, we could probably track them down."

She caught her breath. "What if they don't want to be found?" she asked.

"They did reach out to your parents all those years ago," Evelyn said. "The Caivanos may have gone to their graves believing Ephraim's family wanted nothing to do with Elena or the child. Or they might have wondered if the letter ever reached them."

"But that would be the child's grandparents. Even if they wanted to reach out, it doesn't mean Elena or her son would want that," Beulah said.

"There's a return address in Naples," Annie said. "Why don't we write back to the family, explaining what has happened? They don't have to respond if they don't want to," she said. "This time, we'll have Janice write it in Italian. After all, she'll be here next week," Annie said.

"It was so long ago, the parents will be dead now," Evelyn said. "It would be unlikely to reach the same family."

"Not always," Annie said. "Look at us. If someone wrote the May family on Gibson's Creek Road, it would end up in Grandma's mailbox."

Evelyn laughed. "That's true. It can happen."

"I would like to pray about all this before we decide anything," Beulah said. "It's a lot to take in and I need time."

"Good idea," Evelyn said. "Let us know how we can help."

"It's your decision, Grandma," Annie said.

Beulah looked at them both, feeling deep affection. "Thank you both for being here."

After Evelyn left, she boiled a big pot of greens with onions and ham hock. Then she made a macaroni and cheese casserole and sliced tomatoes from the garden. She whipped potatoes with butter and cream and then baked yeast rolls, and all the while she prayed.

***

With a table laden with food, Evelyn and Jake joined her and Annie for dinner. It seemed there was an unspoken agreement to avoid the recent family revelation. Instead, Jake talked of trying to find more hay for the winter and Annie updated everyone on the progress of the old stone house. Evelyn talked of preparations for the upcoming wedding.

It was a balm to end such a day. Exhaustion settled over her that was far beyond anything physical even though it carried with it a peace of sorts. That night, once she settled into bed, she opened the box and pulled out the last letter from Ephraim.

Both anticipation and dread filled her, as she knew this was to be the last communication her parents had received from him.

> *Naples, Italy*
> *January 21, 1944*
>
> *Dear Mother and Dad,*
> *We are moving out tomorrow for a mission we don't yet know. It's the way of being a soldier. You train and prepare and guess until the day arrives.*
> *There is a somber mood in camp tonight. We have been told to prepare ourselves for battle. The chaplains are here to make it easier for us. There is a church service after supper and I plan to go. I only tell you all this because by the time you get this letter, whatever is going to happen will have happened.*
> *After I found out we were leaving, I went to see the Caivanos to thank them for all their kindness toward me. Elena gave me a picture of herself and I am glad to have it. I left some money for Mr. Caivano to help offset all the many suppers they have shared with me. I plan to see them again when the war is over. I have fallen for Elena. She is different from any girl I have known. I ask you to keep her and her family in your prayers as well.*
> *I must tell you I have acquired a taste for red wine. Only a little, mother, should you think I have turned my back on your temperance ways. But when it is made*

from a man's own grapes, well, it's hard to see much difference between that and our own tobacco crop.

If that were my only confession. This war has changed us all. We are not angels, any one of us. I only hope you can find it in your heart to forgive the things I have done. I have asked God for his forgiveness, but I can't help wanting your forgiveness as well.

I love you both very much and look forward to the day when I will be home and we will be together again. If something should happen, please know I have made my peace with God and trust his will to determine my days.

Love,
Ephraim

She slipped the letter back into the V-mail envelope and placed it in the stack, next to the two letters found in the secret place. This time, nothing was hidden away. Each letter was part of the whole story.

Chapter Seventeen

ANNIE MET LINDY for breakfast at Bill's Diner and shared the contents of the letter from Elena's parents over a plate of eggs, bacon and his famous cathead biscuits.

"You have relatives in Italy?" Lindy said in amazement.

"Apparently," Annie said. "If anyone is left. Elena's child might have died before marrying, so it could have ended there. We've no idea."

"I could do some research," Lindy offered.

"Grandma's not ready to go there yet," she said. "She idolized her brother, and his death really marked their family. I want to give her as much time as she needs . . . How are you?" Annie asked.

Lindy sighed. "Better. If I'd heard Rob was engaged a month ago, it wouldn't have hit me this hard, but it was worse with recently seeing him. I still can't wrap my head around how he treated me here when he was on the verge of getting engaged."

"Maybe it was a surprise to him as well," Annie said, remembering her own awakening to Jake as more than a friend after coming home last summer.

Lindy's expression brightened. "Anyway, I did get a call

from an old law school friend who invited me to Keeneland next Friday for lunch in the Clubhouse and then a day of horse racing. It's something to look forward to."

"Find a nice outfit. Sometimes a girl simply needs a new dress," Annie said.

"I wish it were that simple," Lindy said. "Listen, Annie," and then stopped when the waitress brought their food and refilled the coffee.

"I need to talk to you about my dad."

Annie added Tabasco sauce to her eggs. "Something wrong?"

"Not exactly wrong," she said. "He's just acting weird. I've walked into his office a few times to find him staring into space. That's not totally uncommon. In fact, when he's on a big case he often spends a great deal of time thinking through strategy. We have some heavy stuff going on," Lindy's voice trailed off.

"I'm doing that a lot these days, too," Annie said.

"It's more than that. At home, I found the cereal box in the refrigerator last week. The week before I found the milk in the pantry. What if his mind is slipping, maybe it's the early stages of something?"

"He's only in his fifties, right?"

"Yeah, but I did a little research and it can happen early for some people," Lindy said. "It's not like him. I keep thinking of Bill's wife, Viola, and all they have dealt with after she was diagnosed with Alzheimer's. It would be devastating if something happened to Dad."

Annie remembered hearing about the illness of the diner owner's wife when she returned to Somerville. She had grown close to Viola during her high school days working part-time as a waitress.

As if on cue, Bill bounded over to their table, his white apron dirty with grease and food stains. "How is it?" he asked, bushy eyebrows raised.

"The best," Annie said. "Jake says you're getting the eggs from a local farm now."

"Happy chickens on pasture. Taste better, don't they?"

"How's Viola?" Lindy asked.

Bill wobbled the spatula in his hands.

"Good days, bad days, and I never know which it will be."

"Early on, when she started showing signs, how did you know something was wrong?" Lindy asked.

"I found cheese in a drawer and flour in the refrigerator. Then she couldn't remember how to drive here from our house and we only live three blocks away. It went on from there," Bill said, and heard his name called from the kitchen. "Gotta go," he said.

Lindy looked at Annie, her eyes wide.

***

Annie knocked lightly on the cottage screen door, and then pushed it open. Jake was sitting on the couch, papers spread over the coffee table, and the phone to his ear.

She sat down across from him and he looked up, the frown changing to a smile when he saw her.

"How much do you want for it?" he asked. "Uh huh. How many do you have?" another pause. "I'd like to come down tomorrow and see it," Jake said and began scribbling an address on one of the papers. "Whatever's good for you," he said. "That's fine, thanks."

He put the phone on the coffee table and ran his hands through his hair, leaning back on the couch.

She could see trouble spelled out on his face. "Bad news?" she asked.

"Good news that I found hay, but the price is high due to last year's dry season." He leaned forward and rested his forearms on his legs. "But I don't have a choice. I have to feed cows this winter."

"Will you always have to buy hay?"

"No, but it will take me a year or two to get our pasture in shape for what we need. I may have to do some part-time bank consulting for a while, until I can get everything off the ground."

"Not exactly what you hoped," she said.

He nodded. "Well, there's no doubt my dreams have adjusted to reality over the last few weeks."

"Jake, I had a funny conversation with Lindy this morning. She thinks something is wrong with her dad. Tom's done a few weird things lately, like leaving the milk in the pantry and the cereal in the refrigerator."

"Just like Mom," he said.

"Right. Like Evelyn," she smiled at him and waited.

Jake frowned at her and then sat back on the couch. "Mom and Tom?"

Annie nodded. "Crazy, huh?"

"Are you sure?" he said.

"No, but the signs are there," she said.

He started laughing. "Tom always asks me how she's doing and what she's been doing."

"How do you feel about it?"

"If she's happy, I'm happy. Tom is a great guy. Does Lindy know?"

"I didn't say anything since it doesn't appear to be in the open yet. But I don't want her to worry her dad is losing his mind."

"How about that," Jake was grinning.

Annie looked around the room at the cardboard boxes stacked on top of one another in the corners of the room and even pushed under the coffee table. One stack served as a table and held a lamp. "I can help you with these today if you like," she offered.

"Actually, Joe and I are headed out to Western Kentucky this afternoon to see a goat dairy that's doing a good job with gourmet cheeses. We'll come back tomorrow and pick up the hay on our way back into town. I'm sorry to miss the offer."

He looked around at the boxes.

"Mom is on me to get it all put away. She's worried I won't get to it before we have Scott's family stay here for the wedding."

"I love organizing. Why don't I work on it while you're gone?"

"You really don't mind?" Jake said. "There's a bookshelf in my old room I've been meaning to bring out here. I'll get it before I leave this afternoon and you can decide where to put it."

"Okay, so I'll see you tomorrow," Annie turned to go but Jake gently held her arm.

"Surely I get a better goodbye," he said, drawing her into a hug. Annie melted into the safety of his arms and wanted more than ever to tell him what was breaking her heart.

"Jake," she started.

"Yeah," he said, kissing her head and then her cheek before reaching her lips.

"Nothing," she whispered.

***

Later, Annie had barely settled down to do more reading when Janice called again.

"How's it going?" Janice asked. "I can't stop thinking about your grandmother. I couldn't even sleep last night."

"Hold on," she said, and crept up the stairs, out of earshot from her grandmother who was in the kitchen. "It was a shock," she said. "The only other time I've seen her like that was when my grandfather died. She seems better today, but we haven't talked about it."

"Have you started Googling the family in Italy yet?" Janice asked.

"No, she's not ready. I mean, what if she finds out they are all gone? To find out you have a piece of your brother alive and then to lose it all over again . . . it'd be so hard on her."

"Is she not ready—or is it you?" Janice said.

Annie was pushing her bedroom door shut when she stopped cold.

"What do you mean?"

"You're the one who always avoids any kind of emotional risk. I mean, it's fine if your grandmother is not ready, but be sure you're not projecting your own fears onto her."

"When did you get your psychology degree?" Annie asked.

"When I became your best friend, for Pete's sake. Don't get mad, but we both know you tend to shut down when it gets a little risky."

Annie took a deep breath and exhaled.

"Janice, this isn't about me, honestly."

"All right, all right. Look, I've been Googling, pages and pages. I can't find an Elena Caivano anywhere. There are lots of Caivanos, and they're all over Italy, mostly in the south. When I type up the address in Naples, nothing comes up."

"Too bad. Where do we go from here?" Annie asked, sitting down on her bed.

"Italy," Janice said.

Chapter Eighteen

BEULAH FINISHED SEWING the last tablecloth and folded it neatly, then placed it in a box with the others. She would ask Annie to carry it over to Evelyn's as soon as she had a chance. The rhythmic work and hum of the machine gave her uninterrupted time to think; she hadn't even answered the phone when she heard it ringing.

The question of whether they should find any remaining family members weighed on her. Some things were better left alone. *If my parents were alive today, what would they want to do?* Even more important, *what would Ephraim want?*

As the only family member left from that small nucleus, Beulah was the self-appointed guardian of her brother's memory. What Ephraim might have wanted was more important than even her parents. It was Ephraim's situation after all. She gathered stray pieces of thread and then folded the green Singer sewing machine down until it looked like any other end table.

Now she would do the thing she had looked forward to all day as she sat and sewed. Once outside and into her Mercury Marquis, she headed down the driveway and turned left onto May Hollow Road, then took another left onto Gibson's Creek Road. She passed the driveway to the old stone house, down to the entrance of the May Family Cemetery and slowly up the gravel road to the top of a wooded hill. There was the cemetery, surrounded by the old limestone fence and the creaky iron gate.

Inside, the area was neatly trimmed. Joe had taken it on when he agreed to mow her yard as part of the bargain of leasing her farm for his cattle. The older limestone markers in back were cocked slightly to the left or right as the ground had settled over the many years. The newer ones in front were made of granite and stood straight and even.

Facing her first was dear Jo Anne's grave, Annie's mother, who died when she was only thirty-two. Then there was little Jacob, who was just an infant, Beulah's only son. There was the newest grave, the one belonging to Fred, and next to it, the empty spot where Beulah would be laid with her family.

Beulah's parents, Lilah and William May, were buried in the second row next to their son and her brother, Ephraim. She stood over Ephraim's grave and read again the words on his military footstone: *Ephraim May, PVT US Army, World War II, December 14, 1923 - February 1, 1944.*

Shafts of sunlight filtered through the maple leaves hanging low over the stones giving the grass below a watery illusion. On the wrought iron bench near a walnut tree, Beulah stretched her legs in front of her, and asked God to give her wisdom in making a decision.

The child was Ephraim's responsibility, but with his death, it fell to their parents. What they discussed or even decided to do, she would never know. There was only so much country people could do in 1946. Whatever had happened—or had not—went to the grave with her parents.

Nowadays, the world was smaller, and they might be able to find some answers after all these years. What would Ephraim want her to do?

Come to me, all who labor and are heavy laden, and I will give you rest. The verse came to her out of the blue, as Bible passages so often did. The truth was, she was never meant to carry the burden. *None are perfect; else we wouldn't need the grace of God.* But maybe she had thought Ephraim was perfect, and in the process, she had placed a yoke on her brother he was never meant to carry either.

With renewed purpose and a lighter spirit, Beulah parked the car and went in the back door, where there was no black snake in sight. She hesitated in the kitchen, but there was no need to cook tonight with so many leftovers in the refrigerator.

Annie came down the steps and met her there.

"Where did you go?" Annie asked.

"Up to the cemetery. I needed to sort some things out," Beulah said, pulling a pitcher of iced tea from the refrigerator. "Are you going out with Jake tonight?"

"He's in Western Kentucky with Joe and won't be back until tomorrow," Annie said.

"I'm heating up leftovers."

Annie brought out plates and silverware.

"Sounds good to me."

They filled their plates and Annie said grace. The food tasted better this time around since the night before her emotions were topsy-turvy.

"How are you feeling about everything?" Annie asked.

"It was a good day of thinking and praying," she said, taking a sip of her iced tea.

"I was worried last night," Annie said.

The expression on her granddaughter's face reminded Beulah of when Annie was a little girl with long, dark hair pulled back into a ponytail, eyes wide and wondering.

"Grief is a funny thing. Sometimes it's a nicely contained river you have to cross from time to time and sometimes it floods through like a dam has broken. I guess my dam broke last night," she said, smiling at her granddaughter. "At least some of it was grief, but I was also looking at things wrong," she said.

"How do you mean?" Annie asked.

"Oh, I reckon I idolized my older brother. I suppose I even canonized him if you could do that in the Baptist denomination," she chuckled. "But I realized today I was wrong. He was human and needed grace, just like I do, every day."

Beulah took a breath and went on.

"I also realized we don't need to fear the truth. Not that we won't have emotions or even damage from knowing truth, but it need not be feared when we have God to help us face things. What I'm trying to say . . . please see what you can find out about the

Caivanos. We can still have Janice write the letter next week, but if you can find anything out on the computer, we should try it."

Annie nodded. "Well, good, because Janice has already been searching. And she's reading the Italian sites, which only she could do anyway."

Beulah leaned over her plate of food, eager to hear the results.

"There are lots of Caivanos, all over Italy," Annie said. "There are several *E. Caivanos,* but nobody named Elena is coming up. When she typed in the Naples address, nothing happened. She's even tried sites where you can see the building from the street, but nothing comes up for the address."

"Well, I guess that answers the question," Beulah said, the words coming out in a sigh.

"There's another option," Annie said. "Instead of staying on the farm next week, Janice and I can go to Italy and see what we can find by actually being on the ground."

Beulah pushed her plate away and crossed her arms on the table.

"Oh no, I can't let you spend your savings when we don't even know if there's anything to find," Beulah said.

"Janice has a buddy pass I can use through the airline. If the flight loads cooperate, we can fly free. We won't know exactly when we will be able to leave or come home, which makes it a little risky. But a free trip is worth it. I don't know when Janice and I could manage this time together, so it feels like the right thing."

"But where would you stay? Big city hotels are terribly expensive, or so I've heard."

"Janice has a big family and half of them are in Italy. Her cousin has an apartment in Naples we can use. Another cousin works for a rental car agency and can get us a discount. It won't cost much. Janice is giving us a gift."

It was strange how this was coming about. In Beulah's thinking and praying time today, she had an overwhelming peace God would make a way if they were meant to pursue these old family connections. Here it was. Janice's offer to sacrifice a relaxing week on the farm for travel she did all the time was a gift and Beulah decided to accept it.

"A fine idea," she said.

The surprise on Annie's face nearly made Beulah laugh.

"You didn't think I'd want you to go?"

"Honestly, I thought you'd be afraid to find out they might not be alive or they'd want nothing to do with us," she said.

"Those things might just be the case. Either way, I don't want to go to my grave knowing we didn't try. Janice's offer to translate and take you without much expense, well, it's too good to pass up."

Beulah poured another glass of tea.

"You'll still need food and you may even need other things we aren't thinking about. I'll give you money to cover anything else for the two of you."

Annie looked at her grandmother in wonderment.

"You amaze me," she said. "As soon as I know how you are going to react, you surprise me."

"Sometimes it surprises me," she said and chuckled.

The euphoric feeling of freedom gave way to a taste for something sweet. Then she remembered the chunk of date cake she had frozen for just such a time as this.

Chapter Nineteen

AFTER THEIR EARLY supper, Annie packed up her toothbrush and pajamas. She decided to spend the night at Jake's cottage while he was in Western Kentucky so she could unpack the mess of boxes and take advantage of his satellite television and movie collection. Scott's car was parked in Evelyn's driveway, so she stopped to say hello before going on to the cottage behind the main house.

"Annie," Evelyn said when she walked into the kitchen. Scott's smile was warm when he stood to his feet and he shook her hand when she extended it. Annie greeted Mary Beth, who always had the look of a pretty department store doll, with her porcelain skin and auburn curls framing her face.

"We just finished eating," Evelyn said. "Would you like something?"

"I've had supper, but thank you. I'm staying in the cottage tonight while Jake is gone to get things organized."

"Thank goodness," Evelyn said.

"Everyone is going to so much trouble," Mary Beth said. "We really appreciate it." She looked at Scott.

"We do. It's special to get married here. Annie, did you know

Mary Beth and I met over lunch in this house? It was Evelyn's turn to host and they invited me since I was new in town."

"And me, the first weekend I was alone and without the kids after the divorce," Mary Beth said. "We couldn't think of a more perfect place."

"I knew Evelyn and Grandma's after-church Sunday dinners played a role, but I didn't know y'all actually met here." Evelyn motioned for her to sit down at the table and she did.

"We'll be forever grateful to Evelyn and Beulah and their ministry," Scott said.

Annie hadn't thought before about Evelyn and Beulah's Sunday afternoon dinners being a "ministry," but maybe ministry didn't always mean a tax status. Annie liked Scott with his short dark hair and athletic build. He was warm and approachable, unlike other ministers she had known in her youth. The young Grace Community church had been a refreshing option for both Jake and her after coming back to Somerville.

"I'll let y'all get back to wedding planning."

"Take one of my cinnamon rolls for breakfast tomorrow morning," Evelyn said as she put a gooey roll onto a plate and handed it to Annie. She doubted it would last until morning.

Inside the cottage, she dropped her overnight bag on the couch and stared at the boxes stacked and pushed to the corners of the room. Jake had practically lived out of a suitcase for weeks, ignoring the things he didn't need on a daily basis, which appeared to be very little.

She started with clothing and hung each item in the closet or folded it and placed it in the chest of drawers. Finishing one box of winter clothes, she tackled another.

There was an intimacy to handling another person's clothing. It made her long for these daily domestic rituals with Jake when such things as this would be part of their life together. She was barely able to enjoy the fantasy when a sobering thought barged into her mind: *Did my father feel this way about my mother before they married?*

With one of Jake's shirts hugged to her chest, she sat on the bed. *Did my father long for intimacy before it arrived with such smothering sense of responsibility?* And when the claustrophobia came, did it come on like a sharp pain or muscle spasm? Or did it make a gradual entrance into the relationship, like a rising tide that ebbed its way into the sand?

These were questions she had never thought to ask her father. She never wanted to spoil the little time they spent together with hard questions. Now she regretted that neediness. If she had dealt with those things earlier, maybe they wouldn't be popping up now at the very worst possible time.

***

Later that night, Jake called her as she readied for bed.

"How's it going?"

"The goat farm was educational," he said. "They're making gourmet cheese in an old tobacco barn and the set-up is nice. It's good to see what other people are doing and how they're doing it. What about you?"

"Well, I do have all your clothes put away. I'm leaving the books for tomorrow morning. Right now I'm in my pajamas and looking at your movie collection, which is pretty high testosterone for my taste."

"You're spending the night?" Jake said. "I hope it's a more permanent arrangement soon." She smiled into the phone but didn't trust her voice.

"It looks like Janice and I are going to Italy next week instead of her coming here for a visit," she said.

"Italy?" Jake said.

"Crazy, I know, but it's all coming together."

Annie filled him in on the details.

"Sounds like a good idea," he said. It was a moment of silence before he said, "I'm glad you're getting to the bottom of it, but I will miss you."

The emotion closed around her throat and she could not respond.

"I love you, Annie. Don't ever doubt it."

After she hung up, all her intentions of watching a movie disappeared, ushering in sadness after the uncomfortable phone call. Jake had sensed something was wrong. Of course he did. How could he not?

If she talked to her father, possibly he could answer some of her questions and make sense of everything. It was early morning in Spain, probably not a bad time to reach him. After a brief pause, she scrolled through and found his number.

After several rings, Annie was nearly ready to hang up when a female voice finally answered.

"Hello?"

"Is Ed there?" she said, her voice barely above a whisper.

"Who is this?" The woman had an American accent.

"His daughter," she said, her voice stronger now. "May I speak to him?"

"Daughter?" the woman laughed. "Ed doesn't have a daughter. He's not here right now anyway, but next time you call, you may as well say who you really are."

The line went dead.

Annie sat in stunned silence and stared at her cell phone.

***

Vesta was seated in a wheelchair in the sunroom, her glasses dangling from her neck by a delicate metal chain. Annie pulled a chair up next to her and sat down.

"I read through all the papers and didn't find anything," Annie said.

"Neither did I," Vesta said, studying her. "Are you giving up?"

"Oh no. It's why I'm here. I want to know where to go now," Annie said.

"William Champ, I believe. He's the one I would try next. His letters can also be found at the History Center."

"It will be a while before I can get there. I'm going to Italy in a few days," she said. And then she told Vesta the whole story about Ephraim and his Italian child.

"My, my, what an exciting adventure!" Vesta clasped her hands together and, for a moment, she envisioned the old woman as a young girl.

"Italy was a place I always wanted to go. So much history!"

"It's beautiful, although all of my experience has primarily been in the city of Rome on layovers, so I can't quite say I've seen the country."

Vesta put on her glasses and peered at Annie as if she were a bug under a microscope.

"You don't look happy for someone going to Italy," she said, taking off her glasses. "There's more you're not telling me."

She lifted her chin and met Vesta's penetrating stare. "I'll bet you never had a student lie to you," she said.

"Maybe once, but it never happened a second time," Vesta said.

Annie smiled and she could see the corner of Vesta's mouth crease just a bit, even while she tried to be stern with her.

"It's my name. Around here, I'll always be known by what the Taylors before me have done. Lately, I've worried that I might really be like them . . . like my father." She whispered the words, glad to have finally said them to another human.

Vesta studied her for a minute before she spoke.

"Listen, child, Jeremiah says: 'Can the Ethiopian change his skin or the leopard his spots? Then also you can do good who are accustomed to do evil.'"

Vesta straightened in her chair and leveled a steady gaze at Annie.

"When you come back from Italy, I want a report on what that means to you."

***

Janice had carefully watched the Rome flight loads and she was quite certain they would make the next day's flight. Annie pulled out her suitcase, the one she had used on so many work trips, but now gathered dust under her bed.

While she cleaned it off and began packing, she thought back to the last time she used her suitcase. She and Janice had been on a flight to Rome together when a random conversation with a passenger unraveled Stuart's lies to her. She had just agreed to move in with him and planned to make the move when she landed. Her roommates had already found a replacement. What she learned on that flight made her realize he was not who she thought.

To make matters worse, when Annie had landed, she found out her airline had been sold and she had lost her job. That fateful day had sent her running home to Kentucky and her grandmother. What had seemed like complete devastation at the time ended up being the best. She came home just as Jake was considering a move back to the farm. It had all worked out better than she could have dreamed. If only she could return to those blissful days after she and Jake reconnected and before the ghost of her father's sins began haunting.

Annie packed clothes and toiletries in her suitcase and placed a photocopy of the letter from Lilliana Caivano, and the picture of Elena Caivano, in her purse along with her passport. There were even some euros stashed in her suitcase from that last trip to Rome.

Janice's number popped up on the cell phone lying beside her suitcase.

"Hey," she said. "I'm just packing."

"There's a problem," Janice said.

She sat on the edge of her bed. "What is it?"

"Have you been watching the news on those wildfires out West?"

"Out in California?"

"Right. Jimmy just got called out. He leaves tonight to spend a week out there relieving crews who have been working nonstop. They're sending a whole unit from Brooklyn."

"They use city firefighters for forest fires?" Annie said.

"Jimmy and some others had special training with the military. He's on a reserve list for emergencies like this."

"Yeah, but the kids are gone, right?"

"Left today. The problem is Mama DeVechio. Annie, the last time I had to work and Jimmy was on an overnight call, she invited people we don't know into our house for pasta. Our DVD player went missing along with every small electronic device not tied down. The woman can't stand to be alone. I guess it was growing up in a big family and in a village where everyone did everything together. If I leave her here for a week we'll be robbed blind."

"Oh no, so we can't go?"

Annie couldn't hide the disappointment.

"There is one possibility. What if Mama DeVechio stayed with your grandmother for the week? She can ride buddy pass with me down to Lexington and I'll pick her up on the way back. As long as she has access to a kitchen, she'll be happy as a clam.

I'm sure she would love to see the farm. What do you think?"

Mama DeVechio and Beulah. Annie nearly laughed out loud even though she had never even met Mrs. DeVechio. Janice's stories about her mother-in-law were infamous. It would stretch her grandmother, but Annie had a feeling she would do it.

"Let me ask her and I'll call you back." Downstairs, she found her grandmother in the kitchen, kneading dough.

"Janice called and we have a small problem," Annie said.

Beulah reached for a towel and turned from the kitchen counter. Wiping her hands, she said, "What's wrong?"

Annie explained the situation.

"Janice is mighty kind to do all of this for us. I can only return the favor. Of course, I'd be happy to have Mrs. DeVechio stay. The guest room is ready, and at least this way it will be used."

"Oh, thank you," she hugged her grandmother. "I'm sure it'll be fine. Janice says she's a little feisty, but you both like to cook and you both like having people over to eat, so there are already two things you have in common."

Annie didn't mention Mama DeVechio had invited strangers and Janice and Jimmy had been robbed because of it. As her grandmother had said once, "You don't have to tell everything you know." After all, Mama DeVechio couldn't possibly invite anyone her grandmother didn't already know.

Back in her bedroom, Annie called Janice to tell her the news before she finished up the last-minute packing. With one final check of the guest room to make sure it was in order, she dressed for dinner at Evelyn's.

***

"So what's this Mama DeVechio like?" Lindy asked.

Jake, Beulah and Lindy all sat around Evelyn's kitchen table.

"I've never met her," Annie said. "She moved in with Janice and Jimmy a few months ago."

"How long has she lived in America?" Evelyn asked.

"She grew up in Italy, but I'm not sure when she moved here. Mrs. DeVechio lived with Jimmy's sister until she decided to move to Florida. Apparently, Mrs. DeVechio didn't want to go, so she stayed with Janice and Jimmy for a month and it seems to have worked out as a more permanent arrangement."

"Has she ever been to Kentucky?" Beulah asked.

"She's never been out of the Northeast as far as I know," Annie said, growing aware of how quiet Jake was.

"Well, we'll do all we can to make her feel welcome," Evelyn said. "Beulah, I'll be glad to have her over here for dinner one night. I think it'll fall over your Sunday to cook dinner, but I can bring whatever you need me too."

"I hope it's not too much of a burden on you," she looked at her grandmother. "Janice said she's quite self-sufficient and she loves to cook."

"It'll be just fine," Beulah said. "It'll be nice to have another body in the house with you gone."

After dinner, Jake helped to clear the table while Annie and Lindy rinsed dishes and loaded Evelyn's dishwasher. Beulah and Evelyn retired to the living room with their coffee.

"Jake," Lindy started. "You've been seeing Dad a lot lately, getting his advice on your plans. Noticed anything odd?"

Jake was carrying the platter of roasted chicken to the counter and he cast a glance at Annie. She forgot to tell Lindy what they suspected, with everything going on.

"He's not quite himself. I'm worried."

"Lindy," Annie said. "Evelyn's been doing some of the same things."

Annie glanced at Jake for support.

"I wouldn't worry about it. It's curable," Jake said, looking back at Annie.

Lindy looked at Jake and then Annie, obviously confused.

"We think they like each other." Annie smiled.

"Dad and Evelyn?"

***

After Beulah and Lindy left, Jake took Annie by the hand and led her to his cottage.

"You did a great job," he said, looking around the neatly organized space. "I didn't know it could look this good."

Annie warmed with the praise.

"I enjoyed it," she said. "I wish Grandma would let me get hold of her house, but fat chance."

They snuggled on the couch and she was aware it would be the last time for a while.

"I liked being in your house with all your things around me." She thought about how different it was now than her former relationships. "It was nice to know no matter what box I opened, I wasn't going to stumble into some secret you were keeping from me."

"Some secrets are good," he said. "Finding the letters was a good secret."

"True, but it wasn't always good, or else it wouldn't have been hidden away."

"Since we're talking about secrets, why don't you tell me what's going on," he said.

His eyes searched hers and the intensity forced her to drop her gaze.

"I can't, Jake."

"Whatever it is, it's eating you up. Do you think I don't notice?"

Annie tried to hold it together, to push it down, but the tears came and she shook her head as if too shake them off.

"Trust me to protect you," she whispered.

"Protect me? I'm here to protect you. But I can't do it if you won't tell me what's going on."

Annie stood and paced.

"It's too big. And too deep."

Jake stood and caught her by the shoulders.

"It's not too big or too deep for us to deal with it together. If we're going to have a life together, it has to be this way or it won't work."

"I do want *it*," Annie said, "I want *you*."

Jake's voice was low and controlled.

"If you can't trust me with this, you're not ready."

After an awkward silence, Jake gathered up his keys. "I should drive you home."

"Jake . . ." Annie started.

"Annie, if you can't talk, then we need to call it a night. Otherwise one of us will say something we'll regret later."

Chapter Twenty

"MORNING," ANNIE SAID, as she made her way to the cupboard for a coffee mug.

"You don't look very chipper to be heading out on a big trip," her grandmother said, snipping coupons as she spoke.

"Slept awful."

"I can imagine," Beulah said. "I'd be a mess if I thought I would soon be hurtling over the Atlantic Ocean for eight hours."

Annie tried to smile. If only that were it. The strained conversation with Jake had made for a restless night. Her troubles went far deeper than a little trip anxiety.

"Can you think of anything else I need to do before Janice gets here with Mama DeVechio?"

"Nothing comes to mind. Tomorrow night I'll take her with us to the Country Diner and Sunday to church and then dinner back here. I reckon the rest will play out however it's supposed to," Beulah said.

"I hope it goes well. I'll call when we get there and I'll keep you posted on what we find out. It might be easier for me to email updates to Evelyn," she said.

Beulah reached across the table and put her hand over her granddaughter's.

"Thank you for going. It means a lot to me. God's will be done, no matter what. Don't be afraid to tell me anything, I want to know the truth."

***

Annie accepted Jake's offer to drive her to Lexington and bring Mama DeVechio back to Beulah's house. After she hugged her grandmother goodbye, he loaded her suitcase into the back of his SUV. When they pulled out of the long driveway, he reached for her hand, and the gesture comforted her.

Sometimes a creek is too high to cross, her grandfather used to say about emotions. *Have to let it go down a bit and then you can cross it.*

If only the creek would go down and not turn into a raging river, she thought.

In front of the airport, Jake drew her close.

"There won't be time later for goodbyes," he whispered. "I'm here if you need me."

Her chest tightened. If only she could tell him all her fears.

"I do love you," she whispered as Janice called her name.

Janice stepped off the escalator. Right behind her was Mama DeVechio, a petite woman who wore a bright pink dress, with a mound of salt and pepper hair.

Annie embraced her friend and then turned to Jake.

"Jake, meet Janice," she introduced them.

Jake gave Janice a big smile and a hug.

"Mama, this is Annie Taylor and Jake Wilder," Janice said, nearly a head and shoulders above the tiny woman.

"Hello," she said, extending her arm, "I so happy to meet you," she said to Annie. "And this eez our boyfriend? Oh my, he eez so handsome. Am I to ride with you?"

She's flirting, Annie thought, amused, as Janice cut her apologetic look over the top of Mrs. DeVechio's piled-high hair. And she was an attractive woman, the dress hitting her just above the knee and a scarf tied stylishly around her neck.

"It's my honor, Mrs. DeVechio," Jake said.

"She checked two huge bags," Janice whispered. "I have no idea what all she is bringing. I told her it was just for a week, but she waved me away."

Like a queen, Mrs. DeVechio directed Jake on which bags to pick up from the baggage claim area.

"And, she's got a handbag stuffed full of who knows what," Janice said. They watched as Jake pulled off both of Mrs. DeVechio's very large suitcases. Janice handed the smaller bag to her mother-in-law.

"You'll have to carry this, Mama; Jake's got his hands full."

"He eez *forte*," Mama said, smiling and nodding her approval at Annie.

"Ready?" Jake asked. Janice kissed her mother-in-law on the cheeks. Annie brushed her lips against Jake's but he avoided her pleading gaze. A second later, Mrs. DeVechio whisked him away.

"Be good!" Janice called to her mother-in-law. Mrs. DeVechio answered with a wave of the back of her hand. Jake glanced over his shoulder and grinned.

"I hope this isn't a mistake," Janice said as they went to the airline counter for their boarding passes. "Promise me we will still be friends no matter what happens?"

Annie laughed, releasing the pent up emotions.

"I promise, but I can't speak for my grandmother."

"Mama's not been on a farm since she left Italy," Janice said on the plane to Atlanta. "In the five years she's lived with Jimmy's sister in Chicago and now us in Brooklyn, we've hardly had the opportunity."

"How're you doing with her in the house?"

"All in all, it's working out okay. She's great with the kids and she loves to cook for us. The problems happen when I actually want to do something myself in the kitchen. Then it is as if I've offended her and not appreciated her cooking. If she decides to live with us permanently, we might need a bigger house," Janice said. "But I don't want to do anything until we know the airline is stable after the merger a few months ago."

Annie remembered well the turmoil in April when the airline she and Janice worked for, TransAir, was merged into Patriot Airlines. The months leading up to the announcement were unsettling. It was likely to take a while for the dust to settle.

"How do you think Patriot is doing?"

"I think it will come out a stronger airline, but there are lots of things to work out. I don't want to make any big financial moves right now until we are in a better position. That's partly why Jimmy is taking this work out West. It's good money we can save toward a new house."

Once they were off the commuter flight to Atlanta, they headed to their gate in the international terminal. It was strange for Annie to be with Janice pulling suitcases in normal clothes, since their time together was usually in uniform as flight attendants.

There was a chance they could get to Atlanta and not be able to catch the ride to Rome, despite Janice checking the passenger loads ahead of time. But when they got to the gate, all was well, and there was plenty of room on the flight. They even had a seat between them allowing a bit more comfort in economy class. They could rest better before renting a car and driving south to Naples.

They talked with the flight attendants, neither of whom they had met before. They found out the crew had worked with Patriot prior to the merger. Janice engaged one of the attendants over some of the differences she had noticed coming from TransAir. No longer a part of that world, Annie settled down with a magazine.

As soon as the meal service was over, she tried to sleep. Once they landed in Rome, they would have a full day ahead of them, and she wanted to be fresh for the task at hand.

Chapter Twenty-One

BEULAH WIPED OFF the kitchen counter and realized she was nervous. When was the last time she had a houseguest outside of family? She couldn't remember. Here she had gone and agreed to host a woman who came from a different country altogether; and then there was the dilemma of what to call her? Certainly not Mama DeVechio.

The house already seemed lonesome without Annie. They had fallen into a comfortable routine with each other and the arrangement seemed to work out well. *I've grown to depend on my granddaughter,* she thought, as she folded the dishtowel and placed it over the kitchen faucet to dry.

At the sound of crunching gravel, Beulah saw Jake's vehicle pull into her line of sight from the kitchen window.

Beulah peered out the window and watched as a spry little woman climbed down from the passenger side of the truck. Fashionable even, with black, sling-back heels, a nicely cut dress and a scarf. Why had she pictured a gray-haired woman in a muumuu? Mrs. DeVechio put her hands on her hips and looked around, frowning. Meanwhile, Jake pulled two large suitcases out of the back of his SUV.

"My lands," Beulah said out loud. "I've never seen the like of luggage."

Jake carried the two bags to the back door while Mrs. DeVechio retrieved a large purse from the back seat. Beulah smoothed her hair and took off her apron before going to the back door.

Before she pushed open the screen door, Mrs. DeVechio cried out, "*Mamma Mia!*" and lifted her bag high in the air with her eyes laser-focused on Booger, the old black snake who had made an unexpected appearance on the millstone. Jake, quick as a cat, saw what was happening and dropped the luggage, catching Mrs. DeVechio's bag before it came down on the snake.

Thank the Lord Jake had good reflexes, Beulah thought, her hand to her heart. Booger was like family.

"It belongs here," Jake said, smiling as he took the bag from Mrs. DeVechio. "Beulah keeps him for mice."

Mrs. DeVechio turned and looked at her as if she had a horn growing out of her forehead.

"You need cats," she said. "Not snake. Veepers eez bad."

Beulah looked at Jake for the translation.

"Oh, it's not poisonous . . . This is Beulah."

In a split second, Mrs. DeVechio changed expressions and opened her arms.

"I so happy to be here." She grabbed Beulah and kissed her on one cheek and then the other. "Call me Rossella," she said, rolling her *R* in the way foreigners did.

"Thank you," Beulah said. "Welcome, please come in."

"Ah, the kee-chen. Beautiful. Thees eez where I work," she said, and pointed to the largest bag Jake was pulling. "Open that," she said. "We put here."

Jake placed the bag on the floor and unzipped it. Beulah was astonished to see the suitcase explode with canned goods, a tin of olive oil, produce, vegetables, and even jars wrapped in clothing.

Item by item, Rossella placed each one on the kitchen counter while Beulah stood with her mouth hanging open. At the very bottom of the suitcase were long rolls of clothes lying side by side. Rossella knelt and peeled off undergarments and blouses to reveal a bottle of wine, which she proudly handed to Beulah.

Beulah took it, and held the very thing she swore she would never serve in her house—the demon drink. Rossella continued to unroll bottle by bottle while Beulah was rooted to the floor in shock.

One after another, wine bottles were placed on the counter until she counted six. Beulah finally managed to look at Jake and saw his eyes dance while he pursed his lips, as if he were fighting a grin, which made her know she would have no support from him.

What in the world would she do if the preacher happened by and saw her harboring a gaggle of wine bottles? Pastor Gilliam was known to make surprise visits, and he often showed up in her kitchen for a slice of pie or glass of sweet tea, him being especially akin to sweets despite his struggle with weight.

Forget Pastor Gilliam, what of the Gibson's? Or worse, Woody Patterson. He might stumble if he thought she was partaking. She had to do something now. It was her kitchen, after all.

"Mrs. DeVechio," she began.

"No, not Mrs. DeVechio," she said. "Call me Rossella."

"Rose-ella," she said.

"No, *Rossella*," she said, emphasizing the rolling R. "Try again."

"Rose-ella" she tried again, but her R sounding like a dying June bug. Rossella pointed to the roof of her mouth and said her name once more, getting louder with the rolling R. Out of the corner of her eye, Beulah saw Jake walk out of the kitchen, his shoulders shaking.

"My mouth doesn't work like that. I'm sorry."

"Eez okay, you try."

Beulah felt her face flush hot.

"Let's put your things in the pantry here," she said, pushing aside the curtain that hid the wall-to-wall shelves in the small, dark room just off the kitchen. She could at least get the wine out of sight for now.

"Okay, fine." Rossella handed the items to Beulah and she put the wine bottles on a shelf along with some of the canned items and jars. There was nothing in her kitchen to open the bottles anyway.

Just then, Rossella handed her a corkscrew. *So much for that,* she thought, and placed the gadget next to the wine.

"How about I take these upstairs," Jake said, grabbing the suitcases and scurrying upstairs before she could meet his eyes.

"Maybe you would like to get settled," Beulah said to Rossella, leading her houseguest through the dining room to the stairs.

"*Bellissima!*" she said, looking around and clapping her hands. Instead of following Beulah up the stairs, Rossella wandered into the living room where she looked at each picture, examined the hand-knit doilies from the end tables, and picked up her mother's afghan, drawing it to her chest and squeezing it.

"Okay," Jake said, already back downstairs. "Is there anything else you need me to do?" Beulah wished she could think up something else to keep him here a little longer.

Rossella grabbed his hands and kissed him on both cheeks. "*Ciao.* You come back. I cook for you."

After Jake left, Beulah attempted the stairs again.

"Would you like to see your room?"

"Ah, *Si.*" But when they got to the top of the steps, Rossella went into the other rooms, including Annie's and her own room. Finally, Beulah led Rossella to the guest room where she left her "oohing and ahhing" over her curio cabinet. It was Annie's suggestion to move the cabinet from the living room to the guest room, and it did please Beulah to hear Rossella enjoying her collection of ceramic figurines.

And now, surely Rossella needed a rest. She sure did.

***

Beulah didn't know how long she had been napping, but when she awoke, it was to the pungent smell of food cooking and robust singing. She pushed herself up to the side of the bed. Had she been dreaming? No, there it was, the singing along with the distinct smell of food cooking. She opened her bedroom door and a strong smell wafted into her bedroom. Slamming the door shut, she leaned against it.

Garlic. The one spice she never allowed in her house.

She put on her shoes and ran a brush through her hair before taking the steps slowly, trying to be careful about her healing knee, but wanting to get to her kitchen as soon as possible.

From the doorway, she saw Rossella taking the skins off tomatoes, a steaming bowl in front of her. On the stove, a pan of oil sizzled with what Beulah knew had to be garlic. Rossella sang loudly in Italian as she peeled the tomato skins and dropped them in another pan in the sink. When she saw her, Rossella smiled, and with a knife, motioned for her to come in.

Beulah walked in and saw three plates set at the table, a bottle of wine open and three of her small glass tumblers next to the plates.

"I no see your wine glasses. I use those," she said, pointing again with the knife to the glass tumblers.

"Really, Rossella, you don't have to cook for me," Beulah said. "I meant to cook for you tonight. You're my guest, after all."

"No problem," she said. "This week I cook for you. Tomatoes I found in the garden, still good. Tonight, we have spaghetti *pomodoro*. You like."

Beulah wondered who was going to be the third person? Had Mrs. DeVechio invited Jake?

"You've been to the garden?"

"I walk outside and see what we have. Nice beans, but no arugula. You make big mistake not planting arugula."

Arugula? She had never even heard of it.

Just then, Woody entered the back door, wearing his overalls with one suspender hanging down and smiling with his big toothy grin, the loose upper plate jiggling ever so slightly.

"I was dropping off the wheelbarrow I borrowed when I saw Rossella in the garden. She invited me to dinner," Woody said, obviously pleased with the invitation.

"I love Eye-talian," he said. "Stella took me to a nice place up in Chicago last weekend," he said before realizing his slip.

"Stella?" Beulah asked, forgetting for the moment her kitchen had fallen into chaos.

"Well, yeah, you know I had to go up there to look at some horses, and, well, uh, I remembered she was there and thought maybe we could grab a bite to eat. So we did. . . .Would you look at this," he said, leaning in to smell the concoction, a look of ecstasy on his face. Jealousy seared Beulah upon hearing Woody's admiration for another cook—and right in her own kitchen to boot.

To make matters worse, here they were with a bottle of wine open on her kitchen table for all the world to see. Poor Woody, an occasional Methodist, was likely to stumble at seeing her Christian witness diminished by the fermented fruit of the vine. Well, he had to know she had nothing to do with it.

Rossella pulled fresh-baked bread out of the oven and put it on the table.

"Sit!" she told Beulah and Woody. "I fix you."

For all Beulah's indignation, she knew of nothing else to do but obey Rossella. They sat.

The little woman took the tin of olive oil and poured some of the greenest oil Beulah had ever seen onto the white plate. She cut the bread and gave them each a slice. With a slice in her own hand, she pushed it onto the plate of oil and let it soak. Then she popped it into her mouth.

"You do," she said.

Beulah watched Woody do it first and then she followed suit. The oil tasted earthy, but it flavored the crusty bread nicely. The bread was too chewy for her, though. *Good bread took the right hand, and Rossella doesn't have it,* she thought smugly.

When the tomato sauce was finished, Rossella put spaghetti on each of their plates and then a ladleful of sauce. When she sat at the table, she tried to pour Beulah wine.

"No, thank you," Beulah said firmly.

Rossella just raised her eyebrows and poured some for Woody and her.

If Woody wanted to partake, it was his business, but he wouldn't see Beulah doing it.

The spaghetti was heavy on garlic and Beulah dreaded the indigestion sure to follow later. Woody had second helpings of the spaghetti and of the wine. Beulah dearly hoped the mound of spaghetti would offset the effects of drink.

"Rossella, this was the best meal I've had in a long time," Woody said, and pushed his plate away. Another sting to Beulah's pride since he had just sat at her table less than two weeks before.

"Why don't you stay around a bit? You did have two glasses of wine; maybe you shouldn't drive quite yet." Beulah said.

"I take a little wine every night for medicinal purposes," he said. "I'm kindly used to it, but I believe I might sit outside and smoke my pipe before I head home."

"I sit with you," Rossella said, and then turned to Beulah.

"You no do dishes. I do later," she said.

Beulah was glad to leave her to the pile of greasy dishes. She went upstairs to her bedroom, feeling the garlic roll around in her chest. It was going to be a long night.

No, it was going to be a long week.

Chapter Twenty-Two

WITH A LITTLE sleep on the plane and a light breakfast just before arrival Annie felt reasonably rested and ready to face the day. After de-boarding, they searched for rental car signs in the terminal.

"This is certainly a new experience," she said. "Normally we're working the flight and catching the bus afterwards to the hotel."

"This way," Janice said, plowing ahead.

It seemed a mile of walking through a maze of halls, escalators, and moving sidewalks.

"Are you sure we're going the right way?" Annie asked. "It says to go this way for rental cars." She pointed at the sign.

Janice stopped and pulled out the map.

"Paulo said not to go there. He's sending us to the VIP counter where we don't have to wait in line. He got us a good deal: twenty-nine dollars a day."

Janice pointed to a place on the map and then looked up at the signs.

"Should be at the end of this hall," she said, taking off with her rolling bag. Annie followed and soon they were in a parking garage.

"Here's the counter," Janice said. "I'll go in and get the keys."

Annie sat on a bench to wait and tried not to think how much she would like a shower.

A few minutes later, Janice was dangling keys in front of her. "Can you drive a manual?"

"Sure, but you know how to read the road signs. Wouldn't you rather drive?"

"I can't drive a stick shift. Anyway, I need to navigate," Janice said. "All right, it's in parking space thirty. Over there."

She followed Janice and then spotted the bright red car. Something wasn't right. Annie checked the number again.

"Aw! He's going to get a good Christmas present this year," Janice said.

"You have got to be kidding," Annie said.

"Sweet, huh?" Janice opened the trunk.

"Janice, I can't drive this! It's a Ferrari."

"Annie, if you can drive a straight shift, you can drive this car."

"What if I wreck?"

"Why do you think we have insurance?" Janice asked, heaving her bag into the trunk. "Here, I'll load your bag. Get up there in the driver's seat and get familiar."

"Let's go back and trade it for something normal," she said, and groaned.

"To some people, this is normal," Janice said and grinned. "Let's go."

The low driver's seat practically swallowed her. After driving a truck all summer, it was like sitting on the pavement. In the dark of the parking garage, she squinted at the instrument panel while Janice studied the map. This was surely a bad idea.

Annie turned on the car and put it in reverse. They jerked backward and the car stalled. She tried again and this time let out the clutch slowly while giving it more gas. Janice looked at her with raised eyebrows.

"Remember you asked for it, so no comments."

Slowly down the parking garage ramp, she circled and circled, until they exited the airport parking and entered the autostrada toward Rome.

"Okay, we are going to merge onto the *Grande Raccordo Anulare*," Janice said.

"The what?"

"The GRA. Watch the Mercedes!"

A silver car whizzed by them on the left as if they were standing still.

"Good grief," Annie said. "They fly around here."

"I doubt they expect a Ferrari to be going at a snail's pace. You're driving like a grandma. C'mon, speed it up. Now, stay to the right, the exit is coming up," Janice said.

Muscles tense, Annie longed for a stout Italian espresso. Watching her mirrors, she eased onto the GRA.

"Now what?" she said.

"We're taking the A1, but we'll need to go through a toll booth first. Go to the lane where it says 'ticket'," Janice said.

"Which lane? My Italian brain hasn't kicked in yet."

"*Biglietto*," Janice said, and pointed.

Annie sailed into the lane and then stopped and stalled the car, forgetting to press down on the clutch. She grabbed a ticket and handed it to Janice. When she restarted the car, the motor rumbled and echoed off the concrete tollbooths before she launched onto the A1.

"How far on this?"

"I think a little more than two hours. Oh, I forgot to tell you. My cousin called and someone is using his apartment, so he's putting us up in the Grand Hotel *Vesuvio*."

"Sounds fancy."

"Probably is," Janice said. "He felt bad about the mix up. His wife scheduled somebody else without him knowing about it."

"I had no idea traveling with you meant such luxuries," Annie said. "First the Ferrari, now the hotel."

Janice laughed. "The price is right. And it helps to have a big Italian family on both sides of the pond. Hey, do you want to stop and eat lunch on the way or just go on to Naples?"

"Let's get there. I'd like to get this driving behind us," she said. "Do you have directions to the hotel?"

Janice pulled out several sheets of paper and rifled through them until she found the one she wanted.

"Here it is," she said.

In two hours, they were on the outskirts of Naples after passing the exits for the historic archeological sites of Pompeii and Herculaneum. A view of Mount Vesuvius was in front of them and the natural beauty of the landscape had gradually changed to include heaps of garbage on the side of the road.

"Why does this look so different?" Annie asked.

"It's the Camorra, the local mafia. They've taken over the removal of trash, some of it toxic, and then dump it wherever they want," Janice said.

"Terrible," Annie said, looking at the bags filled with trash, television and computer screens, appliances, and clothing piled on the sides of the road and under the overpasses.

"The percentages of cancer diagnosis are up dramatically in the last few years. It's partly why my aunt and uncle spend half their time in the US. But Naples is their home, so they don't want to abandon it entirely. It's really sad for the people who live here."

"Who knows what's buried or thrown out to sea," Annie said.

"Okay, we are going to turn up here," Janice said, pointing to the right.

For the next few minutes, they wound around streets with the Bay of Naples off to the right and the stunning Mount Vesuvius in front. As much as Annie wanted to enjoy the view, she concentrated on her driving. She was mastering the straight shift but traffic darted in and out, motor scooters whizzed by, and if she missed the turn into the hotel, it would mean another circling around.

"It should be up here on the left, less than a quarter of a mile," Janice said, leaning forward in the seat to see. "Yes, there it is. Just pull into the reception parking."

Annie did, and it was with great relief she turned off the car. A bellman met them and took their bags. Standing and stretching her arms, she felt the effects of the long flight, the stress of the drive, and the jet lag. She gathered her purse out of the car and followed Janice and the bellman into the lobby.

A shiny marble floor, antique furnishings, Persian rugs, and staff standing at attention told her this wasn't like the hotels she was accustomed to as a flight attendant or on her own personal travel. Janice's cousin had gone above and beyond in compensating for the booked apartment.

Janice got the room key and they took the elevator upstairs.

The room was large and had two twin beds in the Italian custom. If they had needed a king bed, the twins would have been pushed together. It was quite practical, she had always thought.

After the bellman was tipped and out the door, Janice turned to her.

"What about a quick bite of lunch in the hotel restaurant, then a short nap? Or do you want to go now to the address?"

"I don't think I could do it now," Annie sat down on the bed. "I'd like to be fresh when we knock on their door."

"Okay, then tonight we'll go out to dinner. Let's get a taxi so we don't have to navigate the downtown streets, since we have no idea where we're going. We can leave early, and let them drive us by the address first. You can decide if you want to stop tonight or we can scope it out and go first thing tomorrow morning."

"Tomorrow is Sunday," Annie said. "It might be a better time to catch a family at home. But I like the idea; let's see what it looks like tonight before dinner."

With a plan in place, they ate bruschetta with tomatoes for lunch along with a green salad, and then retired to the room for naps. By seven, they had both rested and showered and were ready to go. Annie tucked the copy of the letter and the address in her purse, along with the picture of Elena.

They stopped by the concierge and Janice asked about the location of the address. The woman's dark hair was pulled back into a ponytail at the nape of her neck and she squinted through stylish glasses.

"Ah, thees address eez een the historic area of Naples," she said in her heavily accented English. "We are on the edge of it, but this eez here," she said pointed to a place not terribly far from the bay.

"Is there a restaurant or osteria you might recommend in this same area? We would like a taxi to drive us by this address first."

"Oh, no," she answered immediately. "Thees eez not a good area. But I can recommend thees and eetz not too far from thees address."

The woman wrote down the name of a restaurant and an address.

"Would you like me to call a taxi for you?"

"Please," Janice said.

A few minutes later, butterflies danced in her stomach when they set off for the address where the Caivanos lived in 1943. She could not imagine what Naples looked like back then, but certainly the garbage and toxic waste would not have been piled on the roadsides. But it was in the middle of a war, so it may not have looked much better. She did know Mount Vesuvius had not changed remarkably, and the Bay of Naples must have looked the same as well.

The driver took them down toward the bay and she tried to imagine it through the eyes of her great-uncle Ephraim. While she saw a beautiful view of the ocean with Mount Vesuvius off to the left, he would have seen all types of naval ships in port. Finally came the day he saw Naples for the last time, when he loaded a carrier ship for the Battle of Anzio, which would be the last place on earth he would see. Her own eyes welled with tears as she imagined what he might have seen before leaving this place, and his loved one, for good.

The taxi slowed and pulled next to a vacant building with graffiti written on the side. He took the address from Janice and looked again and spoke to her in Italian. She answered and pointed to the building. He shook his head and said something else, then eased back out onto the street.

"Was that it?" Annie asked.

"No, but we are close. I think this area must have looked much different in 1943," Janice said. Buildings on both sides of the street had boarded up windows, graffiti marked the stone fronts and broken glass shards hung in the windows not boarded up.

"He thinks it's the next street up," Janice said.

When he turned, Annie recognized the street name from the envelope. This was the address. The taxi driver pulled up in front of an aged metal door that covered the storefront. The three-story building was vacant and she wished she could see behind the metal covering to the storefront behind, to better imagine what Ephraim would have seen during the war. To the left of the metal store covering, there was a wooden door. She guessed it led to the family's upstairs apartments, just as the letters said.

The taxi driver said something to Janice.

"Do you want to get out? He said he'd wait."

"Sure," Annie said. When she stared up at the apartment building, she envisioned a street alive with activity as people bought and sold, lived and loved, ate and drank in the midst of a war. For a moment, she could feel the poverty, the fear, and even hope as the Italians were freed from the rule of a dictator.

When reality of what existed today set in, she could not quell the disappointment. The Caivanos were gone. Long gone. Annie should have known it would turn out like this when nothing surfaced after all the Internet searching they had both done prior to the trip. With only one address several decades old, how could they possibly track them down now?

Beulah would want to see it, even if there was nothing much to see, so she took pictures of the building and the street.

The restaurant was just a few blocks away and they were both quiet on the drive over. Once they were seated at a table, Janice order sparkling water and a half carafe of the house wine.

The waiter brought a basket of bread and olive oil and they placed their order for a shared antipasto of cured meats, and their individual selections of the *primo piatto,* the pasta dish.

"Are you discouraged?" Janice asked, adding salt and pepper to the olive oil before letting her bread soak in it.

"A little. I didn't really expect to go there and find the store and their apartment just as it was in the 1940s. I did hope it would be an active neighborhood and we might have found someone with a lead on the family—maybe someone who knew them or knew relatives. If we only had a name for Elena's son, it would help so much."

"Yeah, it puts us at a disadvantage for sure," Janice said. "But I noticed a Naples history museum advertised in the hotel stuff. I wonder if that might be a good place to go tomorrow. Maybe we can get a lead on what happened after World War II."

"Good idea," Annie said, a sense of encouragement at having some direction. "And what about going through the phone book, placing random calls to Caivanos to see if we turn something up? . . . If you don't mind to do the talking."

"That's what I'm here for," Janice said.

Chapter Twenty-Three

AS IN MOST of Europe, breakfast was part of the hotel stay in Naples, and usually meant a nice display of cheeses, cured meats, breads and fruit, along with boiled eggs, yogurt and cereal. The Grand *Vesuvio* did not disappoint. Not only did the breakfast boast a delectable spread, the floor-to-ceiling windows in the dining room faced the Bay of Naples and Mount Vesuvius.

"I checked with the concierge and the museum opens at ten," Janice said, laying a phone book on the breakfast table. "And they let me have this. I guess no one puts phone books in hotel rooms anymore with the Internet."

"And cell phones," Annie said, buttering her toast. "While you're making calls, I'll use your laptop to keep searching."

"It's a good thing we're looking for the older generation. I doubt younger folks even have a landline. What would Elena be now if she's alive?" Janice asked.

"Older than Grandma. And her son would be in his sixties."

She thumbed through the phone book. "Caivano . . . Caivano . . ." Annie said, letting her finger trail down the list of names beginning with a *C*. "Here it is," she said. And then her heart sank as she scanned the long list. "There's a hundred or more. But no Elena."

"Finish your toast so we can get started," Janice said.

***

Janice settled into a comfortable chair and began calling while Annie used her friend's laptop to search the Internet once again, something they had both already done back in the states. This time she tried different search combinations to see if any new information might turn up. Meanwhile, Janice called and explained in Italian to each person who answered what she was looking for. "Eduardo," she said at one point, looking at Annie. "*Mille grazie.*" Janice hung up the phone. "*E* for *Edoardo*, not Elena."

On and on it went for more than an hour.

Finally Janice hung up the phone. "No one knows anything about Elena Caivano or the store. I even gave the address and nothing is familiar. Did you mark the ones we called?" Janice asked.

"You called forty, but eight didn't answer. This afternoon might be just as good or better for catching people at home."

"Yeah, we're right in the middle of mass time now, and most families have lunch afterwards."

They left a short time later for the museum. Annie drove the Ferrari slowly downhill to the historic center, bumping over ancient cobblestone streets.

"Turn right," Janice said and she turned a quick right onto a narrow street.

"Not here, the next one," Janice said. "This is one-way!"

A driver barreled toward them. Annie slammed on the brakes and he threw up his hand in disgust. She backed out of the street and hoped for a break in traffic.

"We should have taken a taxi," she said, shifting the gear into first.

After another wrong street, they finally arrived at the large stone structure with a small sign posted outside the door.

"Park there," Janice said, pointing to a marked space just in front of the museum.

"Are you sure the sign means it's okay to park here?" Annie asked.

"It's Sunday; it'll be fine."

Inside, a woman with gray hair sat at the information desk. Janice spoke quickly in Italian.

The older woman smiled and responded, then pointed to the exhibits behind her. Janice spoke again and she caught the words in Italian that meant World War II.

The woman nodded and pointed in another direction and spoke again. Janice translated for Annie.

"There is an exhibit here on World War II and its effect on Naples we can see today. There is a woman who is an expert on the era who she recommends we speak to, but she is not working today since it's Sunday. While we are looking at the exhibit, the woman I talked to offered to call her and make an appointment for tomorrow morning if she is available."

"I'm so anxious, I wish we could meet her today," Annie said as she walked to the entrance of the World War II exhibit.

"Italians take resting on Sunday pretty seriously. I'm a little surprised the museum is even open," Janice said.

"My grandfather always said, 'Work on Sunday, come hard on Monday.'"

"Are we working?" Janice asked.

"We're in Italy. How can anything feel like work here?"

The exhibit showed pictures of Naples during World War II giving her an idea of what the city looked like back then. She learned Naples was the most bombed Italian city during the war. Many pictures showed the destruction. One picture showed an American GI holding a young Italian girl who clutched a pillow to her breast, her expression one of shock. Another showed a young, disheveled mother holding her baby on her knee, sitting next to baskets of onions for sale. There was a street scene with American naval troops milling about and another showed the busy port. Seeing the pictures steeled Annie's determination to find Elena and her child.

When they left the exhibit, the woman from the information desk waved Janice over. They exchanged a few words and she handed Janice a piece of paper.

"We have an appointment at nine tomorrow morning, before the museum opens," Janice said.

"At least it's early so we can have the rest of the day to track down leads."

"There's one more thing," Janice said. "The woman we will meet with tomorrow . . . her name is Elisabetta Caivano."

"Do you think . . . ?"

"I don't know," Janice said, pushing open the museum doors. "There might be a connection."

Janice grabbed her arm and stopped short. "Look!" she said, and pointed.

Annie followed her friend's finger.

"What? I don't see anything," Annie said.

"Exactly. The Ferrari's gone."

The parking space was empty. The red sports car had vanished.

"I knew this was a bad idea," Annie put her hands on her head. "Why do I let you talk me into things?"

"Quit moaning and come on," Janice said, turning on her heels. "We need to report it now while the trail is fresh."

Inside, Janice explained to the information booth attendant. Annie watched and listened as the woman spoke quickly back to Janice and then back and forth. Finally, the woman shook her head and picked up the phone.

"What?"

"Well, I didn't actually read the parking sign. It was a tow zone and she said they are vigilant about towing here. Even on Sundays. She's trying to locate it for us."

Annie waited while endless conversations in Italian went back and forth between Janice and the museum volunteer, then the volunteer and the phone. When the older woman hung up the phone, she wrote something down for Janice on a piece of paper, and then picked up the phone again while Janice walked away.

"She called a taxi for us. We have to pay a fine and we can get it out."

"How much exactly does insurance cover?"

In a few minutes, the taxi pulled up. Janice handed the driver the address and they got in the backseat.

"It'll be fine. It's all bravado," Janice said.

"Bravado? Didn't you tell me this is the home of the Mafia, or some form of mafia, and I think you also said . . ."

"Shhh!" Janice said and then whispered. "Don't say that word around here, they're sensitive to it."

Annie looked at Janice as if she had just grown a second nose. Janice stared back but began smiling. A giggle worked its way through the jet lag and stress. They both began laughing; the predicament seemed suddenly hilarious. The taxi driver stared at them unsmiling when he stopped the car at the impound center. After they paid him and got out, the driver took off with squealing tires, which only made them laugh harder.

Annie sobered as she looked around at the shabby surroundings.

"If our car's not here, we might be in trouble," she said.

"Don't worry," Janice said. "I've got a number to call in case of emergency. Let's go."

The entrance door was locked, but Janice found a button to press and waited for a response. When it came, she spoke back in Italian and waited for the buzzer to sound. The door clicked and they went inside.

Concrete walls, fluorescent lights and a tile floor made the room seem nearly like a prison. The thought made Annie shudder and she pulled her scarf tighter around her shoulders.

"*Buongiorno*," Janice said.

The young man at the counter raised his eyebrows and smiled.

Janice launched into the reason they were there. He nodded, all the while ogling them, up and down.

Disgusted, Annie walked to a window while the conversation went on and looked into the compound area. The red Ferrari was sitting just behind the building in perfect condition. Three young men were standing around it, each taking turns posing for pictures in front of the car.

"Alright, we're paid up. But it wiped me out, you'll have to buy lunch." Janice said.

"Expensive?"

"You don't know the half of it. He offered to waive the fee if . . ." Janice said rolling her eyes. "Let's get out of here."

Chapter Twenty-Four

BEULAH WOKE UP Sunday morning and sat on the side of the bed, discombobulated. In her fuzzy, pre-coffee brain, she tried to go over the disturbing events from Saturday in order to sort herself out.

Saturday had started out fine with Jake giving Rossella a tour of both farms. Beulah had enjoyed the quiet time in her house while they were gone. Then came the disastrous trip to the Country Diner.

With Betty and Joe Gibson along with Evelyn, they had arrived at the diner at the normal time. Once they had settled into their regular table, Rossella tried to order a glass of wine and when she was told no, she didn't seem to understand they lived in a dry county.

"What this mean, dry county?" she asked. Evelyn tried to explain and finally ended with saying, "No wine here." They all ordered the catfish, as usual, but Rossella ordered the spaghetti.

Another disaster. When the dish arrived, along with the green shaker of Parmesan cheese, she lifted the noodles with her fork high above the plate with a look of pure disgust on her face. Then she peered into it as if she were searching for a bug. Finally, she dropped the fork and pushed away the plate.

Beulah was just about to offer her a piece of catfish when Rossella scooted back her wooden chair, walked to the back of the diner and disappeared behind the swinging kitchen doors. For once, even Betty Gibson was speechless. They sat there in silence, appetites gone, and waited. Elmore Letton, the diner owner, was known to be cantankerous, especially with criticism about the food.

They stared at each other and waited for the verbal explosion, breaking glass, or even a yelp from Elmore, but nothing happened. Finally, Joe started eating his fish again, and they all followed suit. Even though they ate, no one spoke, as they waited for Rossella to return while the rest of the diner bustled like normal.

After several minutes, Rossella walked through the swinging doors carrying a plate of spaghetti as if she were displaying the crown jewels, taking it to each table in the diner for each person to see, smell and admire. Then she sat and started eating, twirling the pasta around on her fork, instead of cutting it up like normal folks did.

If that weren't enough, the strangest part followed. The waitress began taking orders right and left for spaghetti. Apparently Rossella had made a big batch while she was at it. Even Evelyn ordered a plate of Rossella's pasta for them to try at their table; all the while Rossella sat like a queen at court and nodded her approval. Beulah took a small taste to be polite, but there was too much garlic and she would not give up another night of sleep.

Elmore came out just as they were about to pay their bill and even thanked them for bringing Rossella.

"Would you like to come and cook this Thursday?" he asked her. "I'll make your spaghetti the special and we'll advertise it on the radio," he asked.

"Of course, I cook. Beulah bring me what time?" she asked.

***

Beulah had to fight to keep Rossella out of the kitchen on Saturday while she made her lunch preparations. And now, here she was on Sunday morning, having to miss her church in order to drive Rossella over to Rutherford for the Catholic mass. At least it was at ten, giving them enough time to get lunch on the table before the others got out of church.

Beulah sat on the edge of the bed while she worked her panty hose on. When the hose was knee high on both legs, she shimmied them up with some difficulty in going over her thighs. She hated panty hose, truth be told, but women of certain ages dared not go without them, at least at her size.

Panty hose had a tendency to put her in a bad mood anyway, but it didn't take much these days after this small Italian tornado had taken over her house and tossed everything willy-nilly.

How can one small woman cause so much disruption?

Routine. That's what Beulah liked and that's what she didn't have right now. Was her desire for routine why she had so few houseguests over the years? But surely every houseguest wasn't like Rossella? Beulah stepped into her beige slip and dropped her Sunday dress down over her head, straightening it in front of the mirror.

Beulah had never even been in a Catholic church. What would her Sunday school class think of her not being there this morning? They would think she was sick and start passing around a sign-up sheet to bring her meals. Or worse, put her on the prayer chain, which would spread the untruth all over town in a matter of hours.

"Lord, help. I am not in any shape for church today, mine or somebody else's. I ought to stay home in bed," she said aloud to herself.

But, she reckoned, a body ought to go to church the most when they were in the worst shape. When she opened her bedroom door, she saw Rossella's door was already open and the bed made. Beulah grabbed her pocketbook and walked down the steps. As she turned into the dining room, she stopped short at the sight of Rossella, standing on a chair, and hanging cream-colored flat ribbons over string that went from the chandelier to picture frames.

"What in tarnation?" she said aloud.

"I make you homemade *tagliatelle*," she announced, and smiled. Rossella placed another noodle over the string and stepped down from the chair. "It must dry now," she said. "Then I make you dish."

Beulah's mouth hung open and she stared at the crisscross of string with dough ribbons hanging like flags across the dining room.

Lord give me strength, she prayed silently. Managing a half-hearted smile for Rossella's benefit, she said, "It's time to go."

***

Beulah had no idea where to sit inside Rutherford's only Catholic church. She had her regular pew in the Baptist church. *Was it the same for Catholics?*

Rossella took charge and selected a pew for them. They sat and Beulah eyed the kneeling bench and hoped it wasn't necessary. Sure enough, Rossella went right down on it before church even started. There was no way she was going to put her recently operated-on knee down on that bench, no matter how much velvet padding there was on it. The Lord knew she was kneeling inside and she could pray just as well while sitting on the pew.

Rossella cut her eyes at Beulah and pointed to the bench. Beulah shook her head "no" and pointed to the scar on her knee visible through the suntan shade of her panty hose. Rossella squinted at the scar and then cocked her head to the side, ever so slightly, grudging agreement.

The service started and they were up and standing, and then sitting. Standing, sitting, kneeling and then standing again. When they launched into the Lord's Prayer, Beulah spoke the words with gusto, happy to have something familiar to her. Suddenly, the whole congregation stopped before the prayer was finished while Beulah rushed headlong on her own. Several of the congregants turned to look at her, and Rossella cut her another disapproving glance.

When Communion time came, the elements were not passed as they were in the Baptist church. Instead, the parishioners filed out of the pews and down the aisle to partake at the altar. Beulah was deciding if she should step out or not when Rossella turned and wagged a finger at her, so she stayed put. When Rossella returned and everyone had taken Communion, there was more sitting, standing and kneeling. At the end, there was kissing. It was the most activity-filled service she had ever attended.

Brother Gilliam could stand to incorporate a little more activity in Somerville Baptist. She imagined it might help reduce his girth.

***

Back at the house, she set about cutting up the chicken and dipping it in the egg and buttermilk mixture. Rossella followed her into the kitchen, and out of the corner of her eye, Beulah saw her rooting around in the refrigerator as if she were hunting ingredients.

"Rossella, I cook for you today, okay?" Beulah heard herself speaking in the way Rossella did in a shortened version of English and was glad no one was around to hear her.

"Okay, yes. I cook for you tomorrow?" Rossella said, holding her finger up in front of Beulah's face, as if waiting for her to give her promise.

"Fine," Beulah said. She would agree to anything to get that woman out of her kitchen today. True to her word, Rossella disappeared until everyone began arriving for lunch. Evelyn came first, and then Jake and Lindy, arriving in different cars but at the same time since they went to Scott's church. Scott and Mary Beth weren't coming this week and Beulah thought they were likely to be around less and less with the wedding coming up soon and making their own Sunday traditions.

Woody filed in, dressed in a suit, and with his wiry hair combed back off his face, exposing his freckled white forehead.

"Fried chicken," Jake said. "Annie's going to be sorry she missed this."

"I'll get the coleslaw out," Evelyn offered.

"We'll have to eat in here today," Beulah said. Usually they ate in the dining room if there were more than six people, but with Rossella's pasta drying on strings that option was out.

"What happened here?" Woody said, pointing to the dining room.

"Rossella made spaghetti and they have to dry," Beulah said, keeping her opinion on the matter to herself.

"No spaghetti," Rossella wiggled her index finger at Beulah.

"*Eez tagliatelle,* no spaghetti. Tomorrow night, I cook," she said. "Come at eight."

Beulah bristled. *Who does Rossella think she is hosting dinner in my house? It's my place to do the inviting.*

Evelyn glanced at Beulah, waiting for her to respond before she accepted. Beulah recovered.

"Yes, please come. But Rossella, eight is a little late for us. Country people go to bed early. Can we make it earlier?"

"Okay, seven," Rossella threw up her hands as if time were of no consequence. Beulah turned her attention back to the frying chicken and tried to compose herself.

"Sounds good to me. Can I bring my dad if there's enough?" Lindy said.

"Of course," said Beulah, feeling a bit more in control. "He's more than welcome."

"Rossella, would you like me to bring a dish?" Evelyn asked.

"No, no, eets fine. I have all," Rossella said with another wave of her hand.

You have it all because you are using my groceries, Beulah thought, feeling very uncharitable. The brazen nerve of that woman rubbed her raw.

"Really, let me bring a dessert," Evelyn said.

"No, no, I do," Rossella said.

After frying the chicken, Beulah made cream gravy while Evelyn got the biscuits out of the oven. With Evelyn's help, they brought coleslaw, green beans and macaroni and cheese to the table.

After being seated at the table, Jake said grace and then the food was passed around the table in family style. Beulah noticed Rossella was picking at the macaroni and cheese and she looked at her.

"It is okay?" she asked, knowing her macaroni and cheese was a crowd pleaser.

"Okay, but no garlic," she said.

"I can't eat garlic, so I don't cook with it," Beulah said as firmly as she could.

"No garlic for you?" Rossella's face lit up as if someone had turned on a light. "Okay, I see problem with you."

Beulah felt the hairs on the back of her neck stand straight up. She was just about to respond when Jake said, "I got an e-mail from Annie."

This got Beulah's attention and she let Rossella's comment go.

"How is she? Any word?" Beulah asked.

"They went to the address on the letter, but it was a boarded up building. She could tell where a storefront had been by the stone work, but it was abandoned."

Beulah was disappointed.

"I suppose it is to be expected," she said. "It was a long time ago."

"They do have some leads. She said she would call as soon as she knew anything. And she said to give you her love," Jake said.

Beulah was a little miffed Annie communicated with Jake instead of her. She was feeling a little sideways in general right now. The sooner Annie and Janice could get the mystery solved, the better for all of them. Then Rossella could go back to New York City where she belonged and Beulah could get her house, and her kitchen, back.

"Rossella, how long have you been widowed?" Lindy asked.

"Too many years now. I no like being alone. But men no want my age, they want young woman," she laughed. "Even though young woman can't cook."

"Beulah ought to have been snapped up, as good as she cooks," Woody said. "And Evelyn, too."

"I don't want a man," Beulah said, feeling a little irritated this issue had come up again so soon. "One was enough for me."

"Maybe that's my problem," Lindy said. "I don't know how to cook."

"You don't have a problem," Jake said. "You just haven't met the right guy yet."

"Have you talked to Stella lately?" Evelyn directed the question to Woody, who seemed embarrassed.

"Well, yeah, I have. I invited her down for Scott and Mary Beth's wedding, truth be told. In fact . . . I was wondering, Beulah, if maybe she could stay with you since Evelyn's got her house full."

Beulah swallowed a piece of chicken whole. Good grief. Another houseguest.

Chapter Twenty-Five

IN THE 1500s, ANNIE learned from the pizzeria menu, pizza was a crusty flatbread sold in the streets of Naples for poor people. Later, toppings such as oil, tomatoes and fish were added. From her travels to Rome as a flight attendant, she knew the authentic Italian version of pizza was very different from the jazzed up American version loaded with cheese and piled on a thick crust.

When the classic *pizza margherita* arrived at their table, it was a light smattering of tomato sauce on a thin crust with a sprinkling of cheese and fresh basil leaves.

"Are we counting carbs?" Janice asked.

"How can you in Italy?" Annie said, taking a big slice. They ate in silence, enjoying the view overlooking the bay. After lunch, Annie took her cell phone out on the terrace and called home.

"Hey you," Jake said, "How's it going?"

"It's awfully romantic here; it's a little wasted with Janice and me."

"I hope there aren't any handsome Italian men around," he said, teasing. They were both trying hard to sound normal, she realized, avoiding the tension thick as sorghum between them.

"I do wish you were here," she said.

"I don't think farming is conducive to much travel. Any news on the Caivanos?"

"Nothing yet. I'm beginning to think the trip is a waste of time and money. It will be a miracle if we find the right Caivanos. Although we are meeting with a World War II expert tomorrow who happens to have the same last name."

Annie told Jake about the Ferrari and getting it impounded.

"Be careful," he said. "You might be better off taking a taxi, at least inside the historic centers."

"How's it going with Mrs. DeVechio?"

"Have you talked to Beulah?"

"No, I was waiting to call when I actually had news one way or the other. Everything okay?"

"Mom said they went to the Country Diner last night and Mrs. DeVechio charmed her way into the kitchen and made spaghetti, which they promptly added as the nightly special."

"Charmed?"

"Maybe elbowed is a better word. Anyway, I think Beulah was pretty embarrassed about it, according to Mom. I don't think anyone else minded. In fact, Mom says they're all quite taken with her and the spaghetti was delicious."

"How is Evelyn?"

"Yesterday, she asked for help finding her car keys. They were in the silverware drawer."

"Nothing's in the open yet," she said.

"Nope. It appears to be another secret."

There was an uncharacteristic note of sarcasm in Jake's voice. What did she expect, she had hurt him, despite all her intentions.

"I miss you," she said.

"Same here." Annie hung up and stared silently out at the Gulf of Naples and the long distance between them.

***

For dinner, they decided to take Jake's suggestion and hire a taxi to a restaurant recommended by Janice's cousin. They sat on the osteria's patio surrounded by greenery and enjoyed spaghetti *alla puttanesca* prepared *al dente*. Afterward, Janice took out a pack of cigarettes.

"I thought you quit?"

"I never smoke unless I'm in Italy. Something about these Italian cigarettes," she said.

"Janice, they're Marlboros."

"Well, maybe it's something about Italy."

Janice put the cigarette to her lips and inhaled, then leaned back in her chair, exhaling the smoke slowly.

"So when are you and Jake getting married?" Janice asked, leveling her gaze at Annie.

"I don't know; it seems early still to me. We've only officially been dating for a few weeks."

"What's this *official* business? You've known him forever. The point of dating is to get to know each other. You two are way past that."

Annie took a sip of red wine. "I just want to be sure."

Janice squinted at her through the smoke of the cigarette and Annie braced herself.

"What are you afraid of?" she said.

Annie shrugged and then to her dismay, her eyes welled with tears. Janice's face softened and she held the cigarette back as she leaned forward.

"It's okay, Annie. It's normal to be afraid to trust after all you've lost."

"Janice, you don't understand. That's what's so awful about this. I'm afraid he can't trust me."

"What?"

"My father left my mother within a year of being married. He couldn't stand being tied down, staying in one place. According to half the town, I am just like him. I feel so bad inside, like I am headed for some destiny and I can't stop it. I'm frozen with fear. I can't bear to be without Jake, but I am scared to death to take a step forward. It's not that I don't want to, I can't. I would never want to hurt him."

Annie's chest tightened and she dabbed her eyes with the cloth napkin.

"Have you talked to Jake about all this?"

"No. I'm afraid it will make it worse. Then he really won't

trust me. How'd you feel if you wanted to marry someone who told you they might have to leave you?" Annie asked.

"You have a point," Janice said.

"Jake knows something is wrong; he knows I'm not trusting him with it. But how can I?" Annie said. "It's eating me up inside."

"Annie, you are not your father. Do you think your father agonized over your mother like this? Do you think he cared so much about her he was bound and determined to protect her like you are with Jake?"

Annie couldn't imagine her father agonizing over a relationship at all. His narcissism overshadowed any concern for others.

"No, I guess not, when you put it like that."

"Believe me, you're not like him. You've let this thing get too big. Let me tell you a story," Janice said, leaning back in her chair.

"My uncle Tony said when he was in elementary school, there was a bully who cornered him every day for his lunch money. The guy was twice his size and Tony gave it up as soon as the bully came his way. Then one day, he got tired of being hungry at lunch, and when the bully came to him for his money, he jumped on his foot as hard as he could. The bully screamed and ran off howling and never bothered him again."

Annie blew her nose. "Who's the bully here?"

"Fear. It gets so big and ugly it controls your life. But there's nothing to it if you confront it," Janice said. "Do you think I wanted to trust Jimmy again after he had an affair? No way. I was ready to leave him. But I realized what I was feeling and even the reason Jimmy had the affair in the first place was because of fear. Our priest counseled us and I remember he said, 'Perfect love casts out fear.' It's in the Bible."

Janice stubbed out her cigarette.

Annie nodded. *Perfect love,* she thought. The very thing she was incapable of giving.

***

Janice asked for Elisabetta Caivano at the museum's information desk and they waited until a middle-aged woman greeted them and introduced herself as Betta. Janice asked her in Italian if she was comfortable speaking English or if she would rather have Janice interpret.

"No, English eez okay," she said and led them to a small office behind a door with a sign that read *Privato*.

Annie explained the story; beginning with finding the letters and then the realization her great-uncle had fathered a child during the war.

Betta's eyebrows rose when the Caivano name was mentioned, but she listened without interrupting. Annie handed her the letter from Lilliana Caivano and the picture of Elena. Betta took them. Annie watched her face, hoping for some sense of recognition.

"Ah," she said, after finishing the letter. "I understand. First, let me say the name Caivano eez," she hesitated. "How you say, common? My family eez not this one. I tell you because you must have been surprised at my last name."

"Yes, actually we wondered if you might be related," Janice said.

Betta nodded. "Yes, I am sure. My married name is Caivano, but my husband's family eez not originally from Naples. They come from Basilicata, which eez another region in southern Italy."

"We were wondering what happened to Naples after the war? Did the people leave for another place? We thought possibly there might be certain villages people went to escape the cities that had been bombed so badly?" Annie asked.

Betta made a clicking sound with her tongue and shook her head.

"Eet's very difficult and might require a long time of much research. There eez not one place where people went. In fact, most people stayed to rebuild the city. But for theez particular family, I cannot speak."

Her optimism sank like a torpedoed ship. They had embarked on an impossible task.

"The most likely possibility would be to ask the older Neapolitans who would have lived in this area, but the ones who are left are elderly now. I can make some inquiries if there is some with thees last name and send information by e-mail if I find anything. Could I photocopy this letter?" Betta asked.

"Certainly," Annie said. It was a private, family matter, but if it could help reunite them with Ephraim's descendants, she knew her grandmother would approve.

Betta stood with the letter and then stopped suddenly.

"Oh, I just thought of something we might try. Come with me," she said. Annie and Janice followed her to a computer on the opposite wall.

"You know there were many occupation babies born here during and after the war," Betta said. "Many, many, here and in other parts of Europe and in the Pacific. After the Internet existed, resources were developed to reunite the soldiers and their children. Many times they did not know of their existence. There are several, but we will try the most popular one for Americans. Maybe someone has reached out. It's just a chance, but we must try," she said.

The computer was up now and she typed *American World War II GI babies.*

Annie never even thought about the possibility of all the babies left behind along with the mothers. It must have been a common scenario despite the military's provision of contraception to the soldiers during the war.

"Ah, okay. Here we are," Betta said. Annie and Janice looked over her shoulder.

"Thees eez one of the databases. There are several resources based on where soldiers were stationed. Thees eez the one for Italy."

Betta leaned into the screen and frowned. "No good."

"What's wrong?" Janice said.

"Eets not possible to search by name, you must go through all postings. There are many, going back many years." Betta scooted her chair back from the computer. "I will get you both an espresso while you search."

"Thank you," Annie said, scooting into the seat. "Janice, why don't you read through it, too, so I don't miss anything."

Janice pulled another chair up next to the screen.

An hour and two espressos later, they were several pages down and into the late 1990s.

"My eyes are starting to hurt," Annie said, rubbing them with the palms of her hands.

"I know. I need a break after this page," Janice said.

"A break sounds good," Annie said, scooting back her chair and stretching her arms.

"Wait, look," Janice said, and pointed to a post at the bottom.

"What?" Annie asked, pulling her chair back toward the screen and squinting to see where Janice pointed.

"Ephraim May, Kentucky," Annie said, hardly believing the words she read aloud.

"Read it," Janice said.

Seeking information on Ephraim May, stationed in Naples, Italy during 1943.

"There's a name, and a city. Here's an email."

Betta joined them. "Did you find something?"

"Yes, can we send an email from here?" Janice said.

"Certainly," Betta said.

"But it will come back here," Annie said.

"I know, but just make sure it still works, then we can send it from your phone," Janice said.

Betta traded places with Annie at the computer screen.

"What would you like me to say?"

Janice looked at Annie. "You have some information and could we please have a phone number and an address," she said.

Betta nodded, typed the e-mail in Italian, and hit send.

"I call you with the information as soon as they respond," she said, and then looked back at the screen.

"Oh, thees eez not good. The e-mail eez back."

"We do have a name, and a place," Janice said.

Annie read it aloud, "Benito Gianelli. Montefollonico."

"The information eez very old," Betta said. "Let's try and search this name in Montefollonico."

They waited while the search engine pulled up information.

"Ah, yes, here is Benito Gianelli, Via dei Colli. It's outside the village, maybe a farm."

"Where is Montefollonico?" Janice asked.

"North. In Tuscany."

Annie looked at Janice and they made a silent decision.

"We'll go to Montefollonico," Janice said.

Chapter Twenty-Six

BEFORE THEY LEFT the museum, Betta searched the Internet for a phone number to go with the street name, but nothing more was listed. Excited to help, she had printed out directions to Montefollonico and had even booked the only hotel in the village.

"Less than four hours drive," she had said.

They checked out of the Grand *Vesuvio*, loaded their luggage, and were driving north back to Rome and beyond to Tuscany. Annie debated calling her grandmother, but it would only be around five in the morning. She decided to wait until there was something concrete to tell later.

"I hope this is not a wild goose chase," she said to Janice, shifting gears, and finally getting the hang of the stick shift. "What if we get to Montefollonico and find out they moved back to the south? To Sicily, for instance?"

"Then we go to Sicily," Janice said.

"What if Benito has since died, and he has no children?"

"Then at least you know what happened. Do you always think of the worst-case scenario?" Janice asked.

"Yeah, pretty much," Annie said, grinning back at Janice.

"You have got to stop. I don't remember you being that way in New York. You're always the positive one. I'm the cynical one," she said.

"I hid it in New York because everything was so predictable."

"How was New York ever predictable?" Janice asked.

"*My* New York was predictable because I had a job and knew what I was doing every day. I lived in the same place for ten years. Now I'm back home, living with my grandmother, without a job, trying to overcome my father's legacy, and terrified to marry the most wonderful man I have ever known. I feel a little as if the rug was pulled out from under me," Annie said.

"You probably needed the rug pulled out from under you. You can't live with an apartment full of flight attendants forever," Janice said.

"Have some sympathy," Annie said

"Well stop this *what-if* business. Those words will put you in a mental health hospital. If you're going to do the *what ifs* go the other way. My high school art teacher always said 'What if is the gateway to creativity.'"

"Okay, okay. Don't you need a nap or something?"

Janice grinned at her and leaned back in the seat.

***

They skirted Rome where the traffic was considerably thicker. Annie found herself driving faster, keeping pace with the other cars. She was getting the feel of the Ferrari and she liked it.

In the last hour of the drive, the landscape changed. Hillsides were covered in vineyards, olive groves, and farms. Walled cities sat atop jutting hills providing protection and giving watchers visibility for miles around. Annie thought how different this was from Kentucky, where towns frequently sat down in valleys next to rivers or creeks, not on the tops of hills away from a water source. But medieval times were different; the ability to protect the towns depended on creating a fortress with long views of the landscape.

"Can we take a smaller road or is it the A1 all the way?" she asked Janice, who was studying the map. "It'd be nice to see more of the countryside."

"Looks like we're getting off about fifteen minutes from here and then it's a small road," Janice said.

The road wound around, up hills and down, passing more olive groves, vineyards, and cheese factories offering tastings of pecorino, the area specialty. Finally, there was the sign to Montefollonico, and they turned onto an even smaller road. Betta had told them it was a very small village—*piccolo* she had said in Italian—but Annie couldn't even see a village. Finally, winding around the backside of a hill, it came into view. Like many of the other hilltop towns, it was surrounded by an ancient stone wall.

"Our hotel is actually outside the city wall, at the base of the village. There's the sign for it," Janice said.

It felt good to get out of the car and stretch. Annie stood for a moment in the parking lot, enjoying the flowers and trees while Janice barreled her way into the reception area.

When Annie finally followed her inside, Janice was bent over paperwork. A blonde-haired woman introduced herself as Carlotta.

"We have your room ready," she said and handed Janice a key. "You will like it. It's a big room with a nice view of the valley. Alfonso will bring your bags. Please follow me."

They walked around to the side of the building. Carlotta used her own key to unlock the door and usher them inside. "It is quite lovely, yes?"

"Oh yes," Annie said. The Val d'Orcia stretched out below them in a stunning display visible from the large window.

"Carlotta, can you tell us how to get to Via dei Colli?" Janice asked.

"*Si*, it's just on the other side of the village, the only road going down into the valley. It's a very long road, beautiful for seeing the farms."

"Do you happen to know Benito Gianelli?"

"No, but I live in Montepulciano. Does this man live on that road?" Carlotta asked.

"Yes," Janice said. "Or we think so anyway."

"You can stop and ask along the way, but I would not go tonight. It will be dark soon and the road is narrow with many turns," she said. "I suggest you have dinner and go tomorrow morning. We have a lovely restaurant here, which is quite good. There are also three restaurants in the village."

Janice looked at Annie, silently asking for her opinion.

"I'd like to go into the village tonight. Perhaps tomorrow night at your restaurant?"

"Certainly. I suggest for your first night in the village, try La Botte Piena. It is in the middle of the square. I recommend a wrap since it can be windy. The other restaurants are good as well, but this is in the center of town. I will put you down to dine with us tomorrow night and you can let me know tomorrow if you need to adjust your reservation. Alfonso will bring you a map of the area. If you need anything, let me know. Otherwise, I wish you good night." They thanked her and Carlotta closed the door as she left.

***

An hour later, they had both showered, dressed, and were walking uphill to the village. They passed a bar serving coffee and libations to customers on outdoor tables. Three old men sat by the medieval gate. Janice said *"buonasera"* to them and they returned the greeting.

Sandstone and brick houses lined the stone streets, the hard surfaces broken by brilliant begonias in terra-cotta planters ranging from red to coral to pink and all shades in between. Climbing vines grew out of pots placed next to the walls. Wooden doors in hues of chestnut brown and walnut had large iron knockers, keeping what lay beyond a mystery to the street traveler.

Iron light fixtures hung from long arms high over the streets. As they walked the stone streets, they discovered a bank, a pharmacy, several churches, three restaurants, and a small grocery store. There were a couple of shops selling everything from small antiques to old jewelry to hand-sewn linens. In less than an hour, they had covered the entire village, walking up and down each street and ending at the entrance to the gardens of the Palazzo. None of the businesses were open.

They sat by the medieval gate and faced the bar, where most of the town's activity seemed to be centered. Men and women were playing cards together; some had glasses of wine or orange aperitifs. Several were drinking nothing, intent only on conversation.

"Do you want me to ask anybody here?" Janice said.

"I don't know how without causing a scene. We're already quite obvious," Annie said.

"Should I ask the bar owner?" Janice said.

"It'd be like going to Bill's Diner and asking him about Beulah. He'd call her immediately and ten other people would hear in the process. It'd be all over town before we have dinner. No, let's wait and ask at the restaurant when we're not quite so noticeable."

"Maybe it should get all over town fast, then we will know sooner than later," Janice said.

"I don't feel right about it. What if Benito is here and he is Ephraim's son. This is a private matter for Benito and his family. Maybe no one knows his father was American. Here we come into town like typical Americans blustering our way through to get what we want and forgetting how he might feel in the process. I want to handle it carefully."

"You're right. Just remember I am a typical blustering American and a New Yorker on top of that, so it seems like a waste of time, but I get it." Janice smiled at her.

"Thank you for suggesting this trip and especially for coming with me," Annie said.

"You're my best friend. What else am I going to do?" Janice said, and then looked at her watch. "Time for dinner."

They were seated on the patio in a corner table for two. Drink orders were taken and they were brought sparkling mineral water and a glass of *prosecco*.

"This stuff is good," Janice said. "Less alcohol than wine and plenty of fizz."

Annie took a sip. "A little like champagne," she said. "But better."

A bag of bread was brought out with much ceremony of rolling down the edges of the bag to make the bread more accessible. Olive oil, aged balsamic vinegar, salt and pepper were all placed on the table.

"*Scusi*," Janice said to the young girl who brought the bread. "*Vive qui a Montefollonico?*"

"*Io vivo a Montepulciano,*" she said, pointing in the direction of another hill across the valley.

"*Grazie,*" Janice said. "She doesn't live here."

A waiter came to take their order and spoke excellent English. They ordered antipasto to share and the special to share, and then each ordered a green salad to follow. The waiter was leaving when Janice asked in English, "Do you live here in Montefollonico?"

"*Si*, yes, this is my restaurant. I live just there," he said and pointed to the upstairs of the restaurant.

"Ah, so you are the owner. Do you happen to know Benito Gianelli?" she asked.

"*Si, si,* I know Benito," he said. Annie held her breath, waiting.

"Great! We're looking for his house on this road. Can you tell us where?" Janice pointed to the map.

"No, no you will not find him there," he said.

Just then, someone from another table called to the owner. "Excuse me," he said and left them. Annie felt like an eternity passed, but in only a few minutes the restaurant owner returned and pointed to the map.

"Benito used to live there, but no more. His son lives there now."

"What happened to Benito?" Janice asked.

"He is just there," the restaurateur pointed down a dark street.

"Down there?" Janice said, pointing.

"Pass the pharmacy, but on same side. A big wooden door, number is fourteen, I think."

"*Grazie,*" Janice said, as he moved away. "He's here," Janice said, hissing the words across the table.

Annie's throat constricted and she closed her eyes. Benito was here.

Janice called for the check and thanked the restaurateur when they made their way out.

"We still don't know who Benito is. We only know he was the one who made the posting," Annie said, afraid to get her hopes up, as they navigated the cobblestone street.

"There you go again," Janice said. "It has to be a family member. Have faith."

Yes, Annie thought. She needed faith. And to pray Benito would receive this news well, if they actually met Ephraim's son tomorrow.

Via Coppoli was the name of the street. They looked for number fourteen past the pharmacy and on the same side. It was just as the restaurant owner said, a big wooden door with an iron knocker on it. Vines climbed from terra cotta pots on each side of the entrance and wound up and over the top of the door. Above the vines, a small, round window showed only darkness from the inside.

Annie stared at the window, wondering about the living and breathing family beyond. She wished them a restful sleep tonight. If Benito were Ephraim's son, what she had to tell them tomorrow would change their lives forever.

Chapter Twenty-Seven

BEULAH STAYED IN her room most of Sunday afternoon, trying to get her composure back. The last few days had taken the cake. Not since Fred died suddenly nearly two and a half years ago had she been in such a state. All because her world had been uprooted by a foreign woman who had come in here and tried to take over.

Or was it really Rossella's fault? Maybe it went back to the whole affair with Ephraim. To have her routine disrupted just as she was trying to sort out what to think about her brother and his long ago indiscretion had just made a hard thing worse.

Honestly, if she looked at the last several months, it had been one thing after another. First, Annie showing up unexpectedly after losing her job; then knee surgery. About the time she recovered from the surgery and worked out a nice routine with Annie, there was the fire in the old stone house.

The paltry insurance check, the disagreement with Annie, Betty Gibson's nosy blathering, and then Annie finding the mysteriously hidden letters. The revelation about Ephraim's son and, finally, the houseguest. Well, it was more than one body could take.

Try as she did to practice hospitality in case she might
be entertaining angels unaware, she was quite sure Rossella
DeVechio was no angel.

***

Monday morning, Beulah drank her coffee at the kitchen
table, hoping for a few moments of peace before the day started.

Rossella planted herself in front of Beulah, hands on her
waist.

"Tonight, I cook for you."

"Yes, we agreed yesterday," she said, growing wary.

"And you not be here while I cook, okay?" Rossella said, now
wagging a finger back and forth.

"You don't want me to help set the table or do anything?"

"No set table, no help cook. No be in kitchen all day."

"Okay, Rossella," she said and sighed. "I won't be here.
When do you want me out?"

"I give you one more hour. Then I take over," she said and
waited for Beulah to nod her agreement. When she did, Rossella
broke into a smile, leaned down and kissed her on both cheeks.
"Good! You like tonight. No garlic."

After Rossella left, she looked around the kitchen longingly.
Just knowing she couldn't be in here today made her want to
cook. Instead, she would look on the bright side. There was a
list of errands she needed to run in Rutherford and that would
keep her busy.

There were only a few days left until Annie returned. If she
could maintain self-control until then, everything would get
back to normal. Whatever normal meant these days.

***

Beulah finally went home when she had run every possible
errand she could think of between Somerville and Rutherford.
As she opened the back screen door, a mixture of spices wafted
from the kitchen. Suspicious, she sniffed again, but did not
smell garlic. Rossella was humming to herself and didn't seem
to realize Beulah had walked in the back door.

Ignoring me, she thought, *hoping I won't come in the kitchen.*

Rossella was busy with her hands and working at something in the sink. Beulah edged up to the kitchen door and peered around the doorframe. A plucked chicken was in the sink and Rossella was using both hands to squeeze out the pinfeathers. A red feather floated to the floor. That chicken did not come from Kroger. That feather belonged to one of Annie's Rhode Island Reds.

Beulah felt her face flush with heat. Enough was enough. She straightened herself up to her full five feet five inches and stormed into the kitchen as best she could with a cane.

"What in tarnation are you doin'?" she said.

Rossella glanced over her shoulder.

"We agree I make deener," she said, turning back to the business of popping out the pinfeathers.

"I never said you could take one of Annie's chickens," Beulah said, and planted her feet and her cane firmly into the linoleum.

"You not say I no take chicken," Rossella said, not even turning to face her. Beulah started to protest, but Rossella's English stumped her for a second. In that brief pause, she realized she was liable to say something she would have to confess later in her prayers.

"Humph!" she said and marched out of the kitchen and into the dining room where she stopped short.

Her white lace tablecloth was spread out on the table and her best china was at each place setting with a matching cloth napkin. Votive candles in teacups sat around the table, lending a delicate ambience, even though they were not yet lit. Crystal water goblets and Evelyn's antique wine glasses were positioned just above the top of each knife. Had she stolen Evelyn's wine glasses, too? If not stolen, then Evelyn was an accomplice.

She had to admit, her table had never looked more beautiful. But just as the thought threatened to soften her, she thought once again of how that woman was putting her in the position of causing someone to stumble by having wine in her home. If Catholics wanted to drink, fine, but she did not appreciate that woman pushing her beliefs off in Beulah's house.

Beulah went upstairs and took a long time getting ready, praying for peace and calm, and finally sitting like a prisoner on the edge of her bed. While she waited for the appointed time, she ran her hands over the metal box that sat on the nightstand next to her bed and wondered how Annie was doing. That was the important thing, and she needed to focus on things that mattered, not petty squabbles with a houseguest. It would all be over soon and her routine would get back to normal. Finally, after the umpteenth time of looking at her watch, she went downstairs and sat in the den, a visitor in her own home.

When the first guest knocked on the door, Rossella dashed to open it before Beulah could even stand from the couch.

"Come in, come in," Rossella said to Evelyn. "Come here and wait with Beulah. I bring you aperitif."

"Did you know your wine glasses are on my dining room table?" Beulah said.

"Yes, Jake ran them over to her earlier today," Evelyn said, her eyes shifting away. At least her friend had the decency to look chagrined.

Betty and Joe Gibson came in, followed by Lindy and Tom.

"Law have mercy," Betty said. "This is fancy, fancy, making us wait in here."

"Well, you may as well have a seat," Beulah said. "Rossella is in charge tonight."

Evelyn and Tom sat next to each other on the couch, with Beulah beside Evelyn. Lindy sat on the arm of the couch next to her dad, Joe took the recliner, and Betty sat in a wingback chair. About the time they all got settled, in walked Jake and Woody.

"Hey everybody," Jake said, freshly showered in a collared shirt and jeans. Woody was also dressed in jeans, but his shirt collar was frayed and so were the cuffs. He even wore a tie, but it hung too short and was cocked sideways. Some men needed a wife more than others, she observed, and Woody was one of those.

There was a reshuffling of the seating arrangement and just as they resettled, Rossella walked in with Beulah's old bamboo tray. She had covered it in two of the lace cloth napkins so it looked quite pretty. On the tray were flutes of champagne. At least Betty Gibson was right here in the middle of it and would be less likely to tell half the congregation.

"*Prosecco!*" Rossella called proudly. She started with Woody and then went around the room, offering a glass to each.

Everyone took a glass and when Rossella finally got to Beulah, it seemed the room fell quiet and waited. After a slight hesitation, she reached for the glass as the room went back to chatter.

Let it not be said I was an ungracious host.

Rossella took the last glass for herself and then lifted her glass. "*Salute!*" Then she took a sip and they all followed. It was fizzy, but not sweet like a soda.

Rossella disappeared and then was back with a tray of small pieces of sliced bread with chopped tomatoes on top. "*Brusketta,*" Rossella said, again with great pride, and then carried the tray around to each person and offering one of Beulah's cloth napkins along with it.

For the next minute, there was only the sound of crunching. Woody dropped half his tomato topping on the floor and bent to pick it up with her white lace napkin.

"Sure is crunchy," Joe said and everyone laughed. There was nothing to do but drink more prosecco, she realized, since the flaky crumbs had to be washed down.

After they had all eaten the bread, Rossella ushered them into the dining room. The room was even more enchanting with the chandelier dimmed and the votive candles lit. It looked like they were walking into a fancy restaurant.

Everyone took a seat and Rossella brought out two plates of thinly sliced meat, one for each end of the table. Had she brought that down with her from New York? It must have been in the suitcase of food, for it certainly wasn't anything out of Beulah's pantry.

"*Antipasto. Prosciutto, salame, mortadella,* and olive.*"

Rossella disappeared into the kitchen again and she realized there was no seat at the table for her. Jake noticed at the same time and when Rossella came back in the room, he stood and offered her his seat.

"No, no, I do for you tonight," she said and then removed the prosecco glasses and opened the bottle of red Chianti. Jake sat back down at Rossella's urging and so Beulah did nothing but allow the Chianti to be poured and take a sip in gratefulness for the gift Rossella was offering. The realization was humbling. Here she was, being resentful and stubborn. It was the old sin of pride rearing its ugly head once again.

Beulah was surprised at how much the prosciutto tasted like their own salt-cured country ham. In fact, it was so much like it she took a second portion.

"This is one thing I would like to do eventually. Learn how to cure pork like the Italians," Jake said.

"What's involved in the process?" Tom asked.

"I would need a barn dedicated to the curing, and the other equipment depends on the types of curing we might do."

Rossella removed the empty plates and then brought out the noodles. "*Primo piatto. Tagliatelle* with lemon."

"What does *primo piatto* mean?" Betty asked when Rossella left the large bowl to be passed around.

"It means the first course, generally pasta," Jake said. "In other words, there is another coming," he said, his eyes twinkling in amusement.

"First course? We've already had bread and ham," Woody said. "I thought the meat was all there was to it, so I had a big 'bate' of it."

"This is delicious," Tom said.

"I taste the lemon and cream," Evelyn added. "It's wonderful."

"Everything is good," Lindy said.

"Are these the noodles what she had hanging in here on Sunday?" Woody asked.

"She called it *tagliatelle,* so it must be," Beulah said.

"You can tell the difference in homemade pasta," Lindy said. "It's so light."

Rossella walked in and there was a verbal explosion of appreciation while Rossella glowed under the compliments.

"I now bring you *secondo piatto*," she said, picking up the nearly empty bowl of noodles. She hoped Rossella had dished some out for herself before bringing it to the dining room, or else she would have slim pickings for her own supper.

Rossella entered carrying the Rhode Island Red on a platter, roasted until the skin was golden brown, and sprinkled with an unidentified herb.

The tray was passed around, everyone taking a bit. She was thankful the chicken wasn't too large with all the food they had already consumed.

"This chicken is delicious. I wonder where she got it," Jake mused, obviously savoring the meat.

"You ought to know, Jake," Beulah said. "You and Annie picked them up."

He raised his eyebrows. "One of Annie's laying hens?"

"I found her plucking it in the kitchen sink this afternoon," Beulah said.

"Well no wonder it's so good," Joe said, and then chuckled. And then Beulah chuckled. And then the whole group burst into laughter.

There was a sound of clinking dishes and running water in the kitchen while they finished the meat. Rossella was not only cooking for them, but cleaning up as well. In a few minutes, she entered the dining room and cleared away the meat and all the plates. Evelyn and Lindy both tried to get up and help, but she shooed them back into their seats. Once the dishes were off the table, Rossella brought small dessert plates and set the stack on the corner of the table. Beulah was stuffed and would pass on dessert.

Rossella entered with a clear glass pan and held it for everyone to admire.

"Dolce. Eez tiramisu."

She then put it on the table and dished servings onto the dessert plates.

When a dessert plate landed in front of her, there was nothing to do but taste it. Never had she savored such a creamy delight. It was both custard and cake in layers. She ate every crumb on her plate and noticed everyone else did, too.

"I'm foundered," Joe said, and pushed back from the table.

"Me too," Evelyn said. "But it was such fun," she said, glancing at Tom.

"It sure was," he said, and looked at Evelyn the way Jake gazed at Annie.

Everything Beulah suspected was confirmed in that one look.

Chapter Twenty-Eight

BUTTERFLIES DANCED IN Annie's stomach when she and Janice walked up the hill to the village at ten the next morning. As long as someone answered the door at 14 Via Coppoli, they would finally know something, one way or the other. They passed the restaurant where they enjoyed dinner the night before, down the street beyond the pharmacy, and then arrived at the address. Annie took a deep breath and reached in her purse for the picture of Elena and the letter, just to make sure they were still there. Janice used the iron knocker first. When no one came, she pressed the button and waited. Finally, the speaker buzzed and a voice said, "*Si?*"

In Italian, Janice explained they would like to see Benito Gianelli.

"*Benito non e qui. Posso aiutarla?*"

"*Si,*" Janice said.

Janice went back and forth with the voice in Italian, and then whatever Janice said made the door click and open for them.

"Benito's not here," she said. "I think this is his wife. She said we can come up and he should be back any minute."

Inside the wooden door, stone steps led up to the living area. An attractive woman with gray hair greeted them and ushered them into a living room with slipcovered couches.

Smiling at Annie, she turned to Janice and asked a question.

"*Si, grazie. Due,*" Janice responded.

Annie looked around the room for framed photographs that might lend a clue to Benito's identity. They were in the more formal room decorated with antique furniture, lace table coverings, and ceramic figurines. She caught sight of an adjoining room and she was about to step into it when footsteps sounded on the stairs and their hostess called out in Italian.

A man's voice responded.

Janice looked at Annie and raised her eyebrows as if to say, *Here we go.*

Footsteps, more Italian conversation, and then the man came around the corner and into the living room. When she saw him, Annie's eyes filled with tears. The man who must be Benito smiled at them and she recognized the familiar gray eyes and her grandmother's nose, straight and with a slight turn down at the end.

Benito had a shock of salt and pepper hair, his skin was weathered and there were deep lines around his eyes and his mouth. But they were pleasant lines, as if they had been earned through lots of laughter. He looked at both of them, but his eyes lingered on her. Annie wondered if he recognized something familiar or maybe it was simply because she was on the verge of tears.

"Hello," he said. "Sorry, no English."

Janice responded in Italian and he smiled and nodded.

"*Americano,*" he said and nodded, looking again at Annie. He motioned for them to be seated as his wife brought in a tray of espressos with sugar and milk.

"*Grazie,*" Annie said.

"Angelina," Benito said and pointed to his wife.

They sipped the espressos and then Janice said to Annie, "I told him you will explain why we're here and I'll translate."

Annie nodded and put down her cup.

"Benito, I have a picture of a woman. Do you recognize her?" she handed the picture to him while Janice translated. Benito's eyes were wide and wondering when he looked up at her with a question on his face that transcended language.

"*Si, é mia madre,*" he said, his voice rising in a question.

Janice spoke again.

"Elena Caivano," he said.

"*E tuo padre?*" Janice asked.

"Roberto Gianelli," he said. "*Perché hai questa foto di mia madre?*"

"He wants to know why you have the picture of his mother," Janice said.

"We found this picture among letters from my great-uncle Ephraim May, who was an American soldier stationed here in Italy. In Naples."

Annie paused to wait for Janice to translate, but she noticed the color had drained from Benito's face when she mentioned her great-uncle's name.

"Ephraim May?" he said, in a heavily accented whisper.

Janice translated the rest. Angelina went to her husband's side and put her arms around him as he put his head in his hands. Annie wiped her own eyes and waited. When he composed himself, he looked up and spoke in Italian.

"His stepfather was Roberto Gianelli, but he adopted him and raised him as his own. His biological father was Ephraim May. He wants to know how we are connected to this man."

Janice spoke in Italian while he nodded, then stopped to speak in English to Annie.

"I told him you are Ephraim's great-niece and how you and your grandmother just learned Ephraim had a son."

Benito was shaking his head in disbelief while Angelina's forehead was creased with worry. Then Annie waited while he spoke in slow and halting words and then again while Janice translated.

"He says, 'I never knew my father. I always knew his name and he was an American soldier. We do not know what happened to him. When I was just three years old, my mother married my stepfather and we moved here, to his hometown.'"

Annie said, "I am sorry to tell you he was killed in the Battle of Anzio, in 1944. Only recently, we discovered this picture and," she said, pulling out the copy of the letter written from Lilliana Caivano, "this letter."

Janice translated as Annie handed the letter over to Benito.

They waited while he read the letter. *"Mia nonna,"* he said, shaking his head, and handing the letter to Angelina.

"My great-grandparents received the letter, but we believe they had no way to translate it and never knew they had a grandson. They hid the letter and the picture away in a box we just found a couple of weeks ago when we were fixing up the house they lived in many years ago." Annie waited while Janice translated.

Benito responded and Janice translated.

"My mother believed him to be dead and she was right. I always thought he might be living and come back one day. My stepfather was good to me, but of course, I always wanted to know my father."

Benito paused and looked at Angelina, grasping her hand. He turned to Annie.

"But, now, I find you are my cousin," Janice repeated and Annie saw a smile breaking through the sea of emotions on his face. Angelina relaxed at this and dropped her arm.

"Yes," she said. "And my grandmother is your aunt, although she is only about thirteen years older than you."

Janice translated and the smile grew wider.

"I have a picture here on my phone." She showed him a picture of Beulah in the garden next to her tomato plants.

"Bella," he said. *"E bella i pomodori."*

"Beulah, my grandmother, wanted me to come here when she knew about you, but we had only the address in Naples," Annie said and then asked Janice to explain how they found him.

His eyes lit with understanding and he went back and forth with Janice, while she explained how they had tracked him down to Montefollonico.

"Bene, bene," he said in approval. *"Molto bene."*

"And Elena," Annie said. "What happened to her?"

Janice translated. "He says he will take us to see her," Janice said. Benito stood and spoke to Angelina.

"She's still living?" Annie said.

"He just said he would take us," Janice said.

"Si," Annie responded.

"Okay," Benito said and spoke again to Angelina in Italian.

"Before we go," Annie said. "Can I take a picture of you both?"

After Janice translated, Angelina smoothed her hair and Benito put his arm around her and they both smiled. She could not wait to e-mail the picture to Evelyn for Beulah.

"*Allora*," Benito said. Angelina carried the coffee cups to the kitchen. Angelina called "*Ciao*" and did not follow when they went down the steps, out the wooden door, and up the street and back to the piazza. Annie and Janice walked with Benito down the cobblestone street and outside the city wall. They were all quiet, each processing the fullness of what had been revealed in the last hour. On they went, down a paved road, until they saw a sign: "*Cimitero*."

Benito pointed to the sign and looked back at them, a great deal of meaning passing through his watery eyes. Annie and Janice exchanged looks, but somehow, it seemed disrespectful to talk.

The cemetery was made up of three walls of vaults in a U-shape, with the cemetery gates closing it in to make a rectangle. Burial sites filled the center. Each grave was marked by a white marble square in the wall with the name, birth and death date, along with a picture of the deceased and a vase with real or artificial flowers. Benito led them to a vault two squares up from the ground and near the middle of the wall.

"*Mamma*," he said and pointed to a square that said *Elena Caivano Maggio Gianelli. Nato 5 Settembre 1924 – Morto 17 Gennaio, 2000.*

"No way," Janice said.

"What?"

Janice pointed to the name Maggio in Elena's name. "This means *May* in Italian."

"They were married?" Annie asked.

Janice spoke the question in Italian.

"No, no," Benito said. And then he spoke for quite a while before Janice translated what he said.

"He said, no, they were not officially married, but Elena said she married him 'in her heart.' They would have married, had the war allowed it, but just as he recovered from malaria, he was shipped off to Anzio. Elena wanted the name on her tombstone since Roberto preceded her in death and it could no longer dishonor him. Benito said his two half-brothers were not very happy about it, but they understood it was her wish."

Annie leaned in and studied the picture of an older Elena. Benito then pointed to the vault next to Elena's.

"*Roberto Gianelli, Nato 16 Marzo 1920 – Morto 26 Guigno, 1995.*" A picture of Roberto showed a handsome man dressed in a suit. Benito spoke again.

"He still misses his mother and his stepfather," Janice translated. "After his stepfather died he posted on the site dedicated to reuniting occupation babies with their biological parent. Benito loved Roberto and would not have done it had he still been living. He told his mother and she agreed for him to do it. She knew of the letter her parents had written and knew there had been no response. But she held no bad feelings since there were many possible reasons why no letter ever came back to them," Janice said.

Annie nodded, humbled by Elena's forgiveness and grace. Annie took a picture of the vault and one of Benito standing next to Elena's stone. Beulah would want to see everything.

As they walked back to the village, Annie said, "Ask him about his children and his grandchildren."

Janice translated and Benito spoke.

"He has a son, Vincenzo, and a daughter, Paola. Vincenzo is married and lives on a farm in the valley near Montepulciano, just a few kilometers away. They have two teenage grandchildren, Luca and Rosa. Paola is not married and lives in London. He wants to take us to meet his son tomorrow."

"Yes, of course," Annie said.

"And ask Benito if he and Angelina would like to be our guests for dinner tonight at the hotel restaurant."

After Janice translated he nodded and smiled. They set the time and Benito kissed both of them, first the right cheek and then the left in the Italian way, before they parted ways.

Annie's heart was full. It was the beginning of a new relationship, one they hopefully had years to cultivate. With technology, the distance across the water need not be far. Annie would send the story over email this afternoon; she only wished she could deliver the news in person.

***

Later that evening, a table for four was set on white linens under the shade of two horse chestnut trees on the patio of the hotel's restaurant. The view was of the distant hill town of Montepulciano, and in between, the Val d'Orcia. The daylight faded to dusk and then dark as they sat around the candlelight and enjoyed a slow meal while Benito filled in the events of his life and Janice translated.

Annie learned Benito had grown up in Montefollonico, and his stepfather was a tailor. Benito met Angelina at school and they married soon after they were out. His father wanted to train him as a tailor, but Benito wanted to be a farmer. He worked on a farm in the Val d'Orcia and bought his own farm eventually. Benito and Angelina lived there until recently when they moved back into the village, leaving their son Vincenzo to take over the farm, which produced olive oil and pork.

His face lit up when he talked of the farm, Annie noticed. He spoke faster and Janice had a harder time translating and they all laughed at one point when Janice said "*piano*" asking him to slow down. Benito was a farmer and had spent his life working the land—just like all the May men before him.

Chapter Twenty-Nine

IT WAS AFTER ten when Annie and Janice got back to the room, but at home it was late afternoon. Evelyn had not yet responded to the e-mail she sent earlier. Annie read and then reread an email from Jake about picking up a new bull with Scott. Annie was glad he had a buddy his own age since there was over thirty years difference between him and Joe Gibson. Reading his words made her miss him to the point of nearly aching. Annie wanted to hear his voice, something to make her feel closer to him with so much that separated them.

When her call went to his voicemail, she left a short message about their connection with Benito and promised more later. The call she had placed to Beulah had gone unanswered.

Janice returned to the room after making her phone calls from the empty hotel lobby.

"The kids are having a great time," she said. "They don't want to come home. On the other hand, Jimmy is exhausted, but said they're getting the wildfires under control."

"I feel disconnected from the rest of the world," Annie said. "It's as if I'm in another era of time right now, reliving Elena and Ephraim's history."

"It's kind of heavy, isn't it?" Janice said, crawling into her bed. "What a strong love she had for him, to have his name written on her tombstone after a whole life with someone else."

"What do you think would've happened had he lived? Would he have gone back to Italy after the war, married her and brought her home to Somerville?"

Janice yawned. "I guess we will never know."

Annie turned off the light but lay in bed and stared out the window. A nearly full moon was rising in the sky. *Luna Bella.*

In only a few hours, Jake would see the moon rise over the rolling hills of Kentucky. It was only a month ago when she had stared blissfully at the full moon after Jake told her he loved her. Then, everything was possible. Now, the beautiful dream seemed impossible.

Annie thought about Elena having that kind of love for Ephraim and then having to part with him. Later, finding out she carried his child and the longing after the war to be reunited with him. After months, when no word came, she finally accepted the dreaded truth that he was gone from their lives forever. Possibly, the young woman lay in her bed and stared at a moon hanging low in the Italian sky on a night like tonight, and made a decision. *Benito needed a father.*

Elena had married Roberto, a good man, a provider, but not the love of her life. The rest of her days, Elena guarded the place that belonged only to Ephraim for the day when she could claim it publicly by attaching their names in death.

Annie turned over and tried to sleep. Vesta's words came to her from Jeremiah: "Can the Ethiopian change his skin or the leopard his spots? Then also you can do good who are accustomed to do evil."

It was impossible to change her family, who she was and what people thought about her. It was possible to do good instead of evil, with God's help. Love instead of hate. Stay instead of leave. Choose truth instead of lies.

Somewhere in the night under the light of the waxing moon, Annie realized that while Elena guarded her heart for Ephraim, she had guarded her heart against Jake. It had nothing to do with protecting Jake and everything to do with protecting herself.

***

"You look bad. Didn't you sleep well?" Janice said, squinting at her from her bed the next morning.

"Thanks." Annie threw a pillow at her. Janice caught it and flung it back. "Terrible night. I'm not sure I slept at all."

"Why? I thought you'd be so relieved at finding Benito," Janice said, and walked to the bathroom.

"I had this overwhelming feeling I was losing Jake forever," Annie said. "In fact, I need to call him."

"You can't call him now, it's two in the morning back home," Janice said, a toothbrush in her mouth. "Did you have a bad dream?"

"It wasn't a dream. It's all this stuff with Ephraim and Elena and how they missed a lifetime with each other. Janice, I'm not like my father. So maybe all this is really about protecting myself, holding back for fear of losing again."

Annie plopped down on the closed toilet seat, feeling herself on the verge of tears.

"This horrible fear is the very reason I could lose him."

Janice spit the toothpaste out. "This is news to you? What've I been trying to tell you?"

"I know, I know. Somehow it came into focus last night."

"Am I your best friend?" Janice asked, the toothbrush emphasizing each word.

"Of course you are."

"Do I love you like one of my own sisters?" Janice asked.

"I know you do."

"Please hear what I am about to say *in love*," Janice said. "I don't think you've ever wanted to let your defense down with another man because of what your father did. It's why you've picked losers in the past, so you'd never be in danger. Jake comes along and you can't resist him. He's the one. You're happy for a while until you freak out because there's no exit door. So you create this whole Taylor-name thing as your way out."

"I didn't create it!" Annie said.

"Okay, wrong word," Janice agreed. "You didn't create it, but you gave it life. You could've laughed off the words of a silly gossip. Instead, you let it become this major thing because you need a way out."

"I feel sick," she said.

"Annie, don't give your father this much control over your future and don't throw this gift away," Janice said, her voice gentle.

"I don't want to throw it away," she said, her voice a whisper. "I love Jake. I'm just not sure how to do it."

Janice knelt beside her. "Of course you don't," she smiled at her. "That's what faith is all about. You take one step at a time."

Annie thought back to a long ago time with her grandfather. They were sitting on the front porch swing, breaking green beans the summer before she left for college.

"I don't know what school will be like," Annie said. "What if it's too hard and I can't do it?"

Her grandfather took the pipe out of his shirt pocket, filled it with loose tobacco from a pouch, and tamped it down. "Sometimes you have to jump off a cliff and grow your wings on the way down."

"What's that?" Janice said and Annie was aware she had mumbled the words aloud.

"Grandpa told me once that sometimes you have to jump off a cliff and grow your wings on the way down. This feels like falling off a cliff for me."

"Then don't fall. Jump," Janice said.

***

After Annie showered, she gave the bathroom over to Janice, and sat on the bed in her robe. The lack of sleep and the emotional morning had physically exhausted her. It was like recovering from a surgery where an abscess had been lanced. While Janice showered, Annie used her laptop to check her e-mail and saw a response from Evelyn.

"Annie, Beulah will be so pleased. I am just getting this and will share it with her Wednesday morning, as soon as I can get over there. I went with Jake and Tom to see a farm down in Tennessee and we just got back. Beulah took Rossella to Lexington today to show her around along with Betty and Joe Gibson. All is well and we can't wait to get you home."

There was no e-mail from Jake. Before she lost her courage, she typed: "I'm ready."

***

Before lunch, Benito drove to their hotel and picked them up in his small car. Through Janice, he pointed out places of interest: an old villa now an *agriturismo*, a hectare of grapes belonging to a certain winemaker, and a friend's large grove of olive trees. Annie noticed the plowed ground was beige, nearly the color of sand on the Atlantic beaches back home, different from the black, fine dirt in Kentucky. When asked, Benito said "the soil drained well, which was good for grapes and olive trees."

They were on a very small road that hair-pinned around the hilltops and gently made its way to the valley below. Benito turned left onto a gravel road that led through a grove of olive trees.

"These are their olive trees," Janice translated.

Soon, a farmhouse came into view, built with the same brick and sandstone combination common in the village and finished with a terra-cotta tile roof. How different from the typical clapboard farmhouses and shingled roofs in Kentucky, Annie mused. But the environment provided the materials, and in Kentucky there was an abundance of wood. Here in Italy, stone, mud and clay to make bricks and terra-cotta came from the landscape.

Benito parked the car and they got out. Two men emerged from another stone building she guessed must be the barn. Father and son, her cousins, Vincenzo and Luca.

Benito made the introductions in Italian. There was much kissing on both cheeks by both Vincenzo and Luca. Vincenzo looked to be in his forties and had the same gray eyes of his father and her grandmother. But he appeared to take after Angelina with his other features. Luca was a handsome teenager, with brown, serious eyes, who seemed past the ravages of puberty but before a boy took on the appearance of a man.

Vincenzo spoke in good English.

"We are so happy to know you. This has brought my father much joy. He says now he can live the rest of his life in peace, knowing about his family."

Vincenzo waited while his father said something in Italian.

"Papa wants to know if you have a picture of his father? If not with you, one you could send him later?"

"Oh, yes," Annie said. "My grandmother has several. We will make copies and send them."

Vincenzo told his father and a wide smile broke out on Benito's face. "He is very happy about this," Vincenzo said. "Now, would you like to see the farm?"

"Oh, yes. And may I take pictures as well?"

"Of course," Vincenzo took them first to see the pigs, which she learned were a special breed called *cinta senese*.

"This pig is native to here and eats in the grass and the forest," Vincenzo said, pointing to the trees that bordered their property. "The pork is the best and has a special taste," he said, passion growing in his voice.

"See the pig is black with a white band around its middle," he said. "The white band is the *cinta*," he said, pointing to a sow with six piglets tugging at her. Annie took pictures of Vincenzo and Luca as well as the pigs, not only for her grandmother, but for Jake as well.

Then they walked a distance away to the other side of the farm where several hectares of olive trees grew in a line.

"We harvest in early November, usually, so we are just a few weeks away."

He plucked an olive and explained how they had to be at the right stage for pressing the oil.

"When they are ripe, we take them down the road a few kilometers to the press. We pay them to press for us, then we have our oil."

After the farm tour, Vincenzo led them back up the hill to the farmhouse. Janice was talking to Vincenzo and Luca while Annie fell in step with Benito. He held his hands behind his back, leaning into the hill, with a contented smile on his face. He caught her looking at him and smiled at her and extended his arm. They walked in step up the hill together, arm in arm, no translation needed.

Vincenzo's wife, Anna, and their daughter, Rosa, had set a table for lunch. More kissing ensued with meeting Anna and Rosa before they all sat down together to enjoy the Gianelli's olive oil and bread as well as Prosciutto, salami, and sausage from their cinta seneses and pici pasta with a pecorino cheese and white pepper sauce, another local dish.

Before they left, Janice took several pictures of Annie with her new family members. They exchanged contact information and made promises for visits, both in Italy and in Kentucky.

Annie brushed off a tear as they waved goodbye. Benito drove away from the hotel—the only male relative left to her. Italy had always been a place she loved, but now Italy held a part of her heart, a heart she hoped would remain forever unguarded.

Chapter Thirty

AFTER ALL ROSSELLA did on Monday night for the dinner party, Beulah wanted to do something kind in return. It seemed that some of the tension had gone out of the house once Rossella had proved her skill in the kitchen to Beulah's friends and neighbors. Despite the stolen chicken, she felt it was her duty as a hostess to offer Rossella a day of sightseeing. She would just as soon have stayed home, but Rossella should see more of Kentucky than the farms on May Hollow Road.

While she was happy to drive around Somerville and even Rutherford, she was no longer comfortable driving up to Lexington with all the traffic. Beulah asked Joe and Betty if they would drive her car and off they all went early Tuesday morning.

Rossella's eyes nearly bugged out at all the manicured horse farms with the dry-laid stone fences, grand entrances, and the thoroughbred barns nice as human homes.

"I know the fella who runs this one," Joe said, turning into one of the driveways that led back to the farm office.

They waited in the car while Joe went in to see his friend. Betty craned her neck from the front seat.

"Land sakes, this is fun! I sure wish Evelyn could have come with us. What in the world did she have to do that kept her from it?"

Beulah knew good and well that Evelyn was with Tom and Jake today but she was not going to be the one to tell Betty Gibson.

"She had more work to do on the wedding," Beulah said vaguely.

"Ha!" Rossella said, with a wave of her hand. "*Amore*."

"What'd you say, Rossella?" Betty asked.

"*Amore*. Love," Rossella said.

"Yes, weddings are wonderful aren't they?"

"I don't mean young couple. I mean . . ."

Beulah suddenly turned to her back seat companion and tried to give her the eye without Betty noticing.

"What wrong with your eye?" Rossella said, and frowned at Beulah.

"Nothing," Beulah said.

"C'mon y'all," Joe said. "Jack's gonna show us a Derby winner."

Beulah sighed in relief. After the horse farm, they toured the Mary Todd Lincoln house museum in downtown Lexington so Rossella could see where the Kentucky-born Abraham Lincoln met his wife.

They had lunch at a sandwich shop and when Beulah thought it was time to go home, Joe suggested a bourbon distillery tour just outside of Lexington, so off they went to Woodford Reserve.

She kept a close eye on Joe Gibson in the tasting room, making sure he wasn't sampling *too* much before driving them all home. As for her own self, Beulah passed on the sampling, having had enough alcohol in the last week to last her the rest of her life.

The subject of Evelyn and Tom had been avoided. If Betty Gibson got hold of that piece of information, especially before Evelyn was even aware of it herself, it would be disastrous. The delicate bud of early love would have no chance to blossom.

***

After such a full day, Beulah slept late the next morning. Rossella's door was still shut when she made her way to the kitchen for coffee. Just after she plugged in the percolator, the wall phone rang. She debated answering it since she could hardly take Betty Gibson's phone calls before a cup of coffee. *But it could be Annie*, so she answered.

"Beulah, I got an e-mail from Annie last night." Evelyn said. "They found Ephraim's son. She has written everything and has even sent some pictures. I'll bring it over now if it's a good time."

"He's still alive?" she said, sitting down hard on the kitchen chair. "What about his mother, Elena?"

"He is alive and well, with children and grandchildren, but Elena is gone," Evelyn said.

In ten minutes, Evelyn was seated at her kitchen table, handing her a photograph of Benito. She clasped her hand to her mouth and shook her head.

"He looks so much like Ephraim. His skin's a little darker but look at those eyes, and his nose."

"This is his wife, Angelina," Evelyn said. "You need to read what Annie wrote to get the full story."

Evelyn waited patiently while she read.

"He was a farmer," Beulah said. "Just like Ephraim, and Daddy and his daddy. All the way back as far as we know," she said. "What about that?"

The wonderment of it all was nearly beyond comprehension.

"Isn't it amazing?" Evelyn said. "Today, they're going to meet his son and grandson on the farm. Annie will send another e-mail later."

Beulah shook her head, unable to speak. Joy, pressed down and overflowing.

"Thank you," she said to Evelyn. "I'm glad you know how to run the computer. It sure does make the world seem small."

She stared for a long time at her nephew and silently asked God to allow her to live long enough to meet him, either here or there. Finally, she gathered up the pages and set them aside, knowing she would pour over it all again in the quiet of her bedroom.

"How was your day in Lexington?" Evelyn asked.

Beulah told her what all they had done. When she finished, she wondered how to broach the subject of Tom Childress.

"And you were with Tom and Jake?" she said.

"Oh, Beulah," Evelyn said, her forehead creasing. "I've wanted to tell you, but you've had so much going on; I didn't want to add anything else."

She reached across the table to take Evelyn's hand.

"What is it?"

Just then, they heard footsteps on the stairs. Rossella walked into the room with her hair perfectly coifed on top of her head and a red sleeveless dress.

"Good morning," she said. "I cook eggs?"

Much to her frustration, they had not been able to get back to Evelyn's problem. Rossella sucked the air out of the room with clattering pans and pulling out butter and eggs.

The end result was delicious as the eggs were flavored with pieces of the salty meat Rossella had served at dinner on Monday night. As good as it was, Beulah resented the interruption.

"I need to leave for an appointment in Rutherford," Evelyn said after breakfast. "Why don't you stop by sometime after three? I should have an e-mail from Annie by then."

Whatever it was would have to wait.

After Evelyn left, Beulah tended to Annie's chickens and gathered a few more tomatoes from the garden while she was outside. The forecast predicted frost any day now, and that would be the end of the garden except for the greens. Later in the morning, she piddled around the house and did some laundry while Rossella sat in front of the television and watched a soap opera.

Lunch came and went with them both taking leftovers out of the refrigerator, and she was relieved to see Rossella more interested in the television than the kitchen.

Finally, the time came around to go to Evelyn's.

"I'll be back in a few minutes," she said to Rossella, who was now sitting in the sun on the back porch reading a magazine. "Don't forget we leave for prayer meeting at five forty-five and then we'll eat chili with the Gibson's after church. So you don't need to cook anything," she said, just to make sure Rossella got the point.

"I be ready," Rossella said, and barely looked up from her magazine, which seemed a bit rude to Beulah.

***

"In here," Evelyn said when she called at the back door. Evelyn was sitting at the computer and printing out papers. "You're going to love this," Evelyn said, handing the papers to her as they came off the printer.

Beulah looked at each face with something akin to greed. Her new relatives! Her nephew Benito, and her great-nephew Vincenzo, his wife Anna, his son Luca and daughter Rosa. Her Italian family. How strange the names seemed on her tongue, yet they belonged to her. By God's grace, they belonged to her.

"Before we talk, go ahead and read Annie's e-mail."

Beulah read it and learned all about her visit to the farm. Pictures completed the story, the family, their farmhouse, the olive trees, and the black pigs with the white circle around their bellies, and even one of the lunch Anna and Rosa had prepared for them.

"It was with great sadness we said goodbye. They want to come visit and they want you to come here."

Tomorrow night, Annie would be home. Rossella would leave on Saturday. Joy of joys, to have her kitchen back by Saturday night. Beulah's cup truly was overflowing. She smiled and looked at Evelyn, trouble spelled out all over her face.

"What's upsetting you?" she said.

"Let's go in the living room where it's more comfortable," Evelyn said, and pushed back from the computer desk.

When they settled into the living room chairs, Beulah saw a range of emotions cross Evelyn's face before she finally spoke.

"It started with Tom returning Jake's calls when he was still living here at the house before he moved to the cottage. Often I answered the phone. We began talking, and if Jake was gone, sometimes we talked for an hour. It's strange, Beulah. I've known Tom the entire time I've been in Somerville, but I've not really known him. He was married and I was married, we only saw each other in passing downtown or at some social function. His wife died not long after Charlie. But he goes to the Methodist church and lives in town and our paths never crossed until he and Jake began a friendship."

"Not unusual in a small town," Beulah said. "We all know each other, but sometimes we don't really know about each other."

"Exactly," Evelyn said. "The more we talked, the more I realized how much I liked him, as a person. He's genuine and loves living here in a small town, but he also enjoys music and art and sometimes travels to Chicago and Atlanta for weekends. His family is actually from Lexington, just like mine, but he settled here when he got out of law school. We've so many things in common."

"You've fallen for him," Beulah said, trying to help Evelyn get to the point, which seemed fairly obvious by the glow on her face.

"We've never been on a date together. We've only talked and then I invited him to the dinner party at my house. He came to dinner at your house on Monday and then Jake invited me to go with them on the farm visit yesterday. I'm afraid I am falling in love."

As she spoke, Evelyn twisted a Kleenex into a tight rope and then unwound it. "I never expected to date again. I wasn't looking for this. Tom hasn't spoken to me about it being anything other than a friendship. What should I do?" she said, an agonized look on her face. "And what about Jake? He was looking for a mentor, not his mother's future boyfriend," she said, laughing. "Then there's Lindy."

Beulah could not keep herself from smiling.

"Evelyn, you know Jake. He won't stand in the way. He'd be happy for you, if it's what you and Tom both want. Lindy as well. You and Tom are adults and must decide if it's worth pursuing or not."

"Should I talk to Jake about it before it goes any further?"

She thought about the challenges of a blended family, even when the children were adults.

"If you want Jake's blessing, then yes, it's probably a good idea. Maybe you should wait until Tom invites you out on an official date. Otherwise, it might be jumping the gun," she said.

"Right. I'm borrowing trouble. If and when he invites me out, I'll talk to Jake."

***

Beulah kept looking at the pictures of her Italian family over and over again and then compared them with pictures of

Ephraim, right before he went into service and as a younger boy. With so many similarities, there was no need for the modern DNA test. It was quite evident from the facial features this family's blood ran the same as hers.

It was hard to tear herself away from the photographs to dress for Wednesday night prayer meeting, usually one of her favorite times of the week. When Beulah came downstairs, Rossella was already waiting for her, dressed in a striking coral dress with a matching headband that circled the base of the piled-high hair. She had never seen Rossella with her hair down and couldn't help but be curious as to the length.

Once inside the church, Beulah led her to her normal pew, six rows back on the organ side. The Wednesday night crowd was always much lighter than the Sunday regulars. Church attendance had nothing to do with being a Christian, but she did value an assembly of believers. She tried to be there every time the church doors were open unless there was a mighty good reason not to. Since she had missed Sunday to go to the Catholic church, it was especially important to attend on Wednesday night in case there was any talk of her joining up with the Catholics. Especially if Woody or Betty Gibson had mentioned her partaking in wine at the Monday night dinner party.

Patsy, one of her friends from the Women's Missionary Union, came over and kneeled on the pew in front of them.

"Beulah, is this the lady who's making spaghetti tomorrow night at the Country Diner? I've been hearing about it all week on the radio and we're planning to come," she said.

Rossella glowed and extended her hand like a princess. Patsy shook her hand and then looked back at a row of women and mouthed, "It's her!" Soon, ladies, chattering and gawking at Rossella, surrounded them.

"You're from Italy?"

"Yes, but now I live in Brooklyn," Rossella said.

"How'd you come to know Beulah?"

Thankfully, the organist started playing "I'll Fly Away," which sent everyone scurrying back to her seat. After a time of worship, Brother Gilliam gave the scripture reading and a mini-sermon. Then he opened up the floor for prayer requests. Congregants raised their hands and shared concerns for prayer when recognized.

"Pray for Jerry Cordier, he's got terrible back pain."

"Remember the leaders of our country and the troops overseas."

"The Durhams down on Puny Branch need prayers, they lost their house to a fire."

"Pray for Esther Ray, her cancer came back."

Pastor Gilliam let it go on for a while and then gave a last call before offering up a prayer for all the requests.

"Any more?" he said, his eyes scanning the crowd.

She heard the pew creak and felt it shift. Out of the corner of her eye she saw Rossella raise her hand. Beulah turned, and before she could swat Rossella's hand down, pastor Gilliam saw Rossella and nodded for her to speak.

"Pray for me tomorrow night," Rossella said. "I have much cooking to do for many people at the Country Diner. Open five to nine. My spaghetti special, six ninety-nine."

Beulah nearly toppled out of the pew in embarrassment.

Chapter Thirty-One

ANNIE THOUGHT HOW good it was to be back on American soil. The trip to Italy was life-changing and there were so many memories she wanted to share in detail with Beulah. Her first priority at home was to scan pictures of Ephraim and email them to her new family in Italy. Benito was anxious to see an image of his father. Her second priority was to invite them to Kentucky. It might be hard with Vincenzo and Luca farming, but if they could at least get Benito and Angelina over, the others might come later.

While Janice waited on the luggage at the Atlanta airport, Annie went to the bathroom to check her face and brush her hair. It was like a first date all over again, she was so nervous about seeing Jake. When she spotted him across the baggage claim, he broke into a grin and seconds later, she was in his arms.

"I missed you, Annie," he said, whispering her name, and holding her tight.

"I have so much to tell you," she said, nestling her face in the folds of his sleeve.

Jake took both their bags and listened, as she and Janice talked nonstop all the way to the parking lot. Jake peppered them with questions which kept them talking all the way to Somerville.

In the farmhouse on May Hollow Road, Annie introduced Janice to Beulah while Jake carried her suitcase upstairs. Rossella reached for Janice, holding her face in both hands and kissing both cheeks.

"Mama, you look well. Farm life has been good for you?" Janice asked.

"*Si, si,*" Rossella said. "*Bene, bene,*" she said. "Good time," she said, as if realizing she had fallen back into her native language.

"I can't wait to hear all about it," Janice said.

"Janice, I can't thank you enough for all you've done," Beulah said, her eyes welling with tears.

"Beulah, it was an absolute joy. You're going to love your new family. They are wonderful."

"I already do . . . Now, you have time for a bath before supper."

"I'm ready," Janice said.

After Jake left and Janice went upstairs, Annie turned to Beulah and Rossella.

"So, you two had a good week?" Annie asked.

They turned and looked at one another and then giggled like schoolgirls.

"What?" Annie said, looking from her grandmother to Rossella.

"It ended well," Beulah said.

"*Si,*" Rossella smiled.

***

At dinner, Annie could hardly keep her eyes off Jake. He had showered and changed from his farming clothes and wore a blue shirt accenting his light blue eyes, along with his standard jeans and work boots. After Evelyn ladled soup for everyone, Annie and Janice relived the trip for Beulah, Evelyn, and Jake with Rossella listening intently and commenting on things about her native country as she could.

Jake was especially interested in the farm visit and the *cinta senese* pigs Vincenzo was raising.

"Several farmers here raise hampshire pigs, which are like the *cinta senese*," Jake said.

"It's the best meat," Rossella said, using her hands to emphasize. "*Molto bene.*"

Beulah wanted to know everything about Benito, from what he had done in his life and how he met his wife, to what his voice sounded like and his mannerisms.

"I took video," Annie said. "We'll watch it later."

Evelyn said, "Janice, you'll be happy to know Rossella has made quite a name for herself at the Country Diner. She was asked to be a guest cook last night and they sold out of the spaghetti by seven-thirty, the first time the diner has ever sold out of anything."

"Mama," Janice said. "You cooked for a diner?"

"Yes," Rossella said. "And I loved it. Today I decide, go back to work," she said and looked at Beulah. Annie saw her grandmother nod. "I need to cook. Every day. For many people. It is my gift and I must give."

"But where?" Janice asked. "Our kitchen's too small."

"No, no. I cook in restaurant. Mario has been asking me, but I no want to leave you since you work. But eez no good for me, cook for four people. I can cook for lunch, and then bring you home supper."

Janice smiled back at her mother-in-law with deep affection. "Fantastic."

***

Annie was anxious for the party to break up so she could be alone with Jake. He had still made no mention of her email and she wanted to tell him in person anyway, just to clear the air. Finally, Beulah, Rossella, and Janice left in the car. Annie and Jake said goodnight to Evelyn and went out the back door, hand in hand, down the steps and across the drive to the servant's cottage under the shade of two maples.

"Is that wood smoke?" Annie asked.

"I made us a fire," Jake said.

They settled on the couch in front of the roaring fire.

"When did you do this?" she asked.

"While you were washing dishes," he said. "It's the first one of the season. I could've had one earlier this week, but I wanted to wait until we could enjoy it together."

"Jake, I'm sorry about how we left things," she said.

For the next hour, Annie poured it all out, from the day she overheard Betty Gibson's words, to all the fear it stirred up in her heart, to a final realization in Italy she had been protecting herself all along.

Jake shook his head. "I've known for years you keep a pretty good wall up after what happened with your dad but I thought we'd crossed that hurdle when we got together. This caught me by surprise." Jake took her face in his hands. "Promise you'll come to me next time instead of holding all that inside."

"I will, I promise," Annie said and he kissed her gently on the lips, his eyes so tender, she nearly melted into him.

He kissed her again before pulling back. "Now, I have a confession to make to you."

"What?" Annie said, and sat up to look at him.

"It was nearly World War III with Beulah and Rossella. Mom and I decided not to tell how you how bad it was so you could concentrate on finding Ephraim's son."

Jake started at the beginning, from Rossella's arrival with wine to Sunday dinner and the *tagliatelle* hanging in the dining room and then to dinner on Monday night, including the Rhode Island Red.

Annie put her hand over her mouth. "Oh, I shouldn't laugh," Annie said, "but the kitchen is her domain. You remember how we battled over the coffeemaker when I first moved back."

"I'm only telling you about what I saw. Who knows what happened between the two of them? Joe told me Rossella offered a prayer request in the form of a plug for her Country Diner gig at prayer meeting on Wednesday night. Joe said he thought Beulah's eyes were going to pop out. Anyway, just so you know, it's not been easy for Beulah."

Annie leaned back on the couch and grinned.

"Poor Grandma, this whole thing with Ephraim, Rossella's arrival on top of it, has rocked her world. Sounds like we need to try and go out for dinner tomorrow night, just to keep the peace."

"I would highly recommend it. Although it does seem like something finally leveled out in the last day or so."

"I'll tell them first thing in the morning before someone starts cooking. How is Lindy? I thought I might see her tonight."

"That's another piece of news. Tom called me and asked if I could come by his office yesterday. He asked my permission to date Mom."

"Finally, they're admitting to it," she said, and then grew concerned. "What'd you say?"

"I asked him what his intentions were," Jake said.

"You didn't."

"I wanted to hear it from him, man to man."

"What'd he say?"

"He said, 'my intentions are for the purpose of marriage, if all parties involved are agreeable.'"

"Sounds like a lawyer," she giggled. "What'd you say?"

"I told him as long as his intentions were honorable, he had my permission. Getting back to Lindy, he said before he proceeded, he was taking Lindy out to dinner tonight to make sure she was okay with it. Lindy knows what he's up to and she's prepared this whole list of questions to ask him. I think she's going to put him on the hot seat before she gives her permission."

"Poor Tom. You two deserve to be siblings."

"He's a big boy, he can handle it. If you marry, you get the whole family, so it's wise to smooth the way on the front end."

With her face pressed against his chest, she watched the dying fire.

"Annie," he said. "You're falling asleep. Let me drive you home."

"I'm fine."

"You're worn out and jet-lagged on top of it," he said, pulling her up from the couch.

"I can drive, you don't have to take me home."

"Don't deny me the joy of taking care of you."

At the back door of her grandmother's house, she kissed him goodnight. After he left, she looked up into the clear night sky and saw the moon, waning now—the same moon from the Tuscan sky just hours before.

Chapter Thirty-Two

WHEN SHE SAW the video of Benito and his family in the farmhouse, Beulah felt like she had a visit with her brother, so strong was the likeness between father and son. They were already looking at the calendar to see when Benito and Angelina might come for a visit in the spring. Maybe she could make the trip to Italy. Knowing there was family on the other end of the long travel made it worthwhile.

It had been an unusual week. Even having Rossella in the house had been a good thing for her, as hard as it was in the beginning.

Beulah thought back to the conversation with Rossella just before Jake brought Annie and Janice home from Italy. Rossella had told her about her joy at cooking for the Country Diner and how much the opportunity had meant to her. Then her eyes had filled with tears.

"After my husband died, I want go back to Italy. But what am I to do with my children and grandchildren here? Eetz been a hard time. I no have purpose. Last night, how you say, special for me. I like cook for many people."

When she put herself in Rossella's shoes, she saw things in a different light. Rossella had been displaced and uprooted after losing her husband. The kitchen was where she had some control over her life. Even this week, she had been dropped in a new and unfamiliar place and it was natural she would try to regain her footing in a place where she was the most confident. Beulah knew these feelings well. Whenever there was a crisis, she wanted to cook. It was like a warm blanket on a chilly evening, or that first cup of coffee in the morning. Pure comfort.

"Is there somewhere close to where you live like the Country Diner? A place where you can cook from time to time for other people?" she had asked Rossella.

"There is Mario's. He does breakfast and lunch and he has asked me to help him, but I can't leave Jimmy and Janice. They let me live with them, so I must earn my keep by cooking."

"Is that the agreement you have with them?" Beulah had asked. "Or what you think they expect of you?"

"It's the right thing," Rossella had said. "I no want be burden."

"Well, what if you brought home food you cooked at the restaurant for their dinner? Then you've cooked for them as well as for others."

Rossella had raised her eyebrows. "Maybe work, I think."

Before Rossella left, she gave Beulah a bottle of wine as a parting gift—and Beulah accepted. In exchange, she sent Rossella home with some doilies she had knitted. Rossella kissed her goodbye on both cheeks. Before Rossella got in the car, Beulah had one final question.

"Rossella, how did you know about Tom and Evelyn?"

Rossella had looked at her and shrugged. "I know love."

There was a twinge of sadness at seeing the car leave the driveway, headed for the airport—only a small twinge.

After everyone left the house, she stood in her quiet kitchen and whispered a prayer of thanks. Having the house back made her want to dance a jig, and she might have attempted it, had her knee been stronger.

***

"Beulah, did Rossella leave? Elmore was talking to Joe and wanted her to come back this Thursday to cook if she was still here," Betty said.

"She's in New York by now," Beulah said.

"I'll bet you are tickled pink to have your house back. I hear you might be hosting Stella for the wedding weekend. Of course, we'd be glad to have somebody, but you know I moved into the extra bedroom because Joe snores like a bear and I wasn't getting a wink of sleep. There're only two bedrooms here, you know. I've never been much on houseguests anyway. Law have mercy, I like to walk around without my bra early in the morning and you have to be all buttoned up with company milling about. We've only got the one bathroom, and of course, Joe and me have our routine and our morning rituals at a fairly set time. At our age, I can't afford to get knocked off my habits. The digestive tract is the second brain—that's what I heard on the morning show the other day."

She frowned, preferring not to hear about Betty and Joe's daily habits. There was such a thing as knowing too much about a person. *Why in the world do people over a certain age feel like they need to talk about it so often?* Even aging celebrities on television were spokespeople for products to help keep them "regular." *It was not polite conversation,* she thought, and attempted to change the subject.

"It sounds like Scott and Mary Beth have everybody placed," Betty continued.

Evelyn's car nosed its way down the drive and she saw her opportunity to break off the phone call.

"Well, I've got company, so I'll let you go," she said, and hung up the phone even as Betty talked on.

"I was on my way to Rutherford to pick up some vases to use as the centerpieces for the reception. Do you need anything while I'm over there?" Evelyn said.

"Come in for a minute." Evelyn smiled as if she hoped for the invitation. Beulah poured her a cup of coffee.

"You have something to tell me?"

"Yes, I do. Tom called yesterday and asked me out to dinner this Friday night. Beulah, he asked Jake for permission first. He also asked Lindy and they both are fine with it. Jake told me he wanted me to be happy and he couldn't pick anyone else better than Tom Childress. I'm thrilled, but I'm also a nervous wreck. I don't know how to do this dating thing. It's one thing to talk on the phone and another to be on an official date," Evelyn said, her face glowing, all the while twisting the strap of her purse.

"Don't borrow trouble," she said. "Enjoy being with him. Get to know him, ask questions and relax."

"Oh my goodness, I never thought I'd be here again, nervous as a schoolgirl," Evelyn said.

Beulah thought back to Charlie's illness and subsequent death, and the heartbreak Evelyn suffered afterwards. A verse came to her mind: *I will restore what the locusts have eaten.*

Yes, indeed, she thought. Sometimes in this life and sometimes the one after.

Chapter Thirty-Three

ANNIE WATCHED AS three stonemasons replaced mortar joints and reset some of the stones. Two other men pulled down charred timbers and parts of the roof truss. A large dumpster sat in the front yard and the damaged materials were tossed into it, making way for the new. It was a relief to see the house getting the attention it needed.

Annie thought back to the day when she found the letters and how it had led her all the way to Italy and back. If the house had been picked apart for salvage and then torn down, the letters might not have been found, which meant Benito would have been lost to them forever.

It had been an unbelievable week. Now, there was a house to restore, a job to find, more research on the stone house's history, and preparations for Scott and Mary Beth's wedding.

Lindy called on her cell.

"I heard all about Italy at Evelyn's yesterday. Annie, it's truly amazing. I'm so happy for you all."

"How do you feel about your dad and Evelyn?" Annie asked.

"Gosh, I love Evelyn, and Jake's awesome, so how could it not be good? I want Dad to be happy. I'm glad to know it's love and not the early stages of dementia, although they sure have some of the same symptoms."

"How're you doing with Rob's engagement?" Annie asked, her voice gentle.

"I heard from a mutual friend he's getting married this weekend," Lindy said, a slight break in her voice.

"No way, already?" Annie said. "I'm so sorry."

"I know. I thought it'd be a long engagement and maybe he'd come to his senses," she said. "Now I have my resolution."

"That is something."

"I'll talk to you later," Lindy said, and hung up.

***

Annie left the stone house and walked to the crossover place dividing the Campbell farm from the Wilder farm. Shielding her eyes from the sun, she spotted Jake bent over a wire coil near the back pasture, at the base of a wooded hill.

"Hey you," she said, after making her way to him.

He looked up, sweat beading his brow, and grinned back at her.

"You got here just in time. Can you hold this for a minute while I tie this end?"

Annie took the spool of wire and watched him work with pliers and wire cutters.

"I talked to Lindy just now," she said. "Rob is getting married this weekend."

"I'm glad," he said. "They want different things."

They were silent a minute as Annie thought about how delicate love was and how the dance before marriage had to be handled so carefully.

"You need to be careful going through the field now. I don't want you to get shocked," Jake said as he twisted a wire.

"What's next after you get the cows set up?" she asked.

"A few goats are coming next week. It's slow integrating and balancing it all, and we're going into winter. Next spring I'll get chickens for the pasture."

"Farming is not immediate gratification," Annie mused.

"Not with a gestation period of nine months for a cow," he

said. "Waiting through seasons for a harvest. But life's meant to be slower."

"Speaking of a slower life," she said. "In Italy, everything closes down from around twelve-thirty to three, or sometimes as late as four-thirty, so everyone can go home and eat lunch, take a nap, whatever else they want to do before going back to work in the evening. It kind of makes sense, to rest in the heat of the day when your body naturally gets sleepy."

"The seasons and cycles tell us what to do. Humans aren't too good at listening," he said.

Jake's cell phone rang and he pulled it out of his front pocket. He looked at the number and she waved for him to go ahead and answer the call.

"It's okay. I can take it later," he said, slipping it back into his pocket.

"I don't mind," she said.

"It can wait," he said, concentrating on the electric fence.

It was only ten minutes later when Jake's phone rang again. He looked at the number.

"Sorry, I need to take this. See you tonight?" he said, and walked toward his truck before he answered.

"Sure," she said, realizing she had been dismissed. When she left, he was talking quietly into the telephone and looking over his shoulder to make sure she was walking away.

***

When Annie walked in the back door, Beulah called out.

"Richwood Manor called and Vesta Givens has asked to see you right away."

"Is something wrong?"

"I don't think so, but it seems important."

"Do you want to go with me?" Annie asked.

Beulah wiped her hands on her apron.

"Yes, I'll go. Give me just a minute to get my pocketbook."

Vesta Givens was finishing her lunch in the cafeteria when they arrived.

"Hello, Vesta," Beulah said, and extended her hand.

"Beulah, it's been a long time," Vesta said, taking Beulah's hand and holding it for a moment. "I'm so glad you came. You'll be thrilled to hear what I have to say."

"Did you find out something about the old stone house?" Annie asked.

Vesta grinned. "Let's go back to my room. Annie, do you mind pushing my chair?" Annie moved behind her, pulled Vesta's chair away from the table and toward the hallway. She went slowly, so her grandmother could walk with them. One of the residents caught Beulah's hand as they passed by, so Beulah stayed back to talk with the woman while she continued to push Vesta down the hall.

"How was Italy?" Vesta asked. "Did you find what you were looking for?"

"Yes," she said. "I have several cousins and they are the nicest people."

"Your great-uncle's love . . . is she still alive?" Vesta asked.

"No, but her child is alive and well. He has children and grandchildren."

"So, your mother and this child would be first cousins. You are his first cousin once removed. You are second cousins to his children. His grandchild would be your second cousin once removed."

"Not sure I can keep all that straight," Annie laughed.

"That's why most people just say 'cousins.' But if you deal in genealogy or legal terms, the distinction is quite important."

At Vesta's room, Annie turned the wheelchair and parked it where Vesta pointed.

"Do you have a report for me?" Vesta said, lifting her chin and raising her eyebrows in expectation.

"About the Ethiopian and his skin?" Annie said.

"Yes," Vesta said.

"What is impossible with man is possible with God," Annie said. "My family name or my history doesn't have to define who I am."

Vesta smiled. "There is always hope. There's far more to the scripture when you examine the historical and cultural context, but that's what I wanted you to understand."

Beulah came into the room.

"Beulah, please sit here on the bed. It will be the most comfortable. Annie, can you hand me those papers over there on top of the bookshelf?"

She reached for the papers and handed the stack to Vesta.

"After you left, I remembered one of my former students who is particularly good at research. She is a professional genealogist and has a vast knowledge of historic documents. I asked her to look into our matter. While you were gone, she mailed this to me."

Vesta handed a page to Annie with two sections highlighted.

"Please read both of the highlighted sections, out loud, so Beulah can hear as well."

Annie cleared her throat.

> *From the letters of William Champ, pioneer and settler of Fort Paint Lick.*
>
> *I had left Logan's Fort on my way home but went round by the crab orchard to see the house of stone. Josiah May and his sons worked that day alongside the Negros he hired from John Douglas. The house raised higher than the tallest man and they were still laying stone. Josiah told me it was the first of its kind in Kentucke territory. I believe it since I have heard nor seen no other. It will make a fine house.*

Beulah's mouth dropped open.

"You found it!"

Vesta's tinkling laugh flowed like water.

"My people were right," she said, nodding her head.

"They were right," Annie said, "and now we have proof. We can apply for the grant."

"And the historical marker," Beulah said. "Honoring both families' contribution to the house."

"Will you help me with the application for the marker?" Annie asked.

"Certainly, if you will do the first draft." Then she looked stern. "But I am a demanding editor, I hope you know. My red pen is itching," Vesta said.

"I'll do my best," Annie said, solemnly. "What are you reading these days, by the way?"

"Christie and Sayer," Vesta said. "After the Russians, I like detective stories. They're like the palate cleanser between courses," Vesta said, her eyes dancing.

"Beulah, do you like to read like your granddaughter?"

"I enjoy magazines and recipe books. I reckon I save most of my reading for the Bible."

"Well, it is another thing we have in common," Vesta said. Then Vesta looked at Annie.

"I suppose you won't be back after we get all this business settled," she said, smoothing out the wrinkles in the lap of her dress.

Annie kneeled down next to the wheelchair.

"Well, there's the matter of the dedication if they grant us the historical marker. You might like to see the old stone house before the weather turns bad, as well. I've also been thinking about reading another Russian author, if you have a recommendation," she said.

Vesta Givens smiled. "Did you know our activities director gave her notice this morning? They'll be looking for a new director," Vesta said.

"Activities director? That has a nice ring to it. I'll stop by and pick up an application on my way out."

Chapter Thirty-Four

EVELYN'S DINING ROOM had transformed into a craft shop complete with glue gun, scraps of parchment paper, scissors, and ribbon in shades of muted pumpkin. Annie examined the ribbon she tied around the wedding program and then handed it to her grandmother who put the finished programs in a basket. Mary Beth and Lindy worked on cutting ribbon while Evelyn went back and forth to the kitchen, making sure everyone had plenty of drinks and snacks.

"The tent arrives on Thursday, along with the tables and chairs." Evelyn said, standing in the doorway between the kitchen and the dining room. "We can set up Thursday night, so everything is ready for the rehearsal on Friday."

"Let's pray for sunshine and no wind," Beulah said.

"When should I pick up the mums?" Lindy asked, placing a vase on the finished side.

"It won't hurt to have them anytime. Jake said you could use his truck," Evelyn said.

"I'm so thankful for you all," Mary Beth said. "With teaching school, it's hard for me to do much this time of year, but this was best for Scott, after the fall kickoff for church activities and before the holiday season."

"What do the kids think about all this?" Annie asked.

"They both love Scott. How they'll perform in the ceremony is another thing," Mary Beth laughed. "Henry was completely against being the ring bearer until Scott told him it was a secret mission and he really needed his help. Now he can't wait. Ellie loves the idea of dressing up like a princess and throwing flowers."

Annie tried to keep up with the chatter, but she couldn't keep her mind from turning over the recent change in Jake. Something was wrong, and this time, it was not her. After getting back from Italy, things were good between them, until just over a week ago. Now it seemed Jake was the one pulling back. They had hardly spent any time together lately. There was always a good excuse: a sick cow, meetings, picking up more hay, setting up the new goats, and on and on it went.

Before, he would make time for a quick visit in the evenings, even if it were late, just to touch base. Now he went straight to bed, claiming to be tired. Then there were the phone calls he obviously didn't want her to overhear. Annie was confused, yet when she said something to him, he assured her everything was fine.

"Annie?" Evelyn was looking at her, waiting on an answer.

"I'm sorry, what did you say?"

"I said I thought you'd probably attended fancy weddings in New York," Evelyn said.

"Not many," she said. "I wasn't in that social circle."

"I love party planning," Evelyn said. "I haven't done anything like this since Suzanne's wedding. I forgot how much I enjoyed it."

"You're good at it," Beulah said. "I am happy to be an extra hand and do some sewing, but organizing is not my strength."

"Lots of details," Lindy said. "It's like conducting an orchestra, every part has to come in at the perfect time."

While they were chatting, Annie heard Jake's truck pull in the driveway and excused herself. They had their first real date tonight since she got back from Italy two weeks ago. She was looking forward to it, hoping it meant everything was back to normal.

Jake was on the phone when he got out of the truck, smiling broadly at the conversation—until he saw her.

"Can I call you back later?" He had already hung up the phone by the time she reached the truck.

"Hey," she said. "I was just wondering what time you wanted to leave for Lexington tonight?"

"You know . . . I need to stick around here and do some things. Can we go tomorrow night instead?"

Despite trying to hide it, she knew her face showed the disappointment.

"Sure."

"Annie," he said, leaving a question in the air.

"I need to help with the wedding stuff tonight anyway. There's so much to do right now." Before he could say another word, she bounded up the stairs.

If she had any doubt he was hiding something before, there could be none now.

***

The next morning, she completed her application for activities director at Richwood Manor and drove it out to the facility. Annie was sent to the director's office where a secretary greeted her.

"Do you have a moment?" the secretary asked.

"Sure," she said, and sat down in one of the available chairs while she waited for the secretary to return.

"The director would like to see you if you have time."

"Of course," she stood and followed the secretary. "Right in there," the secretary pointed to a door.

The office was warm and inviting. Positive quotes about aging were framed and hung on the walls and a middle-aged woman sat behind a clutter-free desk. She stood and offered her hand and her warm smile put Annie at ease.

"I'm Colleen Whitley. Please, have a seat. I hope you don't mind us grabbing you like this, but my secretary knew I wanted to speak with you if you applied for the job," she said. "I've heard such good things about you."

"You have?"

Colleen nodded. "And Vesta Givens doesn't give out her recommendations lightly."

"Vesta is a fascinating woman."

"I don't make any decisions that affect the patients without talking to her first. I call her the Mayor of Richwood. If she's for it, everyone else will go along. If she doesn't like it, well, you can imagine."

Annie laughed again, feeling completely at ease with this woman.

"So Vesta told me you were a flight attendant for ten years. I suppose you've dealt with all types of personalities."

"Passengers make up quite a cross-section of the population. You see them relaxed and under stress," Annie said.

"And you have some emergency medical training?"

"CPR, first aid, flight emergencies, basic stuff."

"Why did you leave the airline?"

"The airline merged and my seniority wasn't high enough to secure a job. Later, I was offered a job, but I decided to stay here."

"So you don't have any plans to leave, to go back to New York or somewhere else?"

"No, I want to be here," Annie said, and there was peace in saying the words she knew were true.

"Aging has a tendency to distill our personalities," Colleen said. "I think someone with your background would be very good with our residents. Simply loving them is part of the job. The other part is coming up with activities for them to do, such as outings, guest speakers, book clubs, anything they might experience if they lived outside the facility. We want to make it easy for them to participate and feel a part of a larger world. If you're interested, we would like to offer you the job."

"Really?" Annie said.

"Really," Colleen said and laughed.

"I accept," Annie said.

There was paperwork to fill out, start dates to discuss, and materials to study from the previous activities director. Before going home, Annie went by Vesta's room, her arms loaded with notebooks.

Annie stood in the doorway and waited until Vesta looked up from her reading.

"You got the job!" Vesta said and clapped her hands together.

"Thanks to you."

"Well, you are the right person for it. God sent you to us. Now, we have some things to discuss." Vesta cleared the reading materials off her lap. "You can put those notebooks on the table." Annie did as she was told and sat down on a chair near Vesta.

"We need to work on the book club. They've fallen into a habit of reading junk. I was thinking of a classical curriculum with . . ."

Annie spent the rest of the day with Vesta, eating lunch with her in the Manor's dining room, taking vociferous notes, and making plans. Annie was excited. The job came at the perfect time for her, now that all her other projects were winding down. Even the work at the old stone house had gone well past her abilities to contribute anything, at least until later down the road when she could begin painting inside.

Driving home, Annie called Jake to tell him the good news, but the call went to his cell voicemail. They were supposed to go to Lexington for dinner, so she would tell him all about the job when they were together.

She saw Jake had left her a voicemail.

"Annie, I am so sorry," he said. "I can't go tonight. It's unavoidable. I'm sorry. I promise everything will be back to normal after the wedding."

Her heart dropped. *Not again.* There couldn't possibly be this many unavoidable things. If Jake loved her, wouldn't he move heaven and earth for them to spend time with each other?

It was past suppertime, but she had missed her daily run by staying all day at Richwood Manor. Since she had no plans for the evening, she changed her clothes and told her grandmother the good news about her job, before starting a run down the long driveway. As she turned the corner onto May Hollow Road, Betty Gibson opened her door and waved her down.

Annie wondered if she could ignore Betty, but the lavender bathrobe and the pink foam curlers sticking out from her head made it impossible. Not to mention the urgent arm-waving that had started as soon as Betty was out her front door. Annie stopped and stretched while she waited for Betty to come down the concrete steps.

"I just heard the news! I am tickled pink. Shirley Updike just called me; she's my friend who works in the nursing home side of Richwood. I am just so proud of you; it looks like you are really putting roots down," Betty said.

Unlike my father, Annie thought.

Betty continued. "Why, I said to Joe just the other day, Annie Taylor is so much like the May side. Solid as a rock." Betty's dimples punctuated her straight white teeth.

"I'm sure I've got a full dose of both sides of the family," she said as she turned to run.

"Jake's been working awful hard on the farm, Joe tells me," Betty called out. Annie paused, turned, and waited for her to finish. "Why yesterday, he worked from dawn to dusk and then had to run to Lexington for dinner last night. I reckon that kind of life is for the young. Of course, it must have been something important to send Jake to Lexington without you," she said, watching for Annie's reaction.

"Sure was," Annie said, waving goodbye over her shoulder.

She pounded the macadam road. Lexington for dinner? Jake cancelled their date in Lexington so he could have dinner with someone else? *Surely not another woman,* she told herself, breathing harder.

Why did he lie to me?

All during her run, she wrestled with the information Betty handed her. Should she confront Jake? *Why would Jake tell Joe Gibson where he was going but lie to me?* None of it made sense.

Annie crossed the pastures to the Wilder's stock barn where she sought comfort with the eight young nanny goats Jake had brought to the farm just a few days before. Annie was drawn to them more than any of the other farm animals. They had grown up with lots of human contact, and as a result they were affectionate and curious, not fearing humans like most of the livestock she had been around.

The goats were in the small pasture next to the stock barn. When they saw her, they ran to her, nearly knocking her over as she quickly latched the gate behind her. Nudging her hand and looking for feed, Annie wished she had grabbed a handful of grain for them. When they saw there was no feed in her hand, they hovered about enjoying whatever attention she doled out.

She sat down on an old tree stump Jake had hauled into the pasture for the goats to jump on. When she did, one of the goats grabbed her ponytail in its teeth and jerked.

"Ouch," she said, wrestling her hair from the goat's mouth.

"Better watch them, haven't you heard they'll eat anything?" Jake was coming around the lot, carrying a pitchfork.

Annie leveled her gaze at Jake, and before she could restrain herself, she fired.

"How was dinner last night?"

Momentary surprise and then recovery all registered in his expression.

"Great," Jake said, forking hay into the goat's pen, avoiding her eyes.

"Must have been important," she said, waiting for him to explain.

He stopped pitching hay and leaned on the pitchfork, this time meeting her stare full on.

"It was important."

"Jake, I don't understand," she said, shaking her head.

"Annie, I can't talk about it right now. After the wedding, everything will be back to normal."

"I'll check on the goats later tonight," she went through the gate. "I know you're too busy these days."

Jake met her on the outside of the gate and touched her gently on the arm.

"Annie, it's not . . ."

"Forget it," she said, walking away.

Chapter Thirty-Five

THERE WAS AN air of excitement on May Hollow Road. The upcoming wedding had set them all scurrying around like mice, everybody hoping to make it a special day for Scott and Mary Beth.

Even though Mary Beth had hired a caterer for the wedding, there was still so much food to get ready for all of Evelyn's house guests as well as her own. Beulah cut out biscuits and put them in an aluminum pan and covered them with foil so they would freeze. Breakfast was the main meal they needed, since Scott and Mary Beth had meals planned out for the rest of the time for their family.

Stella had not been back to Somerville since her stay at the old stone house and the fire that had nearly destroyed it. The renter with the fly-a-way red hair had been in a bad place back then, ready to end her life, and had even tried while she was in the old stone house. Divine interruptions kept her from succeeding. From the letters she had written Beulah after leaving Somerville, she knew Stella was doing the hard work of paying off her debts.

Woody's frequent trips up north had probably not hurt her feelings, either. Woody was picking her up at the airport tomorrow and bringing her to stay with Beulah for the weekend. After having Rossella for a week, Stella Hawkins would at least not be fighting her for the kitchen.

Scott's family from Dothan, Alabama, would arrive today. Some of Scott's family members were staying in Evelyn's guest rooms and the guest cottage while Jake camped out on Evelyn's couch. Extended family and friends were booked at hotels in Rutherford. It would be a whirlwind.

Jake had the Wilder farm slicked up and shining. He and Annie had barely seen each other all week.

Beulah pressed down on the biscuit cutter and twisted, then poked the biscuit onto the tin pan. Another good piece of news came when Annie told her she found a job at Richwood Manor. It was good to see her granddaughter excited about something she was gifted to do. She would be a blessing to all the old folks out there, just as she had been a blessing to her these last several months.

As if on cue, Annie walked in the back door.

"The house is coming along," Annie said. "I want to show Stella since she was so worried about it after the fire. I'm sure it will make her feel better to come back and see it being fixed."

Beulah washed the dough off her hands and wiped them with the hand towel. "What time does Scott's family arrive?"

"Scott and Mary Beth are picking them up around four in Lexington, but they are taking them around to see a couple of horse farms and then to dinner, so they won't get to Evelyn's until sometime tonight. I thought I would go over to help place tables. They should be setting the tent up by now."

Later, she drove the biscuits over to Evelyn. Friends and family of Scott and Mary Beth were bustling about moving chairs and tables under the tent. There was a dance floor and long tables set up for food and such. It already looked festive, even without the tablecloths, decorations and lights. Her heart lifted in joy at all the activity. There was nothing like a wedding celebration.

**

When Woody's truck crunched up the gravel driveway the next day, Beulah took off her apron and smoothed out her dress. From the kitchen window, she watched as Woody came around to the passenger's side and helped Stella out like a real gentleman.

Stella, who walked with hunched shoulders when she saw her the first time, stood straighter. Her frizzy red hair was smoothed back off her face. It was as if her inner peace had turned on her outward beauty.

"Welcome," she said, holding open the screen door.

"Beulah, we're just coming to drop off her luggage and then I'm taking her over to my farm to show her around," Woody said, holding Stella's arm as he steered her onto the back porch. "Booger's not out, is he?"

"No, I think he may be gone for the winter."

"Thank you so much for having me." Stella extended her hand and Beulah took it.

"You're most welcome. I have your room ready upstairs. Woody, if you want to take her up, it's to the left, just above the kitchen here. And show her where the bathroom is, too."

Might as well let Woody do the showing since he's intent on holding on to Stella, she thought. They were soon gone and she suspected she was likely to see very little of her houseguest other than bedtime. Woody had plans to spend every minute with Stella outside of the wedding activities. At least the young woman could see what she might be getting into with Woody early on, just in case she wanted to jump ship.

*****

While Beulah washed the dishes, her thoughts went again to Benito and the letter she was composing to him. Janice agreed to translate it when she was finished. She wasn't accustomed to writing many letters and she wanted to get this one just right, so she was taking her time. Annie had already scanned the pictures of Ephraim and e-mailed them to Benito and his family. Annie said Vincenzo had responded for him, saying how thankful they were, and how much they all thought Benito looked like his father. The resemblance was truly striking.

In the letter, she was inviting Benito and his family to be guests in her home for a visit as soon as they could come. "Practice hospitality," the apostle Paul had written. It did take practice because sharing of a person's space and giving up routine did not come easy. Like practicing anything, the more it was done, the easier it got.

Chapter Thirty-Six

WOODY RAN HIS hand along the hand-hewn studs now exposed in the old stone house.

"Look at the fine work," he said. "Nobody builds like this anymore."

"I can't believe it," Stella said. "I worried about it so much; I was afraid you'd have to tear it down."

"It all worked out," Annie said. "I probably wouldn't have been so intent on finding out the history of the house if it had not been in danger."

Stella pushed her glasses up on her nose.

"It was a good thing for me, too," she said. "I would have probably kept running, and who knows where I would be today," she said, shyly looking up at Woody.

He put his arm around Stella and gave her a squeeze.

"You're here now, and that's the main thing," Woody said. "Now, how about I show you my kids," Woody said, his voice reverberating against the wood floors without furniture or rugs to soak up the sound.

Stella's eyes grew wide. "Woody, you never mentioned children!"

"He's talking about his goats," Annie said.

"Oh, well yes," she said, relief flooding her face.

"Yep," Woody said. "Goats and horses, too. I'll teach you to ride. I've got a sweet little mare called Nutmeg. She's just come into foal, but I can ride you around the paddock on her."

Annie shut the door of the stone house and waved goodbye. The trees were at peak this weekend, the red and yellow maples in full color scattered along the landscape and hills. Needing a few minutes alone before the activity started, she climbed the hill to the cemetery; leaves crinkled and crunched under her feet. At the top of the hill, she opened the iron gate.

It was like a painting with the autumn leaves in various colors, sprinkled on the still green grass, amidst the new granite and old limestone gravestones. She knelt down and laid her open palm on the marble of Ephraim's military footstone. In Italy, she stood beside Elena's grave, where she had claimed her love for Ephraim by taking his name in death. It seemed only fitting to visit Ephraim's final resting place, especially after meeting his son, Benito.

The recent weeks of learning more about Josiah May, who was also buried in this graveyard, made her connection to the land, the old stone house, and to all those who went before her even stronger.

Annie was grateful for Vesta Givens, who helped save the old stone house and brought to light their shared family history. She thought about the word *family* and how shared DNA usually defines it. Sometimes it goes beyond, crossing the boundaries of race and geography.

***

"It's quiet around here," she said, walking into Evelyn's kitchen.

"Annie, come in. I was daydreaming," Evelyn said.

"About Tom?" Annie smiled and sat down.

Evelyn blushed. "Well, he's going to be my date at the rehearsal dinner."

"You'll make a handsome couple."

"As will you and Jake. I've kept him so busy this week, I guess you've hardly seen him."

Annie nodded and avoided Evelyn's eyes.

"It'll all get back to normal next week," Evelyn said, reaching across the table and putting her hand on Annie's.

"Everybody keeps saying that," she said.

For a second, she wanted to tell Evelyn her worries about Jake. The moment passed and Annie changed the subject.

"How do you like Scott's family?"

"They are really nice folks; very polite and helpful. His mother and aunt want to set up tomorrow, so I don't think it will take long."

"I thought you might need help, but it looks like everything is under control."

"Everything is done for now. I'll sit here and daydream a bit longer," she said, laughing. "This is the calm before the storm, so I might as well enjoy it."

***

Jake drove over and escorted Annie and Beulah to the rehearsal dinner at the Old Stone Mill just outside of town. Beulah had resisted going with them, but Annie insisted since Tom was taking Evelyn.

The banquet room was decorated with white lights and candles at the tables. It was the first date Annie and Jake had enjoyed since things had grown so awkward between them. A couple of times, he squeezed her hand under the table, and for those moments, it seemed all was well.

When the evening was over, he took her home along with Beulah, and quickly kissed her goodbye on the back porch instead of staying longer or inviting her to his cottage.

The pit in her stomach returned and she almost dreaded the wedding tomorrow. After it was over, Jake would finally tell her what had come between them.

Chapter Thirty-Seven

SCOTT AND MARY Beth's wedding day dawned bright and clear. Beulah sat outside where she could breathe in the crisp morning air and enjoy the fall color. A wisp of steam drifted up from her coffee. She watched as Annie walked out of the chicken house door in her jeans and boots and waved before heading over to the Wilder farm.

It was a sight how Annie had taken to Jake's goats. When it was time for Jake to move them into the pasture next week to start doing their job, she had a feeling Annie might take one for a pet. Woody said goats need a companion, so that would make at least two or maybe even a horse and a goat. Either way, she could tell Annie was itching for some animals.

Holding the coffee close to her face, she enjoyed the warmth it gave before she took a sip. Today they celebrated Scott and Mary Beth's love for each other. Jake and Annie might be next and what about Evelyn and Tom? Or Woody and Stella? Well, she was happy for them all if it's what God saw fit to do in their lives. As for this old nanny goat, she was quite content alone.

The truth was, she didn't feel alone. Beulah felt God's presence around her and she still was married to Fred in her heart. It was not hard to imagine Fred's comments on daily happenings, the things he would shake his head over, and the things he would chuckle about.

Inside, the heated kitchen warmed her cold bones. Easing down into a chair at the table, her mind went again to her nephew Benito, and when he and Angelina might visit. Spring and summer were such beautiful times, yet she was so hungry to see him it really didn't matter to her, as long as he came soon.

When the time for the wedding finally arrived and Annie came down the stairs, Beulah was nearly knocked over at how beautiful she looked. Her dark hair hung down past her shoulders, a striking contrast against the bright salmon-colored dress she had bought for the occasion.

"My, you are pretty as a picture," she said.

Annie smiled. "Grandpa always said that. He would say the same about you. We need to take pictures tonight."

Annie had fixed Beulah's hair in a style she copied from a magazine where the hair was combed back off her face. *Why not*, she had thought, *it's only for a night*. Annie had also helped her pick out her outfit, a light brown dress with a cream-colored jacket.

Evelyn's driveway was lined with chrysanthemums in wine red and sunset gold and was highlighted by the wash of the setting sun, hanging low in the sky.

"Didn't Lindy do a good job," Beulah said, driving past them to the parking area. Even though they had watched the transformation take place, seeing it now, finished and ready for the wedding, made it look almost magical.

Chairs lined both sides of the sidewalk leading to the front porch. Candlelight glowed from glass globes, guiding guests from the parking area to the seats. Greenery adorned an arch in front of the porch where the ceremony would take place. One of Scott's friends from his church strummed on an acoustic guitar to the side of the arch as the ushers seated early arrivals.

Jake was dressed in a black tuxedo. *He looks like an actor from a Hollywood movie*, she thought. And when he saw Annie, he looked like a man in love.

Another usher took Beulah by the arm and Jake followed with Annie, seating them on Mary Beth's side. The wedding party was small with only Mary Beth's sister as her maid of honor and Mary

Beth's two children serving as the ring bearer and the flower girl. The little boy had a mischievous look on his face, and she sensed Scott might have his hands full with that one.

Scott's brother was his best man, and Scott's father, also a minister, was going to conduct the ceremony. The groom grinned with pride when his new young son came down the aisle bearing the pillow that carried the ring. He beamed again when his new daughter scattered rose petals here and there.

Cued by the music, the crowd stood for Mary Beth, who was escorted by her older brother, and looked lovely in an understated beige gown. Beulah's eyes welled up and stayed that way through most of the ceremony.

After the wedding, everyone meandered over to the reception tent while the wedding party took pictures. Jake found Annie and led her to a table where they sat down together.

Tom had his hand on Evelyn's back and led her to a table. Evelyn looked at Beulah and waved her over. Betty and Joe Gibson joined them.

"Wasn't it lovely?" Evelyn said.

"Your place was a beautiful setting," Beulah said.

"Beulah, can I get you some punch?" Tom asked.

"How nice, thank you," Beulah said, sitting down next to Evelyn.

"Law, law, what a beautiful day. Did you ever dream it would be this nice?" Betty Gibson was showing a little cleavage in a new dress. Beulah fought to hide her indignation.

Woody pointed to the empty seats.

"Are these taken?" he asked, Stella by his side, her fingers nearly white with clutching the small beaded bag in front of her satin green dress.

"Sit on down here," Joe said, pulling out a chair.

The Master of Ceremonies introduced Scott and Mary Beth as Mr. and Mrs. Scott Southerland when they entered the party tent to everyone's applause. Scott was used to handling attention, him being the pastor of a church. Mary Beth blushed, the color accenting the auburn curls that hung delicately around her face.

The food line was open and Joe hightailed it over with Betty in tow as the rest of the wedding guests lined up to go down both sides of the buffet. Cake-and-punch weddings were all she had known, but nowadays the trend leaned toward full meals. *Pity for the bride's parents who have to provide it,* she thought. Beulah hoped surely-to-goodness Annie knew not to count on her if she wanted a big shindig like this. Beulah and Fred had put her through college with Jo Anne's social security. No, if she wanted a big party, Eddie Taylor, Annie's absent father, would have to step up and take his medicine.

Beulah took her plate and was just about to get a crispy fried chicken leg when she felt something nudge her skirt and root its way between her and Evelyn. When she looked down, a furry white face looked back, a tuft of hair trailing from its chin.

"Baaaaa."

"Land's sakes!" Beulah said, looking around for Joe Gibson or Jake. In the minute she hesitated, the goat nudged her arm and her plate dropped to the floor with a crash. A lady in front of her screamed and over the ensuing gasps and clatters, Beulah yelled for Joe. To his credit, he was by her side in a second, scooping up the goat in his arms.

Another scream came from across the room and she watched with horror as a goat pronged from chair to table as wedding guests jumped back. Scott's aunt flew out of her seat, a red shoe flung in the air, as she made her escape. The goat strutted on the table, as if playing king of the mountain, and then twisted in the air like a gymnast before landing on the ground.

Mary Beth's little girl ran in front of Beulah crying, another goat nibbling on the long ribbon trailing behind her dress. In the chaos, she saw Annie, frozen to the dance floor, the color drained from her face. In that brief moment, she knew Annie must have forgotten to latch back the gate. It had taken the goats all day, but they had found her mistake.

"The cake!" somebody cried, and Mary Beth scrambled over the folds of her cream-colored dress toward the two-tiered wedding cake. On the opposite side of the room, two goats stood on their hind legs, nibbling on the groom's confection, until Woody Patterson shooed them away.

When the chaos seemed impossible to control, Jake appeared with a bucket of feed, shaking it to get their attention. The cake-eating goats with chocolate noses followed first, and then the other six trailed along behind him, out of the tent and back to the pasture.

Annie was now on her hands and knees, cleaning goat urine off the dance floor with paper towels. Lindy knelt down to help. When they got it cleaned up, Annie stood, and Beulah saw her granddaughter's dress had a big wet stain near the hemline. Apparently the paper towels weren't the only things that helped clean up the mess.

Chairs were uprighted and Jake was applauded when he came back into the tent. The surprise and tension released into laughter led by Scott and Mary Beth. Scott's aunt was reunited with her red shoe and Mary Beth's little girl was smiling. All in all, no harm was done other than nibbles off the groom's cake.

Beulah looked for Annie and saw Lindy talking to Scott's brother from Alabama. Jake was talking to Scott, but Annie was nowhere in sight.

Chapter Thirty-Eight

THE TURMOIL OF emotions built up inside Annie until she felt like one of the pressure canners she learned to operate last summer; another turn of the heat dial and she would explode. Pressing forward into the darkness, she left the lights and the music of the tent behind her.

How could I have forgotten the latch? It was her grandfather's number one farm rule: "Always leave a farm gate just as you find it. If it's open, leave it open. If it's latched shut, leave it latched." She knew this rule as well as she knew anything, but she had been so distracted with Jake and the chasm between them.

Her heels sunk into the soft ground as she stumbled forward into the darkness. The Wilder dairy barn was just ahead, dimly lit by an old security light. She was nearly there when the toe of her sandal stubbed something hard and she fell face down in the dirt lane. The pain of the fall added injury to insult and she let the pent up tears flow.

How long she lay in the dirt, she didn't know. When she finally pushed herself up, she felt herself being lifted to her feet.

"Annie?"

Jake hardly sounded like himself; his voice was so low and husky.

"What happened? Are you hurt?"

Once on her feet, she pulled away from his grip.

"I'm fine."

"You're not fine. Let's go inside so I can see if you're hurt."

Annie limped into the barn office where Jake pulled a beaded metal chain. An incandescent bulb illuminated the room. Jake turned her so he could look at her, studying her face first, and then taking one arm at a time and running his fingers down each. How long had it been since he touched her so tenderly? Since the night after she got home from Italy.

"You scraped your hands," he said. Then bending down, he said, "Your dress is torn. Your knees are bleeding. Maybe you should take off your shoes."

"I said I'm fine," she heard the hardness in her voice, but what did he expect from her?

Jake faced her, his look asking a question she couldn't answer.

"Sit down for a minute?" he asked, his voice gentle.

She sat on a folding metal chair and Jake sat across from her, their legs touching. Annie wanted to pull away from him but there was nowhere to go. She kept her hands in her lap and stared down at them.

"Annie, I know these last few weeks have been strained between us. You've had some struggles and I've had some things going on too, but that's not all of it."

Barely breathing, she looked at Jake and waited.

"I've kept a secret from you."

Here it comes, she thought. A tear trickled down her cheek, despite the stoicism she tried so hard to emulate. If she could only be more like her grandmother when it came to emotions.

"The phone calls," she said.

"They were important," Jake said.

"Who was it?"

Jake hesitated, his eyes softening. "Your father."

My father? "What?" she said, unable to comprehend the meaning. "Why?"

"I called him to ask his permission."

"For what?" Annie said, the words not making sense.

"To marry you," he said, his voice barely above a whisper.

"Marry me? I thought you were breaking up with me!"

"Breaking up with you?" Jake said, his blue eyes surprised

and then solemn.

Annie shook her head. "Jake, you haven't spent any time with me. You find reasons we can't see each other. And you went to Lexington for dinner with someone else on the very night you and I were supposed to go out. What am I supposed to think? Now you're saying you want to marry me?"

Jake ran his fingers through his hair. "I've screwed this up. Let me explain."

"Please," Annie said and took a deep breath.

"When I got your e-mail from Italy, I was relieved, but I wanted to see you and make sure we had resolved everything. When you came over that night and we talked, I was ready to move forward. I got your father's number from your phone when you went to the bathroom."

"You did?"

"Yep. I called it the next day. The woman who answered said he was working out of the country and to call back later. Anyway, it took me a week to reach him. He called me twice when you were with me out in the field. By the time I got the call to go through, I missed him."

"He rarely answers," she said.

"You told me he's hard to reach, so it's why I tried calling as soon as I could."

"You finally talked with him? What'd he say?"

"He wanted to Skype so he could meet me in person, so to speak."

"He did?" she asked. "I didn't know he knew how."

"Well we did. He has a young woman living with him who is apparently teaching him all sorts of new tricks."

"Hmm. I can only imagine," she said dryly.

"So we Skyped about fifteen minutes and he gave his permission."

"When?" she said.

"A few days ago," Jake said. "But then there was something else I had to do first. I had to see a very special woman."

Annie cocked her head, realizing whom Jake had gone to see for dinner in Lexington. "Your grandmother," she said.

"She gave me her ring," he said.

"I still don't understand why you avoided me so much?"

"I didn't want to take anything away from Scott and Mary Beth's wedding. Once I knew I was going to ask you, I could hardly be around you. I was afraid I wouldn't be able to hold off. Fortunately, Mom had so much work for me to do, it kept me busy. Then you found out I had gone to Lexington after canceling our date." Jake said. "The hurt on your face nearly killed me. But there was no way for me to explain it to you until after the wedding."

"Betty Gibson, again."

"Joe didn't know why I was going or who I was seeing, but he asked me for help with one of his cows and I had to tell him why I couldn't stay. I should have known it would get back to you."

"There are no secrets on May Hollow Road," she said and they both laughed.

"I thought I had this all planned out, but I made it worse," Jake said. "I'm sorry."

"Jake, I sure hope our marriage is easier than the dating."

"It probably won't be, but at least we know what we're in for," he said, taking her face in his hands and kissing her.

"So do you have something to ask me?"

"I sure do." Jake slid off the chair onto the concrete floor of the dairy barn office. "Will you marry me?"

"I will!"

Dirt and the salt of her tears mixed with the long kiss that followed.

"I don't even have the ring with me," Jake said when he pulled away. "It's at Cheney's Jewelry being reset."

"I don't need the ring to know this is real," she said. "But it sounds lovely."

"This was supposed to happen on Monday night. I had it all planned out with a fire, champagne, the ring and a proposal."

"We can re-enact it, if you like. I wouldn't mind looking a little better for the official one," she said, her heart light and filled with anticipation.

"Your father wants to come to the wedding," Jake said. "He wants you to call him when you get a chance."

"Well, he's never participated in any of my life events. Maybe it's time he started."

Chapter Thirty-Nine

LINDY SQUEALED WHEN she heard the news, while Evelyn and Beulah looked on with satisfied smiles. They had been given the privilege of knowing before everyone else, before they had each left for church in the morning.

"Real nice," Woody said, pumping Jake's hand. "You got 'chee self a good one!"

After Sunday dinner, they all sat around and had coffee, replaying the events from the weekend.

"Scott and Mary Beth took it all very well, but Scott's aunt wasn't any too happy. I think she was afraid one of those goats was going to nibble on her Chanel suit," said Evelyn.

"It was a beautiful outfit," Annie said.

"Lindy, you seemed to take up with Scott's brother," Evelyn said.

Lindy smiled. "We danced quite a bit, but I don't think there's a love connection. The truth is, I still have some healing to do and it's okay to just be alone for a while."

"It was lovely to have Stella here," Beulah said, directing the statement at Woody. "She was pleased to see the house in good shape after all that happened."

"Thank you for keeping her, Beulah. I showed her around my farm, and town, even introduced her to my momma, though Momma don't know a thing."

"So what's the deal, Woody? Are you dating her? I mean, don't keep us in suspense," Lindy said.

All eyes turned to Woody.

"Well, we do have us a date two weeks from today. She's taking me to a Bears game," Woody said, smiling. "One of her church members give her the free tickets." His face grew serious. "Can I ask y'all a question?"

"Sure," Lindy said, and the others nodded and waited.

"I was wondering," he said, his face turning red. "Y'all think I should get my teeth fixed?"

"YES!" shouted the group in unison.

***

With Annie's blessing, Beulah called Betty Gibson to share the good news.

"Heavens to Betsy, two weddings all in a row," Betty said. "Have they set a date?"

"Not yet. They're talking it all over. We'll wait and let Annie tell us when she's ready."

"Will they live in the old stone house? It was a good thing you didn't tear the place down after all. You know, Beulah, I told you not to. Why, there's so much history there, and once it's gone, you could never get it back."

She bit her tongue and let Betty prattle on.

"And what did you think of the Alabama crowd?" Betty asked. "Why, I've never heard so much talk of football in all my life. Law have mercy, you'd have thought that's all those people know. I confess, when it comes to basketball season, some folks around here can be the same way. Did you know Scott's father was over here watching Alabama play on the TV with Joe until right before the wedding? He left with barely enough time to get across the road and conduct the ceremony.

"After the wedding, some of them snuck over here to watch more football. Joe loved it, him being the only one around with sports stations. If you remember, I was a cheerleader back in my day, and I could have cheered for Kentucky. But I decided to marry Joe instead."

Betty took a deep sigh, as if it had been her cross to bear.

Beulah decided to jump in then or else it might be another twenty minutes. "Betty, I need to go. It's time to put up the chickens."

***

On Monday afternoon following the wedding, she drove to the May Family Cemetery off Gibson's Creek Road for her weekly ritual. It was nearly November now, and while the trees were still rich in color, a brisk wind would soon blow in the rains and strip the trees for another year. As one season departed, it made room for another.

Next to the old stones, Beulah gave her thanks for the rich heritage her parents provided her, and for the life of her brother Ephraim. In his humanness he had found grace and forgiveness and had given her a beautiful gift, long beyond the grave, through his son Benito and his family.

Even through the sorrows of the graves of her husband, her daughter, and her infant son gone so long ago, she raised her head in thanksgiving for the lives entrusted, even for such a short time.

She gave thanks for Annie, Jo Anne's beautiful daughter, and for God leading her back to Somerville. She gave thanks for Evelyn, and her son Jake, who would now be Annie's husband. She gave thanks for Woody and Stella, Lindy and Tom Childress, Joe and Betty Gibson, and for Janice, who had helped bring about their reunion with Benito. She even gave thanks for Rossella DeVechio, who had helped her see how she needed to receive from others and she shouldn't be so quick to judge.

After leaving the cemetery she parked the Mercury at home and walked to the garden. The killing frost would come tonight. The vines would wither and the tomatoes would shrivel. There was work ahead in putting the garden to bed for the winter. As Ecclesiastes said, "There was a time to plant and a time to uproot," and now was the time to uproot.

The warmth of tears filled her eyes, and it surprised her at how the emotions came so quickly these days. Perhaps with the ending of this growing season and the onset of winter, there was every chance God might see fit to take her home. Nothing should be taken for granted these days, or ever, really. If God allowed, she would love to have more time—to see Annie settled with Jake, to see Benito on the land his father loved.

Time to be a great-grandmother and usher the next generation into this beautiful place. There was a new season beginning and Beulah wanted to be a part of it. She also missed Fred, her children, her parents and Ephraim and realized there was much to look forward to, no matter what God had in store.

The old metal box sat open on the nightstand next to her bed. One by one, she placed the pictures of Benito and Angelina, Vincenzo and his family, all into the metal box, along with all the brown V-mail envelopes, the letter from Arnie Mason, and the letter from Lilliana Caivano. On top of all the letters, she placed the sepia-toned picture of Elena. This time, nothing would be hidden under the false bottom.

There were no secrets left to guard.

Acknowledgments

Thanks to my husband, Jess Correll, who once again saw this book through from the early drafts, eternal cups of coffee and even a trip to Italy.

Thanks to Dr. Brian Ellis for sharing the valuable letters from his great-uncle Samuel Baker, who inspired the letters from World War II. Please see my author's note for more information.

There were two books that provided background and language that helped guide the letter writing from both the 1940s and the late 1700s. *To Hell and Back*, Audie Murphy's classic memoir of World Ward II by America's most decorated soldier and *Westward into Kentucky, the Narrative of Daniel Trabue* edited by Chester Raymond Young. Both are fascinating reading if you want to know more about these topics.

Gratitude for the following people who all provided expertise in their particular areas: Preston Correll, sustainable farming; Joe Hafley, David Cornelius, and Jerry Strehl on house fire damage; Honorable Bruce Petrie, county attorneys; Lynda Clossen, Kentucky history; Spence Clossen, international flight buddy passes; Elisabeth DeRossi, Italian language; Barthenia Brown for cultural guidance. Thank you to Mariella Spinelli for providing a lovely place to write the second half of the book in Montefollonico, Italy; Tina Young and Jay Blount with the American Battle Monuments Commission for valuable information on the American cemetery in Anzio, Italy; the staff at the Anzio Beachhead Museum, who were so very helpful; Rachel Correll, Emma Sleeth Davis, Beth Dotson Brown, and Jan Watson for suffering through early drafts; Adrienne Correll for reading an early draft and also for the Annie photographs; Jason Asa McKinley for the artistic renderings and cover shoot, along with rock climbing insight; Bret Lott, who shared his experience and wisdom to make this book much better; Jason Gabbert for his creative cover design; and McKenzie Reid, for modeling for the front cover.

Finally, thanks to Jenni Burke, my faithful agent; John Koehler, publisher; and Joe Coccaro, executive editor, for all taking a chance on me.

Author's Note

My father, Kenneth Crouch, served with the Navy in World War II. As the youngest son of a farm family, he was a late enlistment; he didn't enter service until August of 1944. By that time, the Allies had taken Italy, and the Normandy landing was just two months prior. Hitler was still fighting back hard, and the war in the Pacific still raged. After training camp in Great Lakes, Michigan, my father went to Solomons, Maryland, for amphibious warfare training.

Later, there was the long train ride across country to Portland, Oregon, and then on to Seattle, Washington, where they waited for their ship to carry them out to sea and battle. During that time, my father contracted a severe respiratory infection that put him in the infirmary. The ship sailed without him, and he was sent to the Naval Hospital in Sun Valley, Idaho, for recovery. I am thankful for that infection. Otherwise, I might not be here today.

My father spoke of his time in the Navy often, and I loved hearing his stories. When I went to Italy the first time, my dad, who never traveled outside the country, said if he could go anywhere it would be Italy. He had a friend who "fell in Italy" during the war and his body was never brought home.

The reality of a trip at that point was too much for him, but when my husband and I returned to Italy on a later trip, we decided to explore some of the World War II sites. We talked with my husband's uncle, Clark Farley, who also served in Italy and was on the trail from Sicily to Salerno to Cassino and on to Rome.

On that trip, we made time for the Anzio Cemetery, the American burial site for all the soldiers who died in the Italian Campaign, except for the nearly forty percent who were returned home for burial by their families.

The peaceful rows of white crosses against the verdant green grass was a visual that stuck with me when I wrote *Grounded*. I included a character, Ephraim, who was long dead but had served in World War II, falling at Anzio. I couldn't get this character out of my head, and even though he wasn't an active character in my first book, I knew there was more to his story that had to be told in *Guarded*.

I also knew that I wanted to tell Ephraim's story through letters. By God's divine providence, I was at a dinner party when the subject of my next book came up. When I shared my plans to research this era and write letters, Dr. Brian Ellis said he had a great-uncle who wrote letters home from the North Africa/ Italy campaign during World War II—and would I like to borrow them? This great-uncle was from a Kentucky farm family, just like my character.

Reading those letters from Samuel Baker, who left his farm in Lewisport, Kentucky, to serve our country in a land far away filled me with the language and thoughts such a boy would have. He often comforted and assured his mother of his eventual return. He sometimes spoke of his current life. Mostly he talked of the farm and peppered the letters with questions of what was going on back home. In some cases, I used the exact language of those letters in order to give readers a sense of what he felt and thought.

The plotline of Ephraim falling in love with Elena, the shopkeeper's daughter, is entirely fictional, as is the character of Ephraim. Samuel Baker survived the war and was able to return home to his beloved farm; he was tragically killed in a car accident by a drunk driver not many years later.

I am very grateful to Dr. Brian and Laurie Ellis, along with his mother, Sue, who had a similar relationship with her uncle that

I imagined Beulah and Ephraim to have. The cover of *Guarded* shows "Annie" holding letters sent home from Samuel Baker.

Before writing this book, I was completely naïve to all the "G.I. babies" that were left on foreign soil by American soldiers. Some soldiers, like Ephraim, were killed and never knew a child existed. Some moved on to other points of battle and may have never known they left children behind. Sadly, some were simply abandoned. There are websites dedicated to reunited fathers with children, although the overlap between the Internet's accessibility and the advancing age of the fathers made for a small window of opportunity. There are success stories, and I cried many tears reading them.

Another outstanding resource for my writing was Audie Murphy's autobiography, *To Hell and Back,* which details America's most decorated soldier's account of the Italian Campaign. The fictional letter from Arnie Mason was written in the style of Audie Murphy. I highly recommend this book for anyone interested in learning more about the Italian Campaign from someone who lived it.

In early 2014, my husband and I returned to Italy to do the on-the-ground research. We started in Morocco, North Africa, then moved to Sicily and then up the coast of Italy, retracing the path as much as we could. All of this was not necessary to the writing, but while reading *To Hell and Back*, I wanted to have a greater understanding of what these brave troops endured and risked. We stood on the banks of the Volturno River and saw what a terrible advantage the Germans had, and then even more up the road at Monte Cassino. We traveled back to Anzio and this time toured the museum and beachhead where the Allies landed and were stalled for several deadly months. Like so many of our boys, this is where Ephraim's journey ended.

We visited again the cemetery at Anzio and the white crosses stretching over green grass. There I found the name of my father's friend, but it was not on a cross. It was on a wall inside a memorial for those whose bodies were never found. Strangely enough, we were there on the 70th anniversary of the Anzio landings.

My father's voice is silent now, like most of our World War II veterans, but I would like to think he would be especially proud of this book.

Discussion Questions

1. When you think of the title, *Guarded*, where do you see that theme carried out throughout the book?

2. The old stone house represents more to Annie than just a building. Why is she so attached to it? What places do you have that are sentimental or meaningful to you?

3. Why does Beulah struggle with the idea of searching for her brother's lost child? Have you ever used excuses to avoid a situation that makes you uncomfortable?

4. Vesta's family and Annie's family are intertwined by history and geography, yet separated by race and culture. Can you think of those possibilities in your own family history? Is there anything you can do—either by forgiving, like Vesta, or apologizing, like Annie—to repair the relationship?

5. Beulah is irritated with her houseguest, Rossella, yet she realizes later they may have more in common than she allowed herself to believe in the beginning. Is there a situation in your life where you struggle to see beyond the irritations of a relationship?

6. Betty Gibson seems intent on stirring up trouble, especially with Annie. Why?

7. Annie's relationship with her father comes back to haunt her new relationship with Jake. How does she finally make her peace with her old hurts? Or has she?

8. How did Jake contribute to the strain between Annie and himself?

9. Beulah's sacred space is in the kitchen, where she feels most in control. She also uses the garden and the family cemetery for reflection and prayer. Do you have places that serve certain needs in your life?

10. Annie experiences small town prejudice against her family name due to the unsavory actions of her relatives. Have you ever experienced this—or possibly been on the other side of it?